Jamaican Sunset

THE BUCCANEERS · 3

Jamaican Sunset

LINDA CHAIKIN

MOODY PRESS
CHICAGO

ISBN: 0-8024-1073-1

3 5 7 9 10 8 6 4

Printed in the United States of America

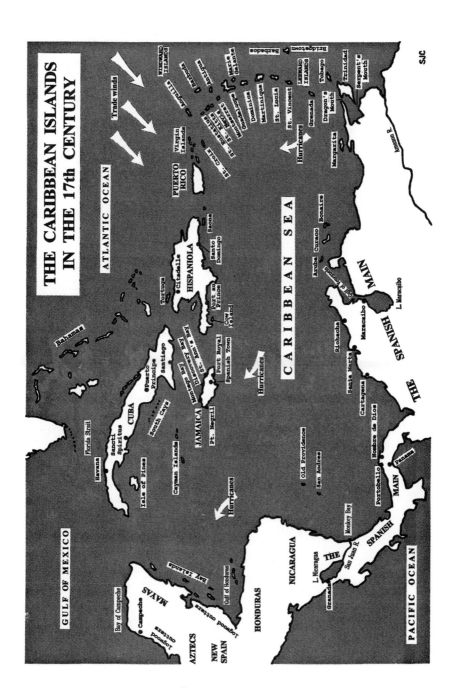

THE CARIBBEAN ISLANDS
IN THE 17th CENTURY

CONTENTS

1

BRIGHT PROMISES

The Jamaican morning sky was boiling with enormous red-gold incandescent clouds.

"Like my heart," murmured Emerald happily as she turned from the small window in the upper loft of the old lookout house on Fishers Row. She fingered the ruby pendant at her pale throat.

The jewel burned with a dark red glory all its own, and she told herself that in possessing the ruby she also possessed the hard-won heart of Baret Buckington. The pendant had belonged to his mother, the woman he esteemed above all others for her martyrdom for the Christian faith.

"Yet, he has honored *me* by bestowing the pendant as a fitting expression of his feelings," she said aloud.

At the moment the ruby was more precious to her than the ornately carved and jeweled gold Buckington ring that he would also give her at their public betrothal at Foxemoore within a few short weeks.

Emerald relived the thrilling moment when Baret had taken her into his arms in the garden at the Jamaican governor's residence and told her that he loved *her*, not Cousin Lavender Thaxton, a wealthy future duchess!

She would hold his disclosure close to her breast and relish every detail again and again, remembering how he had willingly made the decision, speaking the golden words of Proverbs 31: "'Who can find a virtuous woman? for her price is far above rubies.'"

Emerald's emotions were tender, and musings came easily as she indulged the moment of youthful promise, drinking in and savoring the realization that he now believed in her chastity and honor, despite the lies that continued to dog her steps.

"I'm to actually wed him within a year!"

The idea of marrying a viscount left her distracted. Could she live up to this new status that would now be her mantle? With each day bringing new responsibilities, she wondered how she would fit into the customs of royalty and the upper class.

Matters had changed rather drastically for Baret these last weeks. Following Baret's victory over the Dutch Admiral de Ruyter near Barbados, his grandfather Earl Nigel now proudly received him. And the High Admiralty was willing to smooth over the piracy charges that were weighed against him, at least for the duration of the war with Holland. If Baret could locate and free his father and retrieve the hidden treasure of the *Prince Philip*, he might freely return to Whitehall and be received by King Charles.

And I'll be on his arm, bowing to the king, she thought, shaking at the thought of the role she must learn to live in order not to shame Baret. How dreadful it could be to be received at Whitehall, to be requested to sup with the king, and then forget to say or do something important!

Baret would help her, she decided. He knew exactly what was required. He would teach her how to behave at royal events. She could envision the knowing smiles hidden behind jeweled fans, though, and the jealous mean words spoken behind her back.

Emerald shut the distant future from her mind and concentrated instead on the wonders of the present. The Lord was her stay. She must never forget that.

Last night she had returned to her father's lookout house on Fishers Row in a romantic daze. She had sent Baret away when he hadn't wanted to leave, nervously laughing off his insistence that she reconsider and marry him before he sailed with Morgan. The romantic change that had come over him was astounding. She hadn't been able to sleep for thinking about his ardency. This was a Baret Buckington she had never seen before, and she contemplated. She must be careful to keep matters between them from becoming too amorous until the year of engagement was over.

He had left her, leaving behind a guard and assuring her he would return in a few days. She had been so absorbed with these thoughts last night that she had tried in vain to fall asleep. She had also been basking in the astounding news that her beloved father was alive. Sir Karlton was a galley slave aboard a Dutch ship and in danger, yet she was thankful, nonetheless, that he was believed to be alive.

And this morning she would go to Foxemoore to free her cousin Minette from slavery in the cane fields.

Indeed, the bright change in her previously dark circumstances was almost too much blessing to handle in so few hours. The Lord had been so good and gracious to her that she felt like the "sweet singer of Israel," who had written, "My cup runneth over."

She turned, hearing a loud rap on the front door below and Zeddie leaving the cook room to answer it.

Who could that be? Emerald came out of the loft used as a bedroom and peered down the steep ladderlike steps into the small room below.

A young lad stood in the doorway, whom she recognized from the *Regale* as Jeremy, Baret's bosun. He offered a warm grin to Zeddie and, seeing her on the steps, swept off his hat and bowed low.

"There's boxes for Lady Harwick. All from Cap'n Foxworth—I mean, his lordship. And where would ye like 'em all?"

Zeddie, who had returned a few hours earlier from Foxemoore with news of Minette, straightened his golden periwig and went out to help bring them inside. Soon, the warped and creaking floor was piled high, and Emerald stood staring.

"A good mornin' to ye, Miss." Jeremy tipped his hat again. "I'll be telling his lordship you're looking fair." And he backed away from the door and left.

Emerald came rushing down the stairs, amazed at the sight. Boxes sat everywhere, dozens of them. They proved to be full of astounding gifts that left her oohing and aahing like a bewildered child at Christmas. Frocks made of lush velvet, sateen, and silk—the velvet in her favorite color, royal blue. There were crinolines. And even silk stockings! She blushed to think he would dare to send them, but the blush did not last long once she held them and felt their smooth, rich texture. There were slippers too. She could only wonder how he had known her size, for they fit perfectly. He had noticed more about her than she had thought.

"I must be careful," she lectured herself. "We're not married yet—even the engagement isn't for two weeks. Some would

11

say I shouldn't be accepting gifts—but, oh!—Baret isn't a rogue like that odious Sir Jasper. I can wear them safely enough. And anyway, I'll die if I can't!" And she held up a pair of adorable black satin slippers with tasteful buckles.

Zeddie chuckled. "Aye, m'gal, ye've got yourself a treasure chest of fancy things, to be sure. Captain Foxworth knows how he wants ye to be lookin', that's plain to see. Next thing is jewels, but ye'll be gettin' them in England at Buckington House, I'm thinkin'."

Once Emerald and Zeddie had carried all the clothes up the steps to her loft, she spent the next hour trying them on and admiring them, while Zeddie, singing, left the lookout house to catch some fish for their supper. She was humming and looking at herself in the mirror when she heard a horse whinny and the call of male voices below the front steps. She rushed to the window and leaned out, looking below, and a moist warm wind tossed her dark hair.

Two men were leading a magnificent horse, whose neigh greeted the morning like merry laughter.

"Ho, there!" came the lead man's voice. "Anyone home?"

The large bewhiskered man looked up to the window and, seeing Emerald, swept off his battered straw hat, showing a tangle of gray-black waves. "A fair mornin' to you, Miss. Kennedy at your service. His lordship Baret Buckington bade me to make a delivery to his soon-to-be bride." He settled back on his heels and shifted his glance to the ramshackle house. "But I be thinking a wee mistake is made. We're lost to finding the proper abode. 'Twas wondering if ye might tell us where to find a miss called Lady Emerald Harwick."

Emerald's cinnamon-brown eyes twinkled, for they obviously didn't expect to find a viscount's "lady" living in a lookout house. "I'm Lady Emerald Harwick," she said with a laugh. "Do you wish to speak to me, Mr. Kennedy?"

The man was rabbit quick to redeem himself. Clearing his raspy throat, he looked up at her with a grave face so as to hide his contrary thoughts. "Aye, I shoulda known, m'lady, 'twas you," came the polite voice, and he fished in his pocket and withdrew a sealed envelope, which he held up. "This be for you, m'lady, from Lord Buckington. Will ye come down to fetch it?"

She smiled. "I'll be right down, Mr. Kennedy."

12

A moment later she stepped out onto the front porch where the Port Royal morning welcomed her with sea breezes laden with brine. Gulls screamed their familiar cry over the wharf, where the port's water tugged and sucked at the pilings. Accepting the envelope, Emerald gazed at the seal bearing an elaborate "B."

Before she could open it, Mr. Kennedy explained. "The mare and buggy are a gift, m'lady," and he gestured across Fishers Row.

Another gift? Curiously she looked across the narrow cobbled street to see a charming little horse-drawn buggy with a blue fringe top dancing in the breeze.

"Oh! It's stunning," she cried.

Then she read the brief message: "One so lovely should ride home to Foxemoore in style."

"Home." Emerald lingered over the brief but warm, telling words, smiling wistfully. She was overwhelmed by Baret's thoughtful gift, for his was no pauper's generosity. She knew something of horses, and this mare was a fine-blooded specimen. She laughed to herself. She would certainly make a stir returning to Foxemoore now, wearing blue velvet and lace, a ruby pendant, and driving a new buggy drawn by a blooded mare! She suspected Baret knew as much and had done so deliberately.

She read his concluding remarks: "I shall join you as soon as the captains' meeting with Morgan is concluded. If Pitt gives you any more trouble, tell him I'll hang him myself."

As the men left, Emerald affectionately rubbed the nose of the mare and patted her graceful neck. "You're a worthy gift, but coming from Baret, you are a sweet prize indeed."

Then she saw Zeddie coming up the beach with a gunnysack of fresh fish. The tall gaunt man, garbed in faded blue coat with tarnished gold lace, was whistling as he trudged up to the steps. She knew his two big boarding pistols were loaded. In his younger years he had been a crack shot, as he always liked to announce. He had fought in the Civil War in England, where he had lost an eye. He'd been sent to Barbados as a political prisoner in the days of Cromwell, and her father, who had known him in England, had found him on Governor Modyford's sugar plantation and arranged to buy his freedom. Zeddie ever remained a strong ally and served as bodyguard to Emerald.

He straightened his black eye patch, and his whistled tune

turned to a low note of exclamation. He examined the mare, then looked across at the waiting buggy, whose fringe still jiggled in the tropical breeze.

"I'm thinking old Pitt will have his eyes poppin' when he sees you, m'gal. 'Twill be sweet to boot the cunning shark out of Karlton's bungalow." He dropped the gunnysack of fish and rubbed his hands together with exaggerated anticipation. Then he tapped his dyed purple-leather baldric, and his one keen eye turned as hard as a smooth ocean pebble. "Pitt's got himself a bit of luck that his lordship isn't coming with you now—his neck will be spared. Wouldn't take much to have his lordship hang the rat-toothed scoundrel."

"I'm in no mood to hang anyone today, Zeddie, not even that treacherous Mr. Pitt. This isn't a time for vengeance. Don't you remember how David treated his enemies when he became king of Israel? Why, he could have had old Shimei cut down with the sword for cursing him when he left Jerusalem during Absalom's rebellion. Instead, he let him go free when he returned as king."

"Aye, but it ain't no fun! Not where Pitt goes."

She laughed and handed him the reins. "After having landed Baret Buckington, I've grace enough and to spare for the meanest of wretches—" her smile faded and her eyes grew determined "—as long as he doesn't contest my good plans."

"Now you're talking, m'gal."

Hiking up her skirts about her ankles, Emerald rushed up the creaking wood steps to change. She stopped in front of the door and looked down the steps at him. "I'm anxious to dress and be on our way to Foxemoore. This is Minette's shining hour too. Next time Sir Erik Farrow sees my cousin, he'll wonder indeed."

Zeddie chuckled, as delighted by it all as though *he* were the inheritor of good fortune.

She looked over at her new buggy and sighed. It was just the beginning. This would be her first arrival at Foxemoore since the slave uprising and the tragic death of Great-uncle Mathias. She wondered what her beloved minister uncle would think if he knew she was going to marry a Buckington. Well, he had more wonderful things to occupy him now. He had looked upon the fair face of the Lord Jesus Himself, for the apostle Paul had written, "Absent from the body . . . present with the Lord."

Inside the loft she chose a cool silk dress of palest lime color with lemon flower buds on the neck and cuffs and readied herself for the trip inland. There was a matching hat with a trailing yellow ribbon and a dainty white lace parasol. She noticed that all the colors flattered her dark hair and brown eyes and that there was a certain sweetness to the styles. She knew Baret well enough by now to understand the kind of woman he found attractive. No low-cut dresses such as they wore shamelessly in London.

A half hour later she looked at herself in the mirror. Her eyes glowed as warmly as the tropics, while her ivory skin bore little evidence of having experienced the burning sun. Her thick dark tresses were arranged at the back of her neck, and in place of the prized silver cross embedded with pearls that her mother had given her, and which she carried in a little sachet near her heart, the ruby now glimmered at her throat where Baret had placed it the night before under the mammoth yellow moon.

She surprised even herself by the change. A stranger would think her a great lady indeed. Oh, dear! She didn't want to make Lavender jealous, but she surely would, for it was in Lavender's heart to be envious and spoiled to the point that she resented happiness coming to anyone else. And to have captured Baret's heart away from her . . .

Emerald frowned worriedly. Dealing day by day with Cousin Lavender might prove as difficult as dealing with Mr. Pitt. *May the Lord give me discernment and wisdom to know how best to fill my new position without rubbing brine into Lavender's wounded pride.* It took as much spirituality to be gracious to others when in blessing as it did to endure the filth and injustice of Brideswell.

I know how to be abased, but do I know how to abound?

With the shares her father owned in the sugar estate and the shares that Baret possessed—including the extra shares recently granted him by Earl Nigel—she and Baret would own more of Foxemoore than even her father's cousin Geneva Harwick Buckington. Geneva had been recently married to Baret's nefarious uncle, Lord Felix, who considered himself the rightful owner of all the Buckington inheritance. She wondered how the conflicts would eventually work out. Baret was in no mood to submit to Felix, whom he blamed for the imprisonment of his father on the Main.

She remembered Minette and grew sober. She had already packed a pretty new frock for her cousin, with all the essentials, intending to stop at her father's bungalow on the plantation before they entered the Great House together, so that Minette could bathe and change. They would enter side by side as blood cousins—unless her courage gave way in the end like a wet bag and she was left void of resolve. In which case, she might remain in the bungalow until Baret arrived and escorted her and Minette to the main house to meet with Lady Sophie Harwick. Perhaps it would be better if she waited, so they wouldn't think her flaunting.

Emerald shivered, thinking about entering through that ominous front door alone. Minette's presence would undoubtedly anger Lady Sophie. *Lord, give me wisdom to behave wisely*, she prayed. *All this blessing and change in my life is a gift from You. Help me to use it as You would have me do. Not for self-seeking but for the good of us all.*

A short time later she and Zeddie prepared to leave her father's abandoned lookout house. The place resembled the old lighthouse that had once awaited her homecoming with fore boding silence when she left Sir Jasper and the hacienda in Spanish Town. At that time, Emerald had been certain she could feel within its tall narrow walls the harbinger of trials to come. Those dreadful times did come, including her incarceration in Brideswell. The treachery had been intensified by the belief that her father was dead. Now, the sun was shining on her path. Happiness beckoned like a playful child for her to follow.

She looked at Zeddie, who offered her an elegant bow, extending her his arm. His good eye shone. "Coming, your ladyship?"

She smiled and looped her arm through his, and they walked out of the lookout house. The structure's plank flooring creaked beneath their feet. Her ears—soon for the last time—heard the water slapping against its pilings sunk deep into sand.

And then they were seated in the new buggy, and the mare pranced and shook her mane as Zeddie sat tall and straight-shouldered. He gave a flick to the reins.

Leaving Fishers Row behind, they were soon on the back road leading inland to Foxemoore. The sunlight caught the ruby pendant at her throat, and it glowed warm and crimson. She looked at Zeddie and smiled.

"Ah, Missy, if your father could see you now, he'd be a happy man."

A pair of seagulls lifted together on white wings and rose above the crystal blue Caribbean.

2
RETURN TO FOXEMOORE

The sultry morning throbbed with birdsong, and green and blue parrots lodged in the branches of the Spanish breadfruit trees as freckled sunlight filtered through. Emerald breathed in the scent of moist warm earth and trumpet vine and tried to digest the awesome fact that if she married Baret she would become a wealthy heiress, not only of Foxemoore but of land and houses in England.

With a wink, Zeddie, whistling a sprightly tune, settled his tall black satin hat and gave a light flick of the reins to the mare, who trotted proudly down the brown roadway bringing them closer to Foxemoore. On the other side of the road, tall cane rustled in the wind like green waves, and Emerald listened to the rushing sound through the stalks. Above the miles of cane stretching toward the lush Blue Mountain Range, the sky was the color of a topaz.

Today she found nothing but pleasure in the familiar sights and smells surrounding her on the estate where she'd been brought as a small child from the notorious pirate stronghold of Tortuga.

Emerald sighed. "Zeddie, I must be dreaming. Just think, all this unexpected happiness and heaven too. Is it possible God could bless me so?" she mused, amazed at her recent circumstances.

He turned the buggy from the road onto the smaller one that led into Foxemoore. "See that weather vane?" He pointed to a wooden rooster that turned toward the unsettled breeze from the Caribbean. "No matter which way the wind blows, God is good. Say, m'gal, we ought to paint those words on the rooster. Then, no matter how he points, in storm or fair weather, he'll be telling out the truth." He looked at her. "But I'm still mean enough to dream on till I see old Pitt sent a-packing."

18

The very mention of Mr. Pitt brought Emerald a nervous pang. She peered ahead, lifting a hand to shade her eyes, and listened above the sighing green stalks for the sound of the slaves hoeing.

They rode toward the familiar cutoff at the end of the road, which brought them to the main carriageway, lined with fringed palms shaking in the wind. A quarter of a mile ahead, the planter's Great House stood on a grassy knoll facing windward, renewing both distressing and happy memories. On the far side of the carriageway lay a sweeping view of the green cane fields.

Emerald's heart swelled painfully. "Pull to the side," she said quietly. "I want to look at it a moment."

Zeddie brought the buggy under the dense shade of an overspreading hickory tree. She gazed up to the planter's Great House. Its white columns and red tile roof stood as she remembered from her childhood, with serene and superior aristocracy. Its magnificence still awed her and threatened her courage until she touched the ruby pendant at her throat. Someone, at least, believed in her—the earl's grandson!

Foxemoore had belonged to the Harwicks and the Buckingtons since before the days of Oliver Cromwell. During the great Civil War in England, several Harwicks fled to the West Indies, where they had built the sugar estate with money loaned by the great earl Killigrew Buckington. The Buckingtons themselves had gone to France with the exiled King Charles and returned during the Reconstruction to reclaim their title and lands.

Earl Nigel Buckington was now here and, for reasons of his own, was favoring the upcoming betrothal between her and Baret—at least until Lavender and Lord Grayford Thaxton were married. The earl then expected Emerald to return the Buckington ring and melt quietly away into the Jamaican sunset. But when she had told this to Baret, he had laughed, because of his serious intentions to marry her. His confidence bolstered her own, yet she remained uncomfortably uneasy at times.

What would Lady Sophie Harwick say when she walked through the front door, bringing her cousin Minette with her?

"All right, Zeddie, let's go find Minette," she said quietly.

He drove the buggy off the carriageway onto the narrow work road that ran for a great length between the cane fields.

Emerald found that the familiar scene brought many

unpleasant memories, like clouds of stinging flies. She remembered an emotionally dark day several months ago when she had come down this road to keep her meeting with Mr. Pitt over the arrest of Cousin Ty. She remembered how she had failed to gain his consideration for a reprieve. Pitt had threatened that unless she came up with a bribe—the family jewels from her French cousin Rafael Levasseur—Pitt would haul Ty before the Jamaican magistrate to be branded as a runaway.

Emerald's eyes narrowed beneath her thick lashes as she relived the frustration of having no one to turn to for help, to have every door she knocked on bolted. Heaven had seemed brass to her prayers, and members of the Harwick family had turned a deaf ear to her pleas. In the end, Ty had indeed been hauled to the town pillory and branded on his handsome forehead like a steer branded by a rancher.

Emerald moved on the leather seat, trying to hold down the eruption of angry tension from bubbling forth like a volcano. Her eyes closed. It would do no good to get angry now. *It is too easy to hate Mr. Pitt,* she confessed to the Lord. *Help me to leave past injustice to You.*

What had happened in the past could not be undone. What mattered today was to find Minette and take her from the fields.

There was another reason for going to the manor house first. She wanted to search her father's trunk to see if she could locate the much-talked-about deed to his shares of Foxemoore sugar.

Whether or not such a deed existed had always been a matter of some question to Emerald. Her father, Sir Karlton, however, had insisted it was so.

"If I do not legally own a large share of the sugar production," he had said, "then why does Felix not take it to court? He'll not take the matter to law because the man knows I hold a legal document. And not simply a lease either, but I hold it free—and will forever! It is signed by the deceased Earl Esmond Buckington himself."

A legal document, mused Emerald, as they drove along the cane, growing tall beside the narrow red-brown road. Did such a mysterious parchment actually exist, locked away in some box, or was it her father's spurious invention?

One morning he had brought her to his chamber to unlock

a small pirated silver treasure box and fish out a folded deed to show her. The paper might have been anything, since Emerald, twelve years old at the time, had been too young to appreciate its validity. Trust in her father and the official-looking gold seal had convinced her that his claim was true.

Until Lord Felix Buckington had married her father's cousin Geneva Harwick, the Buckingtons had been absentee sugar magnates, living as blooded nobility in England and serving the court of His Majesty King Charles II, while the Harwicks, who were gentry, had run the estate.

But under Felix, all that had changed for the worse. Foxemoore was now doubling as its own merchant, using family ships to haul sugar into the American colonies and Quebec. Felix was also bringing back slaves to work land bought from a neighboring planter. Zeddie learned that the smaller planter had quietly been "encouraged" by Sir Jasper to sell out to Foxemoore against his will.

The knowledge disturbed Emerald. If she married Baret, that would allow them to control what went on in the plantation. Baret told her he would stand by her in making certain changes, especially rebuilding and enlarging the singing school of Greatuncle Mathias. But dare she contest some of the decisions made by Lord Felix? After all, she wasn't Baret's wife yet. She was inexperienced in the ways of ruling, and in Baret's absence, Felix would be sure to point this out on every occasion that proved her wisdom inferior to his.

She would need to move slowly when it came to making decisions that previously had been left to Lady Sophie, Geneva, and now to Felix. Lady Sophie, especially, would resent what she would mistake as "meddling." Nevertheless, there were some matters hot within her heart that Emerald would not compromise: the future of her cousins Minette and Ty and the translation of the slave chants in order to bring the slaves their own Christian hymns. She must locate her father's deed, which Baret had asked her about at the governor's meeting two days ago.

Resentment stirred from slumber as she remembered that Pitt had dared to move into her father's house and sleep in his bed. No doubt the loathsome brute had searched everything. Not that he knew or would care about the deed. What Mr. Pitt was interested in finding was a map showing the location of the Spanish treasure taken from the *Prince Philip*.

He would look in vain among her father's things. Baret had told her aboard the *Regale* that *he* had the map and that the treasure was stowed on the Spanish pearl island of Margarita. But Pitt didn't know that. She wondered if Baret had ever gone to the island. That was doubtful, since he had been fully occupied with a Spanish don he'd taken as prisoner from a galleon. Don Miguel was the son of the planter who had bought Baret's father as a slave. Though there'd been too much happening recently to ask Baret what he had learned from Don Miguel, she suspected he had managed to gain the information he needed. He appeared confident in his quest of finding his father, planning to sail with Henry Morgan under Governor Modyford's sanction.

Zeddie slowed the buggy. Emerald shaded her eyes beneath her sun hat and looked ahead across the cane fields where the slaves were busy at work under the watchful eye of an African foreman. Mr. Pitt was nowhere in sight, but she believed him to be somewhere in the area. He often rode his horse through the fields to make certain those in charge of the cane workers also toed the line.

She leaned forward on the seat as the fringe danced on the buggy top, glancing about anxiously for a sign of Minette. Zeddie had been sent to locate her on the evening of the governor's dinner in Port Royal. He'd reported back yesterday that although he'd been unable to find her, Ngozi had managed to get a message to him telling him that Minette was working in the cookhouse near Mr. Pitt's stockade for disobedient slaves.

Emerald was quite aware of what the stockade was. There had never been one when her father managed Foxemoore, but Lady Sophie knew little of what was going on, and she trusted Mr. Pitt. Cousin Geneva was ill, and Lord Felix, if he did know, wasn't likely to be disturbed as long as things on the plantation remained quiet. One uprising several months ago was enough, and Lavender's mother had died in that brief horror. There was little sympathy for the slaves on Foxemoore right now, as long as Pitt did his job.

The boiling house was working at full capacity when Zeddie brought the buggy to a stop in the work yard. The steam from the huge kettles and the heavy smell of burned sugar and molasses, which would be sold to make Jamaican rum, hung like sticky vapor on the air.

Emerald's eyes flickered with pain as several African women walked by, carrying pots on their heads. They were unclothed from the waist up, and it infuriated her that the women should be treated with such indignity! Before Great-uncle Mathias had died, she and Minette had worked with him to make certain that clothing was distributed. But beside being cruel, Mr. Pitt was a lustful man. He enjoyed debauchery and kept several women for his selfish use. *There will be a quick end to that!* thought Emerald.

The slaves were busy at work as Zeddie parked the buggy in the clearing of rust-brown earth near several wooden frame buildings and the cluster of huts used as receiving stations for Mr. Pitt's paperwork. She was gathering her skirts to climb down when Zeddie laid a hand on her arm, his one eye grave.

"Maybe ye ought to wait and let me bring Minette out."

She knew why he said this. The scene would not leave a pleasant memory.

"I've been here before with Mathias many times. I know full well 'tis an ugly, brutal sight. But I want to see. The Lord has blessed me far above all I could expect or hope for, and in my blessing I don't want to become like Sophie and Geneva, aware only of the pleasantness of the sugar estate. We must never forget the cost in human suffering and indignities."

Zeddie's pride in her showed, but he looked worried just the same. "Don't forget, m'gal, you're but a sweet child compared to clever slavers and businessmen like Lord Felix and Sir Jasper. If you aim to take 'em on where it hurts, you'll be needing Captain Buckington at your side. And while the betrothal takes place in two weeks, it's also true he'll be gone at sea with Morgan for a year or more after that."

She smiled. "I have you, don't forget. And I've rare plans for Ngozi. And maybe Ty too, if I could get word to him in the Blue Mountains." She gazed off briefly toward the lush tropical ranges standing against the clear sky. "I wonder if Ngozi would know how to get word to him?"

"If there's a way, Ngozi be the one, all right. And from the way he treated me the other night, he's as loyal to you as they come. But Lord Felix is the one I worry about. There's nothing worse than a roaring lion except a wily serpent hiding in the tall

23

grass. That's what Lord Felix is, if you don't mind my saying so. He won't sit back and let a young woman marry his lordship and meddle where he has stout plans."

"I've no plans to start a hurricane," she said. "I expect to start out cautiously. But concerning Minette and Ty, there'll be no compromise—" She stopped, seeing his expression change and feeling his hand tighten on her arm. He was looking past her toward the boiling house office.

"Speak of trouble, m'gal, it's come to meet us."

Emerald turned her head and saw not Mr. Pitt but a handsome, muscled African, bare from the waist up. Sempala wore soiled cotton britches cut off at the knees and a hat of dried woven cane leaves. He had apparently come from inside the boiling house. He was followed by two other Africans who served him as law enforcers, which meant that they were big enough and strong enough to crack down on any worker who might decide to rebel under his workload.

Sempala looked toward the new buggy and then at Emerald's expensive finery. He must have recognized her at once, for he removed his hat in deference. She could tell by his sullen expression that he was not a happy man. He must know she had come for Minette. Sempala was Mr. Pitt's chief foreman, whose name he had changed to "Big Boy" to show contemptuous authority over his fellow Africans. Though Pitt had chosen him, Emerald knew he had no liking for Sempala. He was merely useful in carrying out Pitt's orders.

It was unfortunate, thought Emerald, that overseers like Pitt were allowed to choose the slaves they wanted to have authority over the other workers. To guarantee their own better treatment at the hands of an overseer, many were obliged to use whatever tactics necessary to keep order in the fields and at the boiling house. Like Pitt, Sempala carried a short whip, and a machete hung on a leather thong belt.

She recalled that he had once asked to marry Minette. Her cousin had refused him and later told Emerald that Sempala had never forgiven her. That he might now dislike Minette with the same intensity with which he had "loved" her was a frightening thought. He had once called her a "White Heart," meaning that she had betrayed her own people and was good for little else except humiliation.

24

Emerald's throat tightened, and for the first time she entertained the horrid thought that Minette might have been compromised. The thought turned her hands cold. Gathering her skirts, with Zeddie's help she climbed down from the buggy seat.

Zeddie straightened his baldric with its two big dueling pistols and cocked his roosterlike eye toward Sempala, as if to warn in advance that the slightest insult would mean trouble.

"It's all right, Zeddie," she whispered. "By now they've all heard about the upcoming betrothal."

"Don't forget, Pitt has Lord Felix on his side."

"I'm not forgetting. But we have Baret."

She walked across the hot dusty yard, and Sempala came to meet her. For a moment the noise of the slaves ceased, and silence prevailed. Eyes shifted to the contrasting sight of sweet loveliness in lime green silk and lace invading the world of squalor, sweat, and torment.

Emerald stopped and waited in the intense sunlight. Most of the slaves went back to work, but one young African girl stood barefoot, staring.

Sempala stopped a few feet away, holding his cane hat. "Welcome home, Miss Emerald."

"Thank you. Where's my cousin Minette?"

The deliberate use of the word *cousin* wasn't lost on him, and his gaze shifted to the dirt. "Out back of the boilin' house. Mister Pitt wants an eye on the molasses at night. Says slaves been stealin' syrup."

Emerald looked scornful. "I suspect he is his own thief. He always did smuggle it to pirates at Chocolata Hole."

"Yes, Miss Emerald. If you say so."

"Is Minette in the cookhouse?"

He hunched his broad shoulders as though to loosen the taut muscles and glanced away. "She was."

Alarm set in. "Was? Where is she now?"

"Sick. She's been sick days now."

"Sick?" she repeated, her alarm increasing as he avoided her eyes.

"Got sweating sickness."

"Where is she?"

He shifted his feet. "Out back, Miss."

"Out back *where*? Quickly, Sempala!"

He moistened his lips and kept his eyes on the ground. "In my hut."

Emerald's jaw tightened. Zeddie took a step forward, but Emerald laid a hand on his wrist. She handed him her closed parasol and, picking up her skirts, began to run across the yard toward the cluster of huts and buildings, ignoring the slaves, who again stared in silence. Some moved out of her way, knowing Minette and Ty were her cousins.

Sempala groaned as he trotted just behind her, followed by the scowling Zeddie, who had drawn a long-barreled pistol. His temperature was obviously rising.

"I didn't hurt her none!" Sempala protested.

Emerald stopped in the midst of some huts, breathing hard. The sweltering sun beat on her head. "Which hut?"

He pointed. "That one."

Emerald walked briskly toward the small round thatched shack whose door already stood ajar. Flies were drawn to the shade. A sickening odor filled the stifling air. She looked at some naked children squatting in the shade of a breadfruit tree.

The sweating sickness. She hesitated before going in, fearful of the condition in which she might find Minette. Mustering her courage, she prayed silently and then stepped through the doorway into the hot, dimly lighted hut.

Emerald held to the door frame for support, staring down at the thin figure drawn up into a fetal position on a dirty blanket in one corner of the floor. She found herself protesting the sight. This girl couldn't be Minette. Not this scrawny sick figure in a tattered tunic.

Emerald went toward her and sank down beside the blanket, unmindful of the luxurious folds of her silk skirts. Her eyes anxiously searched her cousin, as close to her heart as any sister could be.

"Minette," she whispered, reaching for her gently, noting the torn calico slave frock and her bare dusty feet.

Minette moaned in terror. "Don't touch me—"

"Minette, it's Emerald. Don't be afraid. I've come to help you—to take you away from here." She smoothed back the wild honey-colored ringlets that stuck to Minette's face. Her skin was terribly hot, and her frock was soaked with sweat.

Minette's amber eyes stared upward, dazed. She tried to speak, but her throat seemed parched.

"It's going to be all right now," whispered Emerald.

"Em—" Then came a cracked hysterical cry. *"Em—rald!"* Tears ran down her face, leaving little trails in the layer of dust.

Heedless, Emerald grasped her frail quivering body to her own as Minette sobbed.

"Oh, Emerald—"

"Hush, it's going to be all right now. I'm taking you away. You're going to be better soon."

But would she? Emerald looked into the thin face. What would she do with her? She couldn't bring her to the Great House yet. She must take her to the manor house, where she could nurse her until Baret arrived in a few days.

She laid Minette back down on the blanket and disentangled her weak grip. "It's all right," she repeated. "Lie still. We're leaving here. I'll call for Zeddie."

Minette tried to clutch her, to keep her from leaving, but Emerald stood to her feet and hurried to the hut door, holding back her dismay.

Zeddie stood waiting out in the hot bright sunshine.

"Zeddie! Can you carry her? We'll bring her to the manor house."

"Aye. That scurvy shark Pitt," he grumbled between his teeth as he walked in. A look of pity showed on his face as he neared the old blanket and looked down at the girl. He stooped and gathered up Minette to carry her away. "Looks like plague fever to me—and if it is, she won't be the last to come down with it."

Plague! Emerald held back a wince of horror. If it was, the sickness could indeed sweep the plantation, leaving few, if any, alive, including the family in the Great House.

"The doctor will know," she said worriedly. "Geneva's personal physician is likely to be rooming in the house."

Emerald came out the hut door, followed by Zeddie carrying the childlike figure of Minette.

Sempala loitered nearby and shifted his stance as his eyes followed Zeddie.

"It wasn't me who did this to her. It were Mister Pitt. He wouldn't let me call for no doctor—"

27

Emerald was more concerned over the kind of sickness that was ravaging Minette's body than she was angry. Sempala was right. If anyone was to blame it was Mr. Pitt—Pitt and the family in the Great House.

"Have you told me the truth about not touching her?" Emerald demanded, looking him evenly in the eye as he towered above her.

"Yes, Miss, I told the truth. When she got the fever, Mr. Pitt got mad and told me to take her. I been looking after her, me and the old woman Ngozi sent. Said he'd skin me if I touched Miss Emerald's cousin. And that pirate been asking for her too. Farrow was his name. But I don't trust him neither, so we didn't tell him where she was. He thinks she run away to the mountain."

A silent breath escaped her. *Thank you, Father, for protecting her.*

"Then you need not worry, Sempala. You're right about who's to blame."

He lowered his voice. "You come at a high time. Seeing your cousin Ty is down from Blue Mountain. He is in a heap of fire. Good thing you is dressed like a chieftain's daughter, 'cause Mr. Pitt is plannin' himself a skinnin'."

Emerald whirled toward him, her eyes meeting his deep gaze, unsure whether she had heard him right. Did she see friendliness in his eyes or secret contempt?

"Ty?" came her dread whisper. She held the sides of her skirts. "He's here?"

He glanced over his shoulder in the direction of the boiling house, where steam fumed up like clouds of sulphur mist.

"Ty was a fool. He come for his sister, but Pitt found him. Nobody escapes Mr. Pitt and his hounds."

Emerald's fear grew like the disease that threatened to suck the life from Minette—until she remembered who the new Emerald Harwick was. Pitt *couldn't* hurt Ty! She wouldn't allow it. Not this time.

"Where is Ty?" And her voice sounded steady.

Sempala looked toward the dusty road. "Mr. Pitt has him at the stockade. He and Minette was goin' to try to run away to a pirate ship with that Cap'n Farrow. Pitt, he learned about it."

Emerald's heart chilled with fear and loathing. She knew well enough what it meant that "Pitt has him at the stockade." Without a word she hurried after Zeddie.

Zeddie brought Minette to the buggy and was laying her down on the small backseat when Emerald approached.

"Bring her to the manor. Then go to the Great House for a doctor, will you? I've got to loose Ty!"

Zeddie turned. "Loose Ty? M'gal, the sun's gone to ye!"

"Pitt has him in the stockade!"

"Good mercy, I ain't lettin' you go there alone. Captain Buckington would call me to the yardarm for neglect."

Emerald climbed into the seat. "Then hurry. We'll bring Minette to the manor first. Oh, I wish Baret were here. He'd know what to do."

"You're doin' fine, m'gal, and you've got his name to shield you."

As Zeddie drove the buggy away, Sempala came to stand near the road, holding his whip in one hand and Minette's hoe in the other. A beaten look showed on his tired face, as though he was resigned to knowing he would never see Minette again.

3

TURNING TRAGEDY
INTO TRIUMPH

Fringed palm trees bit their tall slim trunks up through the warm brown soil of Jamaica and stood like pillars against the August morn.

Some distance ahead the manor loomed into view—a tall, narrow white house with a profusion of red roses crawling up toward Emerald's window. She remembered dreaming as she'd sat alone at that window, arms on its sill, thinking of her father sailing the Caribbean. She had imagined him coming home with treasures enough to sweep her away on his horse and ride her up to the front porch of the Great House, where the family would welcome her. It hadn't been her father but Baret who had put substance to her dreams.

She hurried up the steps to the door. It was unlocked, and she went in, followed by Zeddie carrying Minette. Mr. Pitt had made few changes in the manor, she saw, but his presence could be felt, and she resented him all the more.

Emerald hurried across the room over the woven cane floor mats. The heavy window shades were drawn to keep the heat out, and she stopped at the hall table to light a carrying lamp. There was a steep flight of short steps covered with indigo-dyed hemp, and she began the climb, leading Zeddie with Minette.

"It ain't likely Lady Sophie will send Miss Geneva's physician. More'n likely I won't get past the front door. Maybe I should ride to Murdock's plantation. That old indentured midwife he has can come help."

"I want a physician."

The upper hall was quite narrow. She walked past the small gallery that her father had built, remembering the first time Baret had come to Foxemoore and how she thought he had come to see her father about family debts. Baret had crossed the room below and stood just beneath the crow's nest gallery to study the wall-length tapestry in the same manner in which she had seen her father do so often, moodily meditating. She saw that the tapestry, depicting the battle of the Spanish Armada of 1588, was gone. It had been her father's favorite. Fire ships were floating toward the galleons, culverain were exploding, and the English and Spanish swordsmen were boarding ships as hundreds of seamen were falling overboard.

Had Pitt sold it?

Her room waited in musty shadows, airless and hot.

"Put her on the bed, Zeddie, then go up to the house and ask for the physician. By now everyone knows about Baret and me. They won't refuse."

She drew back the hemp shade and opened the window, letting in fresh air and the chatter of parrots. Little had changed in her old room, but it seemed an aeon had passed since she was last here, just after the slave uprising. As she had expected, Pitt had made a shambles of her room in his fruitless search. Her bureau drawers were upside down on the braided oval rug, and her old trunk with its broken latch had been emptied. As if she would sail for England and leave behind anything as precious as a property deed or Rafael's jewels, she thought wearily. Greed made the man blind to his folly.

"Emerald, is it really you?" came Minette's feverish whisper. "Am I dreaming? You look like an angel . . ."

Emerald went to the bed and sat on its edge, taking her hand, aware of the blisters and calluses, broken nails and scratches. These were the hands of a field slave.

"It's me," she said gently. "I've sent Zeddie up to the house for the physician. You're going to get better soon. Are you thirsty? I'll go to the kitchen. Pitt must eat sumptuously," she said a little bitterly. "I'll see if I can find something." She stood, hesitating as she looked at the filthy tunic. She had to get Minette bathed and into clean clothing at once.

"I can't eat . . . water, please—" She raised herself to an elbow, anguish written on her heart-shaped face. "Pitt has Ty in the stockade again. We almost escaped, Ty and me. Then he found us with the hounds—" Tears spilling from her amber eyes as her memory reviewed their nightmarish capture spoke far more clearly than words.

Emerald gripped the worn bedpost. "I'll take care of Ty as soon as the physician arrives."

Minette stared at her through feverish eyes. "You? But how?"

Emerald managed a smile. "I've so much to tell you, but it must wait. Only—oh, Minette, I'm going to marry Baret Buckington!"

Minette blinked dizzily as though trying to fathom what was happening. "Marry—" she repeated. Her voice faded, then her eyes widened, and a weak smile came to her lips. "Vapors! No wonder you look so beautiful—"

"You're going to look just the same before this is all over," Emerald assured her. "Horrors, that tunic is filthy. I've got to get you cleaned up. Oh, why didn't I think to tell Zeddie to bring Jitana to help me?"

"Married to Captain Foxworth," murmured Minette, with a far-off look in her eyes. The news appeared to send a sudden surge of strength rushing through her veins, for she managed to sit up. "Why, you'll have as much to say at Foxemoore as Lady Sophie and Miss Geneva."

Emerald's eyes gleamed. "Yes, I will, won't I? If Baret backs me up."

"He will. He wouldn't have said he'd marry you if he didn't want to stand with you."

"We'll talk later. I've a hundred plans! But now—" She hurried downstairs into the back cook room.

The smell of stale pig fat clung to everything, and she grimaced when a huge cockroach darted across the table. Pitt had turned Jonah's spotless kitchen into a slop house!

Gingerly she searched the floor cabinet for food, but it was too much to expect of Pitt to keep his food in order. A loaf of brown bread sat out on the round butcher table, the honeycomb had left a sticky mess, and there were ants. She supposed he merely flicked them aside when he ate. Nothing seemed to bother him. And he fancied that he could become a great planter and host the governor. The thought brought a laugh to an otherwise sober moment.

Continuing her search, she located overripe mangoes, bananas, and soft crab apples, all clouded by fruit gnats. In tropical weather, food spoiled quickly. The screen door had been left

32

unlocked, and outside on the porch a slab of smoked pig hung on a rope from the roof. Flies droned sleepily, content with abundant feasting as they settled over it. Emerald's thought of carving a slice for a sandwich surrendered to loathing. If the choice was between flies or ants, she'd take a few ants with the honey.

At least there was a covered barrel of clean water, which had recently been filled. There would be more than enough for Minette's bath before Zeddie needed to refill it. She remembered Ty in the stockade and hastened to fill a small jug to temporarily quench Minette's thirst and wash her face. As soon as Zeddie came back, she would take the buggy and confront Pitt.

Cautious footsteps sounded, and she stopped. Zeddie couldn't have returned this soon. Still carrying the water jug, she left the cook room for the front hall. The door was open, and a familiar African slave stood there, a dignified old warrior with the eyes of an ancient elephant and a weaving of gray at his temples. His tan shirt was torn and damp with sweat.

A smile appeared on Emerald's face, and relief swept over her. It was Ngozi. How long ago it seemed that she had hidden him under her bed on the night of the uprising, when Pitt and other armed planters had ridden up with muskets. Twenty slaves who instigated the rebellion had been hanged the next morning, a memory that even now brought a sick feeling to her heart. But the Lord had helped her save Ngozi, and he had not forgotten her kindness.

Before she had left Foxemoore to meet Jamie Bradford, expecting to sail with him to the American colonies, Ngozi had come quietly to the manor and left her a gift. It was still among her treasured keepsakes, an item that reminded her of a spiritual victory. He had left a blue head scarf with his name written on it with dye. The name *Ngozi* meant "Blessing," and on the cloth was an African lion decorated with beads and woven pieces of dyed hemp.

"Ngozi," she said.

His broad face, glistening with sweat, softened. "Yes, Miss Emerald, it's Ngozi. We come to help you. Me and Yolanda."

Out from the shadows came the old woman who had once cared for Great-uncle Mathias in his illness. Yolanda had come to faith in Christ through Uncle Mathias. Her head was covered with a sun-faded yellow bandana, and she carried a battered

33

woven basket that Emerald was acquainted with from the past. She knew it contained African cures for sickness, dried herbs and salves made from bark and other secret ingredients.

She smiled wearily at Emerald. "You bring me to the child, Miss Emerald. I'll take care of her. You'll get yourself all mussed up in that pert gown. Ain't nothing I wouldn't do for you nor little Minette. None of us forgot what you and Mr. Mathias did for us. The singing school was a lighthouse in a dark place. We still mourning 'cause it got burned down. Every Sunday some of us visits the grave site of Mr. Mathias and Jonah too, and we pray the singing school will live again." Her eyes gleamed expectantly. "Now that you be home, maybe the Lord answered our prayers. All of us know how you'll be moving up to the Great House."

She took the water jug from Emerald and started for the steps, and Ngozi went out back to carry water up to the bedroom for Minette's bath.

Emerald turned to Zeddie, "I've a call to make."

"Stab me, lass, you can't go prancin' out to the stockade alone in that fancy buggy. You'll be needing me to train my pistols on old Pitt."

"There will be none of that," she assured him with new confidence, and her eyes sparkled. "Don't you see? Pitt, my dear Zeddie, is now under my authority."

"Bless me, but I want to see how the buzzard takes it."

"He won't go easily, I assure you. But do stay here, Zeddie. I want you to be with Minette until I arrive. I'm not going alone to free Ty—I'm taking Ngozi." She smiled, for secret plans were already blooming in her mind. She knew just what she wanted to do.

"All right," he grumbled. "But I'd feel a mite easier if you'd take one of my duelin' pistols, just in case."

She accepted the pistol, more to soothe Zeddie than because she thought she needed it, placed it in a shawl, and wrapped it up to take with her.

Ngozi was hauling water to refill the barrels when Emerald appeared on the back porch.

"Ngozi, can you handle a horse?"

His formidable face cracked with a smile. "Yes, Miss Emerald. I can handle most anything."

34

"I'm counting on that. I want you drive my buggy. I need an escort, and Zeddie needs to run errands for Dr. Milner."

He wiped his big hands on his dirty shirt. "You wanting to go now? Where to, Miss?"

Emerald smiled. "The stockade. To confront Mr. Pitt."

Down the long avenue between golden walls of cane standing eight feet high, Ngozi drove the buggy with ease. They passed slaves, who turned their heads to stare at him, their shock evident. He sat straight, his eyes never straying from the red-brown road.

Emerald had in her lap the shawl with Zeddie's big pistol wrapped inside. She took it out now and saw Ngozi turn his head sharply.

She looked at him. "Zeddie insisted I bring it. Do you know how to use it?"

"Yes, Miss. But if'n that thing was found on me, I'd be whipped or hung for the crows for sure."

She smiled triumphantly. "Not if I give the order."

He gaped at her, taking his attention from the road. "I'm forgetting you're the new mistress of Foxemoore."

"Not quite yet, and I won't own it all, but the viscount, my husband-to-be, will own a bit more than Lord Felix and Miss Geneva. I suppose I'll own as much as Lady Sophie, maybe more," she breathed, awed again by her own words. And for a moment the dignified demeanor left her as she contemplated the position her heavenly Father had placed upon her.

Ngozi smiled, and sweat sparkled like tiny diamonds on his black face. "Now I know the true God in heaven listens to His children."

They came out upon the green plateau and drove toward the stockade and boiling house. As usual, the work yard was noisy with the sound of boiling kettles. The same heavy smell of molasses filled the afternoon breeze. Ngozi stopped the buggy in the dirt beside some wooden frame buildings. Mr. Pitt's office hut was ahead. The stockade was a hundred yards to the left.

Emerald climbed down from the seat, and Ngozi followed like a protective shadow in the blazing sun. Again, slaves turned to look but dared not cease their work. Tension hovered in the air.

"He's seen you, Miss," whispered Ngozi, his eyes glittering.

Emerald stopped and waited, her heart beating faster, her eyes riveted ahead.

Mr. Pitt emerged from the cane field astride his gray gelding and rode toward them, the dust rising beneath its hoofs. A minute later he stopped his horse and swung down, tossing the reins to the African who followed him everywhere. The moment was not lost on Emerald. She saw the exchange of glances between the "boss men," who served Pitt, and Ngozi. They knew they might soon be losing their positions. They carried whips, but they now carefully held them behind their backs.

The men serving Mr. Pitt as both bodyguard and captains of slave crews looked uneasily at Emerald. Who was this young woman in lime green silk and pretty hat who came to change things? Oh, yes, they had seen her about Foxemoore from the time Sir Karlton brought her as a little girl from Tortuga. But they didn't know this woman. They had only heard how she and the pirate-rascal viscount Baret Buckington would end up owning as much of the sugar as Lord Felix himself. Their furtive eyes pulled away from Ngozi's even stare to look at the overseer, Mr. Pitt. The showdown was here, and they weren't at all sure who would win.

Emerald stood looking at Mr. Pitt, trying to quiet her heart by reminding herself of who she was. She no longer needed to fear his leering suggestions. But did Pitt know this yet? He was nasty enough to pretend he didn't until receiving word from Lady Sophie that he was to hearken to Miss Emerald's wishes.

Mr. Pitt removed his wide panama hat, soiled with dust. His grizzled red hair brushed the wide shoulders of his canvas shirt. He bowed his head, hat at heart.

"Welcome to Foxemoore, Lady Harwick—or should I say Lady Buckington, eh?" He offered a chuckle, as though they shared a secret, but his hoarse voice only rasped an irritating noise.

"I've come for my cousin Ty," she stated tonelessly.

"Sure, Miss Harwick. I've been expecting you," he said with a smile. "I've him all ready for you." He turned. "Hank! Bring the lad!"

Emerald didn't know what to expect. She didn't trust him, but at the same time Pitt was the sort who could fawn and grovel once he knew he couldn't bully. Naturally, he'd want to please her now that she could make him feel the sting of his own whip.

36

She looked toward the stockade, expecting Ty to come from that direction in shackles or at least with a rope tied about him. To her surprise he was escorted from the overseer's hut, walking free.

Ty's French-African good looks had developed in the months he'd been hiding in the Blue Mountains, and he looked strong and lean as a panther. His buccaneer shirt and tight black trousers appeared to be freshly laundered.

"See, I was expecting you, Miss Harwick. There isn't a lash on his fair body anywheres. Nay, not a hair singed, seeing as how he's your cousin and all, and you soon to be the pretty bride of the viscount."

She ignored Pitt, remembering too well his cruelty in the past and what he had done to Minette, as well as the lie he'd told about her to the magistrate at Brideswell.

Emerald walked to meet Ty and put her arms around him while the slaves watched, alert.

"Ty! You're all right?"

He smiled, his white teeth flashing against his tanned skin. "I am now. All it takes is a cousin marrying a Buckington. Suddenly Ty the runaway slave is Tyrone Levasseur." He threw back his dark head and laughed, then turned to the overseer.

"Ty—" began Emerald. But she didn't need to come between them. Ty held up both hands and stepped back from Pitt, but his sarcastic smile was as sharp as any rapier.

"Would I hurt Gentleman Pitt? No, I ain't going to hurt him none. But maybe he's got a branding coming before I set sail."

Pitt's prominent pale eyes glared. "Remember one thing, Ty, Miss Emerald may be about to marry Buckington, but you're still a runaway slave till the family says you're a free man."

"You can be sure the decree will come," said Emerald. She looked quickly at Ty and saw that his smirk continued. "Ty, wait for me in the buggy, will you, please?"

"Don't worry, Emerald. I'm not giving anybody an excuse to arrest me. Not yet. But there's something I must see to before I meet you and Minette at the house. I'm going into Port Royal. I'll be back tonight."

There was a warning in Ty's voice directed toward Pitt. Then he looked at the Africans hovering uneasily in the background, and he walked toward them.

"Ty!" Emerald called again.

He looked the Africans up and down, then spat in the dust, whirled on his polished calf-length boots, and strode toward the buggy. "White trash."

They looked at him sulkily, then their eyes lowered.

Mr. Pitt glared after him angrily, but there was fear in his taut features too. "That young lad is going to end up in worse trouble than any runaway if you don't talk sense into him. He's planning to join a pirate ship."

Ty's plans to become a buccaneer were not new to Emerald. Even before the branding incident at the town pillory, her cousin had spoken of escaping to Tortuga to join his French kin, the Levasseurs. Ty had always been attracted to the lifestyle of Rafael and, unlike Emerald, had been friendly with him over the years. She wouldn't tell that to Pitt, however.

"You best worry about yourself right now," she said quietly. "You've many sins to answer for. What you've done to me doesn't matter now, but I won't easily forgive you for the harm you've done Minette."

"Harm? I haven't touched the wench—" He stopped, catching himself. "She's worked in the boiling house. It could have been worse. I kept Sempala from getting to her. It's me you got to thank for that. If it wasn't for me, the girl would be his woman now and pregnant."

Ngozi took a step forward, but Emerald held out her arm, holding him back.

Her eyes met Pitt's evenly. "I'll thank you for nothing. Your cruel and evil ways have been a curse on Foxemoore. I'm removing you as overseer. You can take your things out of the hut and move in with Jonnie Franks in the indentured servant area. And—" her eyes narrowed "—if you set foot again inside my father's manor, I'll have you sent to the stockade."

His mouth dropped open, and he stared at her. Evidently he hadn't thought she would dare go so far.

"What did you do with my father's tapestry of the Spanish Armada? If you sold it, you'll receive no wages until its value is restored."

"W-what tapestry?" he stammered, wiping the back of his arm across his sweating face.

"You know very well which tapestry. It was my father's favorite, and I want it back."

"Of them ships? His lordship Felix sent a servant for it. Said he had a hankering for it above his chamber desk. If you don't believe me, you'll see it when you get there. I got no cause for a tapestry."

Felix! Why would he *want it?* she wondered.

"Now, Miss Emerald, you'd not be serious about taking the overseership away from me, now would you? I've always done my work well enough, and Lady Sophie has no complaints!"

"If she has no complaints, it's because she pays scant attention to life on Foxemoore outside her sheltered world. Yes, Mr. Pitt, I am removing you as of this moment."

"You can't!"

"I can, and I will."

"I'll go to Lady Sophie or Lord Felix!"

"You may, of course, but it will be Baret Buckington who will decide in the end."

"Baret Buckington!"

"Yes, Earl Nigel's grandson. The earl has awarded him a large portion of Foxemoore, and he will decide how things are run here."

"You won't get by with this," he snarled.

"You make a threat against Miss Emerald?" came Ngozi's cold voice.

Pitt shot him a bitter look, and Emerald gestured for Ngozi's silence.

"My servitude here on Foxemoore is about over anyway," Pitt gritted. "I'll be having my own plantation. You'll change your tune when I'm a respectable gent."

Emerald smiled. "Until that far-off day, Mr. Pitt, you can take Ngozi's place in the boiling house."

His mouth hung open. "Take—"

"Yes, that's right. Your new job is in the boiling house until your servitude on Foxemoore is over." As Pitt stared at her, mottled with rage, she turned gracefully to Ngozi and saw the laughter in his otherwise sober face. "Ngozi? Will you kindly bring Mr. Pitt to his new position?"

"Now, wait a minute—"

"There'll be no arguing, Mr. Pitt. If you wish to contest, you can speak to Baret Buckington when he arrives in a few days." She turned her back to leave.

But Pitt's self-control left like an erupting volcano. His eyes flared wildly, and his sweating face turned red. He cursed her. Then his whip leaped out to wrap like a biting viper about her arm, jerking her backward into the dirt.

"You'll not treat me like this, you high and mighty wench—"

Ngozi seemed as stunned by the surprising action as Emerald. But in the seconds that he stood as though dazed, the African slaves who had once been Pitt's bodyguard sprang at him and wrested the whip from his hand. Muscular arms coiled firmly about him, and in a moment he was powerless, his wrists pinioned behind him in a leather thong.

"Shall we tie him up in the stockade, Miss Emerald?"

Stunned, Emerald held her hand to her torn sleeve where a trickle of blood showed from the stinging lash.

Ngozi stooped to help her to her feet, then started toward Pitt with murderous rage in his eyes.

"No, Ngozi! Enough! All of you!"

They stopped. Dead silence encircled them as the sun beat down on their heads.

Pitt tore his eyes away from hers, breathing heavily.

"You'll take your position in the boiling house," she repeated with a calmness that she didn't feel. "Ngozi, you're to take Mr. Pitt's place as overseer."

"Miss Emerald . . ." he breathed.

She turned to walk away again, pausing briefly to look at the bitter face of Pitt and at the slaves who held him bound. Then she said to Ngozi, "You'd best stay and see that things are all in order. I'll drive the buggy back. Report to me this evening on how things are going, will you?"

Ngozi, flabbergasted, nevertheless managed to keep his dignity. "Yes, Miss."

Emerald walked across the dirt toward the buggy, refusing to look at the slaves who were craning their necks to stare first in her direction, then in Mr. Pitt's.

Her arm stung. Already she heard the buzzing flies trying to land on the wound, but she walked straight ahead to the driver's side of the buggy, climbed up to the seat, and, taking the reins, gave them a snap. She turned the mare toward the manor house. She blinked hard against the perspiration that ran into her eyes, but she kept her show of dignity until away from the work yard.

While driving down the avenue between the cane, feeling weak from the ordeal, she slowed the mare, then brought her to the side to rest a minute. If Baret found out what Pitt had done to her with the whip, she was sure he would deal with him too harshly. She decided to keep the matter from him. The shame Pitt was now feeling, before the slaves he had treated so inhumanely, was punishment enough for the likes of him. His loss of position would sting more than any whip to his back. Taking orders from the slaves he had once abused would be a bitter pill to swallow. She must make certain to order Ngozi not to harm him. Now that Pitt was just another worker, he was prey to the enemies he had made. Pitt had enjoyed making the slaves cringe and beg for his mercies, and more than one of them would enjoy silencing him permanently.

A few minutes later, she slapped the reins and drove on toward the manor house.

4

RECEIVED INTO
THE GREAT HOUSE

The sun dipped toward the horizon over acres of cane fields while the faint promise of an evening breeze rippled musically among the stalks. The otherwise breathless late afternoon settled in lazily. Emerald's heart seemed to beat painfully slow. If this return to Foxemoore to declare herself a great lady by meting out justice gracefully was her moment of triumph, it didn't feel like it.

She sat wearily in the buggy, musing over what to do next. The dust lifted beneath the mare's hooves like a woman's face powder, then settled again. A waft of air smelling of hot ripe earth, burned molasses, and the Caribbean Sea stirred together and tugged at Emerald's hat. Her perspiring skin cooled, and she drove on, her emotions mollified by all the familiar things on Foxemoore in the advancing twilight.

She drove toward the cutoff that turned sharply toward the manor house. She passed a fence post where a black crow perched and then cawed as it flew eastward. She heard horse's hooves from the palm-lined avenue of the Great House. Zeddie was riding toward her.

"Lady Sophie is askin' to see you—to come at once."

She glanced up the wide avenue to the planter's house, a mansion of white with a red tile roof, looking stately and undisturbed in the twilight. This response from her father's aunt was surprising. Emerald had not wanted to enter the house until Baret arrived and she came as his betrothed. Why was Lady Sophie asking for her now? Did a cold upbraiding await?

"Did you explain about Minette? And how I preferred to stay in the manor house and look after her?"

"Jitana told her, m'gal. But what her response was, I'm not knowing. I was kept standing on the porch. But I saw Lady Sophie in the drawing room doorway. And sink me sails, I thought she might turn the hounds on me."

Emerald's fingers tightened on the leather reins. She needed the doctor for Minette, and there was no choice except to face the lions, even if it was an old lion with silver hair and sedate black sateen dress. She'd come close to being devoured before, and entering the den again was a risk she must endure. The Lord would want her to remain gracious and respectful to Lady Sophie, a woman in her seventies. And if the queen lion had made up her mind to devour her, there was little to do but commit her way to the Lord and move forward, trusting in His provision. He had guarded her this far; surely He would not abandon her now.

She drove the mare toward the main avenue. Zeddie turned his horse and rode ahead, leading the way as though Emerald were visiting royalty. His dusty black hat bounced on his golden periwig.

The vast estate of Foxemoore had not changed in the years since Emerald had been brought here from Tortuga. The walled boundaries traversed miles along the outer road, fringed with tall palms.

The English planters on the colonial Sugar Islands of Jamaica, Barbados, and Antigua sought to build their great houses on knolls facing windward. Emerald now had a clear view of the white-pillared mansion with its red tile roof and of Port Royal Bay. Because of the coral reefs, the water sometimes appeared different shades of blue, green, amber, and even red, and on her left was a sweeping view of the green cane fields as far as her eye could see.

She drove the buggy in front of the wide front porch, and a barefoot slave emerged from the dark shadows near the side of the house to help her down.

Zeddie dismounted and took possession of the buggy, and the slave led the guest horse to its place beneath the shade of a large pepper tree.

Emerald drew in a breath of courage and looked up at the forbidding house. Its door was solid oak, a door that had been firmly shut against her from the time she'd been brought from Tortuga as a small child. Now, as the earl's grandson's future betrothed, she walked across the yard, past its heated shadows and fragrant shrubs, and up the wide front steps.

43

Even before she could pull the bell cord and announce her arrival, Jitana opened the door wide. The older African woman, who was head housekeeper, smiled.

"Evening, Miss Emerald," she whispered, glancing cautiously over her shoulder toward the drawing room on the left. "I cain't do a thing with Lady Sophie! She's sprouting thistles over you and his lordship's betrothal."

"I'm certain of that, Jitana. Where is she now?"

The cool dim hall was empty, the discreet house quiet. Most of the family would be napping in their rooms before the cooler winds arose and supper was served. From the back of the house near the cook room, she could hear the muffled voices of servants readying the crystal glasses and chinaware for the dining room table.

Emerald remembered the times she had visited Lavender and had to come and go by the servant's route through the kitchen to her cousin's grand bedroom, as required by Lady Sophie. Lavender was her darling who could do no wrong, and she had wanted Baret to marry Lavender. Yes, Emerald could understand why Lady Sophie Harwick was "sprouting thistles."

The drawing room was on the left side of the entrance hall, and its tall double doors stood open to receive the cooler breezes from the Caribbean.

"I'll tell her you's here."

"There's no need," came Lady Sophie's crisp voice. "I saw the buggy arrive from the window. Come in, Emerald. I've been expecting you."

Emerald turned toward an elegant woman in her seventies. She wore her immaculate white hair in a heavy coil at the back of her neck, and her bristling pale eyes were emphasized by her dark satin dress with stiff white lace collar at the throat and wrists. The appearance of this elegant but distant woman had always overwhelmed Emerald, perhaps because Sophie had never spoken more than a few sentences to her at one time in all the years she had grown up on Foxemoore. And yet, here she was now, facing Aunt Sophie not as an illegitimate waif from the pirate stronghold of Tortuga but as the soon-to-be betrothed of a prized nephew.

The frosty gray eyes in a porcelain white face gave no hint of what was on Sophie's mind, since the woman's demeanor was

44

normally crisp. As always, Emerald held the notion that she should curtsy, as if Sophie were royalty. There had been a time when she had deeply wanted recognition from Lady Sophie, so badly that she used to dream of the elegant woman smiling at her the way she had seen her smile proudly at Lavender. There remained a deep unmet need in Emerald's heart. It was a quest for love, of acceptance, a sense of worth that only the Lord could ultimately satisfy.

The drawing room offered the finest of gold drapes, matching velvet settees, ottomans, and a large olive green divan with gold tassels. The hardwood floor sounded beneath her slippers, but her footsteps softened when she stepped onto the woven rug, thick and plush and brought from the Main.

Lady Sophie's skirt rustled stiffly as she walked to the front windows facing the carriageway, where red hibiscus bloomed below the windows.

Emerald readied herself for a scathing denunciation, but when Lady Sophie turned to confront her, her frosty demeanor had melted into an expression of tense apprehension. Emerald was bewildered. She could only respond by watching her great-aunt in silence.

Sophie cast a glance toward the closed doors as if to make certain they were alone. "We must speak before he arrives."

"Before who arrives?"

Her eyes swerved back, apprehension turning to loathing. "Felix, of course. He's not here now, but he'll soon be. I want you to speak to Geneva before he returns. She's awake now, and waiting, but before I bring you upstairs, I want to make certain of your help."

Emerald was totally unprepared for this. Lady Sophie was reaching out to *her* for emotional support?

"You've always been strong, Emerald. I suppose hardship is a virtue. It can develop character, the will to survive the worst of things."

Emerald scanned her. "Yes, when there is hope," she agreed, wondering what she could possibly have in mind. "Without hope," she continued, thinking of her past situation, "there is little incentive to keep on struggling for survival. But why, Madam, do you bring this up now? I've come because of Minette—my cousin. She's quite sick. I'm sorry I've disturbed you, but it's

45

urgent. If Cousin Geneva's physician could be spared a short time to come to the manor house, I wouldn't need much of his time and perhaps only a morsel of quinine."

"If you think he can be trusted, yes, by all means."

For a moment Emerald's mind stumbled over the suggestion gleaned from her startling words. "If . . . he can be trusted."

The once balmy refuge of the drawing room became restrictive, and it seemed Emerald no longer saw birds with pale yellow and red plumes but heard the distant cackle of a crow. She walked toward Lady Sophie, whose face was now in shadow.

She stared at the woman, trying to fathom the extent of the casual, yet blunt, warning, as if Sophie were seeking confirmation of her own uncertainties. By asking Emerald here, she appeared to be actually seeking to gain an ally within the family structure rather than making Emerald feel she was an inappropriate choice for Baret.

"If Geneva's doctor can be trusted?" repeated Emerald in a low voice. "Why shouldn't he be?"

"He's a Spaniard." Her eyes snapped. "What else needs to be said?"

Perhaps a great deal, but Lady Sophie was not inclined to explain now. She moved toward the doorway with a rustle. "Come along. Geneva's asked to see you."

A Spaniard. So many questions converged on Emerald's mind at one time, but it was the hacienda at Spanish Town and what Baret had told her about Lord Felix and his daughter, Carlotta, that commanded her attention. Until then, she had never guessed that Carlotta *was* Felix's daughter or that he had ever lived in Cartagena.

She thought back to her meeting with Geneva at the town house. Had Geneva suspected her husband even then? But suspected him of what?

Emerald recalled the conversation she had overheard between Geneva and Lady Sophie the night before Geneva's wedding to Lord Felix, a conversation about how his first wife in London had died prematurely and suggesting that Felix may have hastened her death. A chill ran through Emerald.

She followed Sophie into Geneva's large bedchamber, and her senses were struck by its loveliness, the opulence of reddish-brown mahogany, the overflowing yards of cream-colored sateen spilling from the four-poster bed, the windows, the vanity table and bench. A terrace occupied one side, providing a view of amber twilight and lavender blue from distant Port Royal Bay.

Her father's cousin, Geneva Harwick Buckington, sat propped up against lace-trimmed pillows in her bed. Its silk mosquito netting was drawn to one side. Her reddish gold hair, prettily groomed, hung across each shoulder. Her pale face was thin, and there were purplish smudges streaked beneath her silvery eyes. Though apparently in delicate health, Geneva didn't appear any worse than when Emerald had last spoken to her at the town house on Queens Street.

Emerald cast a brief glance about the room. Neither Lord Felix nor the doctor was present. Had Cousin Geneva asked to see her before they returned? *Geneva must suspect them of something,* thought Emerald tensely. Why else would she ask to see her now with such urgency instead of waiting for Baret?

Lady Sophie neared the side of Geneva's bed where there was a settee upholstered with ivory brocade and tiny pink rosebuds.

Geneva lifted a folded sheet of stationery from beside her. "Baret tells me the betrothal will take place in two weeks."

So Baret had sent her a message. That said something about the kind of man he was and that he must hold Geneva's opinion in high regard.

Lady Sophie swished her palmetto fan. "Two weeks is hardly enough time to adequately prepare for a tea, let alone the betrothal of a future earl!"

Emerald felt a sting. The pressure was on her for a postponement, all in the name of adequate preparation. She might have told them Baret had gone so far as to wish to hold the actual marriage ceremony in just two weeks, without a publicly announced engagement, but that would not help the situation now.

"Baret wished to announce the betrothal before sailing with Captain Morgan," Emerald said.

"Henry Morgan." Lady Sophie sighed. "Another error. Baret is beside himself."

"I doubt it matters much what anyone wishes in the matter of the betrothal, except Baret," said Geneva.

"He's a scamp if there ever was one," Sophie agreed, swishing her fan. "Worse than his father, Royce, if you want my opinion."

47

Was it Emerald's imagination or did the mention of Royce Buckington bring a flinch to Geneva?

Emerald was embarrassed by their open disapproval. After the ordeal she'd been through with Mr. Pitt, she didn't care to prolong this.

"I understand it must come as total surprise," she began, striving to keep her voice from fumbling into an apology.

But Geneva's thin face offered a smile. "Not altogether a surprise, if I recall what you told me at the town house. And just what is this French pirate Rafael Levasseur going to do about it? Call Baret out in another duel?"

Emerald was surprised by the keen awareness in the gray eyes so much like her father's.

Lady Sophie groaned at Geneva's words. "Pirates. Oh, the scandal!"

"I don't think, Madam, that Captain Levasseur will dare show his face, seeing that Baret has bested him on several occasions."

"Good mercy, I hope not."

"Anyway," Emerald hastened to add, embarrassed, "what my French cousin may think is of no concern to me or to Baret. Rafael is an odious and bloodthirsty knave."

"Well, we agree on something," said Lady Sophie.

Emerald walked to the foot of the bed and stood between the two sturdy posts, wishing the older women were protectively on her side instead of against her. How she missed not having had an honorable woman for a mother while growing up. She looked from one to the other. It had not been her intention to become involved in controversy without Baret present.

"I had no intention of coming here now," Emerald said. "I didn't want to appear as if I were boldly affronting the family. I don't expect the matter to come to satisfying terms easily. Baret should be here to speak for himself. As soon as he concludes his meeting with Morgan, we expect to see Earl Nigel as well."

"Nigel is still in Port Royal," said Sophie, as though that made a difference.

"I wouldn't want you to think—to think—that—"

Geneva interrupted abruptly. "You needn't apologize to either Sophie or me. If Baret's made up his mind he's in love with you, and I'm certain he has, there's no detouring him now.

And I would remind you, Sophie, Nigel is behind them in this. You know he wishes Lavender to marry Grayford."

"I wouldn't trust Nigel. He has his ambitions where both Baret and little Jette are concerned. He wants them in London at his side, to carry on the earldom. And Emerald, dear girl that she is, is hardly the—"

"And Sophie, this is hardly the time. The reason I wish to speak to Emerald . . ." She looked from Sophie, who had raised her, to Emerald, and her face softened. "Neither Sophie nor I have any intention of making your entry into the family difficult, dear. You'll find life hard enough in London as Baret's wife without the Buckingtons' and Harwicks' opposition. Every woman of title will be anxious to rip your reputation apart, and, believe me, nobility can be wolfish."

Emerald remembered that Baret had told her much the same thing about the biting tongues of London's blooded nobility.

"We haven't asked you here to discuss pirates or your betrothal. All that must wait."

Lady Sophie sighed painfully and lowered her palmetto fan into her lap as if to surrender.

"Geneva is right. We'll all need to get along, and we do need you now. At least you have strength, which Lavender pitiably lacks. And I don't think having you in the family will rival the catastrophe of having Felix."

It was no compliment to Emerald, nor meant to be. Lady Sophie was known for the honesty of her pungent tongue, but Emerald believed that the slightest movement by the woman must be deemed a small victory. Until now, she'd been treated little better than Minette.

Cousin Geneva closed her eyes wearily and leaned her head back into the pillows. "Are we back to Felix again?"

"I'm afraid we will always be back to Felix."

Yet, Geneva showed no suspicion over Felix. *Then I must have been wrong about her response at the town house,* thought Emerald. *At that time I was so sure Geneva suspected Felix of ulterior motives.*

"I came about Minette. She's sick with fever. Is it too much to ask that your physician come and treat her?"

"It would be the kind thing to do, especially if you expect to move into the house with her."

49

Lady Sophie dropped her palmetto fan. "I won't have a half-breed living here like family!"

Emerald turned to face her, but Geneva headed them off by sitting up. "None of that now. We won't discuss who her mother was, Sophie!"

As Sophie's face went rigid, Geneva turned to Emerald. "I'll ask the doctor to visit the manor house as soon as he and Felix return from Spanish Town. They should arrive within the hour with Carlotta."

So Geneva knew about the secret daughter from Felix's first marriage to the daughter of a Spanish don in Cartagena. Perhaps after the ugly incident at the hacienda between Baret and Sir Jasper, Felix had decided he could no longer keep the matter hidden, especially now that Emerald knew so much and would marry Baret. Felix must think that he needed to deal with her as well, if he expected to carry on at Foxemoore as though the incident of her father never happened. Of course, Felix didn't know that the assassin he'd hired to dispose of his own nephew had betrayed his involvement before he died. And as far as Felix knew, Sir Karlton was dead.

"Spaniards," protested Lady Sophie. "Wealthy planters or not, the family of Don Miguel Vasquez are loyal to Madrid. Bringing Carlotta here can bring no blessing to Foxemoore, and that goes for Minette."

"Carlotta won't be here long—only a few weeks until we can sail."

Sail? Emerald looked at her, but Lady Sophie had retrieved her fan and was waving it energetically.

"Felix may dabble all he wants in the medical expertise of Porto Bello, but the very idea of going there is positively scandalous!"

"Sophie, dear, please don't be so dramatic. There's nothing at all inappropriate with my visiting the Spanish estate of Carlotta's future in-law, especially since he's related to Dr. Vasquez."

"Rubbish. I've only to look at you to see your condition has worsened since Felix brought the man to see you. Since when can we trust a Spaniard loyal to King Philip of Spain?"

"Since Dr. Ricardo Vasquez received acclaim for his knowledge in London," said Geneva wearily.

Emerald's surprise could not be concealed. Carlotta's relative was Geneva's physician? She wondered when and how he had arrived. She didn't recall seeing a doctor at the hacienda, but then she had not been given freedom to move about. Even Carlotta's presence there had come as a surprise the night Baret shot Sir Jasper in their duel.

Geneva must have read her expression, for she offered an explanation. "It was fortunate for me that Ricardo came to Spanish Town when he did. He's confident he can help me regain my health at the estate in Porto Bello. I'll accompany Carlotta there with the doctor and Felix."

Covering the thoughts that rampaged through her mind, Emerald said nothing for a moment, but Lady Sophie spoke up indignantly. "Carlotta ran away, and her marriage was postponed. Some pirate helped her to reach Port Royal. She's willful, I understand, and determined to marry Sir Jasper."

Emerald knew, of course, who that pirate was who had helped Carlotta avoid the wedding arranged between the two wealthy families of Spain. Baret had taken her fiancé, Don Miguel, from a Spanish galleon voyaging to the island of Margarita. Evidently no one knew this as yet except herself and Carlotta. And there was also the question of just what Baret had done with Miguel, his prisoner. Emerald assumed that the dashing Spanish soldier was still cooling his heels somewhere under Baret's decree, perhaps on one of the islets or even on the *Regale*.

Emerald tried to look innocent, but she felt a prick of guilt under the direct gaze of the two other women.

"You're being too cautious, Sophie," said Geneva. "Carlotta is a fine girl, just high-spirited."

"Am I being too cautious? Then why didn't Felix tell you about her *before* your marriage? Who knew he had dealings on the Main? Or that he'd fathered a child by the daughter of a don?"

"We're past that," Geneva said, but whether that was true was questionable, Emerald thought. "I confess surprise, yet not disillusionment. Carlotta can be a rewarding young girl in many ways. I don't mind being a stepmother. She needs whatever emotional support I can give her. And my going is not altogether unselfish, since Ricardo can best treat me at the family hacienda. Naturally, I'd prefer to seek a cure in England, but the war has put a pretty end to that."

51

"A good turn of fortune for Felix, I would say."

"Nonsense. Ricardo was willing to voyage with us to London to Buckington House. How can you say they're luring me away? He's being generous in asking us to visit the hacienda."

"Generous!"

"I'm convinced I should go, and it will only be for a few months. I'll have time with Carlotta before her marriage to Miguel and be treated by Ricardo at the same time. But lest you swoon, dear Sophie, I promise not to make final decision on the matter until I hear what Nigel may say. If you're so adamant that mischief awaits me, you can always come with me."

"To Porto Bello?" She whisked her fan. "The idea is horrendous. And certainly no less so for you. The war with Holland is just the beginning. You heard Governor Modyford. We'll be fighting Spain soon. You'll be an English woman trapped on the Main."

"Don't be silly. I'm going in excellent company, and the Vasquez family is highly esteemed by the Spanish governor there."

"You make light of this, Geneva, but I don't see it so. I'm not forgetting what happened in London to Felix's first—"

"That will be enough, Aunt Sophie."

In the strained silence that followed, Emerald felt her heart pounding. *Porto Bello?* It was the Vasquez family that Baret suspected of holding his father there, Viscount Royce Buckington!

Geneva went on in a casual tone as if trying to convince herself of the appropriateness of her decision as well as to convince Lady Sophie, who sat looking pale and distraught. Visiting the relatives of one's husband was not unheard of, and Carlotta *was* young and dreadfully unhappy about her arranged marriage to Miguel. Her stepdaughter needed sympathetic support from an outsider.

Observing her, Emerald concluded that Geneva didn't know that Royce Buckington had been sold to Miguel's father. Royce's safety depended upon Felix's believing him to be dead.

She would explain all this to Geneva, she thought desperately, but first she must tell Baret that Felix was planning to bring Geneva to Porto Bello. Geneva would be more likely to believe Baret than herself. Why did Felix want Geneva to visit the hacienda with Carlotta? And how much did Dr. Ricardo Vasquez know about Baret's father?

Emerald held tightly to the bedpost, her mind unsettled. So much was happening, and none of it had been anticipated. Remembering that Lady Sophie had suggested earlier that Geneva wanted to speak with her, she wondered what she had intended to discuss, if not the betrothal.

"What do I have to do with all this?" she found herself asking, uncertainty in her voice.

Both Geneva and Sophie turned to look at her, but before Geneva could answer, Zunsia, her personal maid, stirred from her unobtrusive position across the chamber and walked to the terrace railing.

"They's here," she called. "Lord Felix, Dr. Vasquez, and that Carlotta."

Emerald crossed the room to where Zunsia stood. A sleek carriage was parked below, and two men in black broadcloth and white ruffled shirts stood waiting while the driver assisted down a girl wearing a red ruffled dress. Emerald recognized the Spanish beauty she had last seen aboard Baret's ship off the coast of Cumana. The tall man was Lord Felix Buckington, and the lean swarthy-faced Spaniard with the short pointed beard had to be Dr. Ricardo Vasquez, uncle of Don Miguel—Baret's prisoner. Suppose he found out?

Emerald's emotions dipped and swayed as precariously as a ship on the storm-tossed Caribbean.

Trouble, she thought, awaited them all.

5

UNEXPECTED NEWS

Emerald stood her ground. Soon she would be living in this house. To turn now and flee like a scolded rabbit would disappoint Baret as well as convince Lord Felix that she could be intimidated and controlled by stronger personalities in the family. She hadn't wanted this confrontation now. It would have been far wiser to be brought into the domain of Baret's disapproving family through his initiative rather than her own.

But I've walked into a trap, and now there's little I can do but see it through, she thought, quaking in her shoes. All because of Mr. Pitt and his treatment of Minette! *If he hadn't bullied her, she wouldn't be sick and in need of a doctor. And I wouldn't be caught in the complexity of Cousin Geneva voyaging with Lord Felix to Porto Bello.*

What were Felix and Dr. Ricardo Vasquez up to? Was Geneva at risk, or was it little Jette? But Earl Nigel would never permit Jette to voyage to Porto Bello with Geneva and Felix, would he? Certainly Baret wouldn't! But could it be stopped in time? Felix might wait until after Baret sailed with Morgan, in which case, who was strong enough to thwart Felix? Most anything could be done in the secret of midnight while Earl Nigel and Sir Cecil Chaderton slept.

Her tensions rambled on, growing as strong as the roses climbing the trellis. If Felix guessed that she knew about his dark involvements at Porto Bello with Baret's father, what might his reaction be? He had already tried to have assassins eliminate Baret and her father. What of Geneva? Or herself? If she tried to explain all this to Geneva, would Geneva believe her or think her as imaginative as she did Lady Sophie?

A moment later she heard low voices speaking in Castilian as they came down the hall toward the chamber. Emerald glanced at Geneva to see her response to the voices, but she was looking expectantly toward the door. That she *wanted* to go to Porto Bello was surprising to Emerald. It might be impossible to convince her of the risk.

Lady Sophie had left before Felix entered the house, but Emerald was waiting near Zunsia on the other side of the room when Felix came in with Carlotta and Don Miguel's uncle, Dr. Ricardo Vasquez.

Lord Felix walked to the side of his wife's bed and, leaning down, kissed her forehead. He took her hand. "Hello, darling. Feeling any stronger?"

Emerald concealed a shudder and glanced toward Carlotta to see her response to her stepmother, but the raven-haired young woman showed nothing. When she noticed Emerald, however, her dark eyes flashed with recognition. There was no hint of apology in that look for the lies she had told Baret about a relationship between Emerald and Sir Jasper. Those lies had nearly severed her from Baret. Only later, when he had questioned Carlotta's maid about Emerald's stay at the hacienda, did the truth of her innocence come out. Carlotta had finally admitted the deception, but until then, Emerald's reputation had been greatly tarnished. The ruby pendant at her throat symbolized what Baret now thought of her.

Carlotta lifted a shoulder defensively and turned her head away. In a quick gait, red skirts swishing, she swept out onto the terrace by the climbing roses.

If I didn't know she was in love with that rogue Jasper, I might think she's as jealous about Baret and me as Cousin Lavender is.

A slight movement of the satin bedcover beneath Geneva's large four-poster arrested Emerald's attention. Her gaze shifted there just in time to see a child's foot draw back. Jette! How had he sneaked in here and managed to hide without Geneva's knowing? And why? She suspected he had climbed up the trellis and entered by the terrace when Geneva was drowsy from her medication. He was clever enough to accomplish such and fool Zunsia too.

She glanced at Zunsia to see if she had noticed the shoe, but the maid apparently hadn't. She was fanning herself languidly as a breeze smelling of roses rippled in through the terrace.

Emerald masked her concern. The child had been in here all along, so he knew about the voyage to Porto Bello. He probably knew much more as well, since he would have overheard the conversation between Geneva and Lady Sophie before Emerald arrived. No doubt Jette knew that Sophie didn't trust Felix. Perhaps he even knew that she suspected his uncle of hastening the death of his ailing first wife.

Jette's knowledge was an added complication. He had already told her he didn't like Felix. Perhaps of far greater concern was Jette's wish to run away with Baret to locate their father. Knowing that he might be asked to go away with Geneva and Felix could trigger the boy into doing something rash!

"I still think Jette should voyage with us," Lord Felix was telling Geneva in a fatherly tone. "It will do the boy good to visit a Spanish colony and view its culture and people from a friendly perspective. The English, my dear, can be such insufferable bigots when it comes to anything with flavoring from Madrid." He smiled with wearied sarcasm. "He's heard so many tales of horror from his brother that every Spaniard has horns and carries a pitchfork. Baret's dislike is fanatical. See for yourself. We're at war with Holland, and does he sail against Curacao? No! Instead he's meeting with Henry Morgan for an attack on the Main."

Geneva reached a hand toward him. "You best watch your tongue, dear. You're forgetting Emerald's presence."

"Not for a moment," he said glibly. Smiling, Felix walked toward her with both hands held out as though she were a long-lost daughter returning to gain his favor.

"Ah, Emerald, welcome to Foxemoore. I'm sure by now that Sophie has laid out the velvet carpet for you?" His bright blue eyes were maliciously amused. He knew the struggles she must be going through.

Emerald couldn't call his bluff, though she knew his welcome was not genuine. She permitted him to take her hands in his and lean over to brush his lips against her cheek. She struggled not to stiffen, for it was this man who had plotted her father's "accident."

"Hello, your lordship," she managed rather stiffly and met his startling blue gaze without wavering.

Felix's eyes flickered as though he saw through her behavior and knew she neither liked nor trusted him. Yet he kept up the pretense and continued smiling, forcing her to do the same.

"'Lordship'?" he teased. "Call me Felix. Has that scoundrel nephew of mine been forcing his future bride to acknowledge his future earldom by addressing him by title? Shame on him. I suspect your marriage, my dear, will be one full of surprises once he brings you home to England. The king, you know, has a roguish reputation for taking interest in his earls' pretty wives. Knowing Baret's temper, he might end up in a duel and run off buccaneering again. You best tell him to settle down here on Foxemoore, where such a pretty girl will be safe."

Emerald knew he meant to embarrass her. She fumed inwardly and managed to keep herself from flushing.

"Even Foxemoore isn't quite safe, Lord Felix, as I can attest, having been brought up here—but on the other side of the plantation," she said quietly but meaningfully. "And my cousin Minette has been treated more shamefully than I. That's why I've come—to speak to Geneva about my cousin's health. She is sick and needs a doctor."

He lifted both brows as though all this was dreadful and scandalous news, and he quickly offered assurance of help and security for her and Minette.

"Naturally, my dear, you'll want to move into the house at once, and your ailing cousin Minette as well. I'll have everything arranged today. It's fortunate that Ricardo specializes in diseases so prevalent in the Caribbean. He'll know how to treat your cousin, and she'll be on her feet again in plenty of time for your betrothal ball."

Emerald could find no quarrel with his words or his outward manner. Felix's behavior was warm and helpful. He was going out of his way to make clear that she was accepted into his prestigious family. But she didn't believe him for a moment. He still wanted Lavender to marry Baret, so that if anything happened to Baret she would be left heir, just as Felix would be heir should Geneva die of her mysterious illness on the way to Porto Bello.

"It's fortunate, my dear, that Baret is concerned for the well-being of Jette. Has he spoken to you about matters yet?"

Emerald came alert. Something in his smile warned her to be on guard. "Was he to speak to me of something important?"

"Ah, then you haven't seen him since the dinner at Mody-ford's residence," he stated with confidence. "Well, no matter. He's taken up with Morgan for a few days but will come to Foxemoore this weekend. He'll explain then."

"Explain what, Lord Felix?"

57

"He's willing to sacrifice his personal desires in order to have you accompany us and Jette to Porto Bello for a few months while Geneva recovers. Naturally, we'll not sail until after your betrothal. It wouldn't be fair to you to visit the Main without the Buckington ring on your hand." He reached over and kissed her forehead, his eyes grave and amused all at once. "Your care for Geneva and Jette will be a sacrifice we won't forget."

Stunned by this unexpected revelation, Emerald looked at him, speechless.

Then Lord Felix escorted her down the stairs and across the hall, where Jitana opened the door.

"I'll send one of the servants to bring you and your cousin here to the house." Felix held her arm, leading her onto the wide porch.

The sun had set twenty minutes earlier. The sky was ablaze with vivid golds, purples, and reds, all blending together across the distant sky. The winds blew warm, ruffling Emerald's hair.

"Thank you, but I'd prefer to stay at the manor house until Minette has recovered. By then Baret will arrive." She didn't tell him that she preferred to have her meeting with Earl Nigel with Baret present, but Felix apparently understood.

"My father wholeheartedly approves of this betrothal. You can rest assured there's nothing Sophie or anyone else can do to stop it."

She noticed that Felix hadn't said that the earl approved of the *marriage,* only the betrothal. Originally, the betrothal was agreed upon to keep his grandson and Lavender from marrying. Did the earl still believe it was temporary? Baret had suggested that his cooperation with Earl Nigel prompted his grandfather's permission for the voyage with Morgan—a voyage on which he would embark with the secret objective of locating his father.

She touched the ruby at her throat and took solace in its cool touch. Baret's pledge of love was sincere.

Felix had said there was nothing anyone could do to stop the betrothal. *If* he *could stop it, he would,* she thought.

Zeddie was waiting with the buggy to drive her and Dr. Ricardo Vasquez to the manor house.

Felix handed her into the buggy and then turned to the doctor, saying something in low Castilian.

Zeddie frowned at Emerald, who looked away.

Then the horse trotted down the carriageway toward the main road, lined with palms. Their fronds rustled in the evening twilight.

Emerald, seated in back beside the Spaniard, turned to him pleasantly, hoping to learn a thing or two now that they were unobserved by Felix.

"So you are from the Main, Dr. Vasquez?"

"Madrid, Senorita Harwick. I came to the Spanish Main five years ago to be with my brother, Don Miguel. I have much concern for your cousin, Lady Geneva. Her illness is a rare tropical fever best treated in Porto Bello, where I have cured many of His Majesty's governors. We have a long history of the fever and the cure, for Spain ruled the Main for hundreds of years before the English came as pirates. No offense, Senorita, of course."

"Yes, of course, Senor Vasquez. Being friendly with Lord Felix, you would know that not all Englishmen are pirates." She smiled.

His black eyes sparked, and he, too, smiled politely. "I see you are not only lovely, Senorita, but also wise."

"Is it so necessary for Geneva to seek cure in Porto Bello? Can you not treat her here?"

"I could, if I were staying. You will understand that my presence is not regarded with favor by your Jamaican Council of Planters. Now that England is at war with the Dutch, they often favor a cause for which to turn against Madrid. I would not wish to be here amid plundering pirates soon to dock their vessels in Port Royal again."

"I understand. It may also be said the same for Lady Geneva voyaging to Porto Bello."

"Ah, yes, but she is the stepmother of Carlotta, the soon-to-be-wife of my nephew. Therefore Lady Geneva is considered one of the don's esteemed family on the hacienda, and my friend as well." He smiled with a hint of tried patience. "You see, not all physicians of renown abide in your England."

"I agree, Senor. And perhaps it is not 'my England' after all but 'my Jamaica.' I was born and raised in the Caribbean. But I'm interested in Carlotta. Felix was married, then, to her mother?"

His eyes hardened, but it wasn't clear whether he was thinking of Felix or was irritated by her question.

"Yes. To Anna Maria Alvarez . . . she died giving Carlotta birth."

"I am sorry to hear that."

"Carlotta has missed having a mother. Her grandmother perhaps was too strict with her."

"Carlotta does not seem the manner of girl who was held back with a disciplined bridle. She is willful."

"She is sometimes unwise. Marriage to Sir Jasper, an Englishman, would have turned into tragedy. She is unhappy now but will grow wiser once the marriage to my nephew takes place. In marrying Miguel, Carlotta Maria Alvarez marries into a respectable ruling family on the Main."

The casual haughtiness to his voice stated simply that superiority rested with Spain.

"Miguel is an honorable soldier of His Majesty, newly appointed captain-general at Margarita. She is favored to have such a marriage arranged." He looked impatient. "She has caused the family much harm and sorrow in running away like this to Port Royal. She could not have accomplished it without friends in Jamaica."

Did he know that Miguel had been abducted from the galleon off the coast of Venezuela?

"You are very proud of your nephew, I see."

"I am, Senorita Harwick, most pleased with Miguel. Unfortunately, the galleon he sailed on was attacked by pirates while on its way to Margarita, and Miguel is being held captive for ransom. We have not told Carlotta yet, not wishing to alarm her further. Arrangements are under way to buy his freedom."

Emerald was relieved that the twilight hid her faint blush. "Oh, how dreadful, Senor Vasquez. Pirates!"

"The scum of the earth, Senorita."

"You have made contact with this particular pirate *capitan* who abducted Don Miguel?"

He leaned into the comfortable leather seat, folding his arms across his chest. "Ah, yes, and before it is over we shall deliver him to the governor of Porto Bello."

Emerald watched him.

His gleaming dark eyes were unsmiling as they fixed upon her. "Forgive, Senorita, I have upset you. You must not become troubled with talk of morbid things. You have a betrothal to dream of, a wealthy esteemed family to marry into, and, like Carlotta, you have much to occupy your mind."

He couldn't know she knew about Miguel or that Baret Buckington had been one of three buccaneering captains who had taken the Spanish galleon with his nephew aboard. No one knew the *Regale* had been involved, not even Felix or Governor Modyford.

"I fear for your nephew, Senor Vasquez. Have you any idea where the pirates are holding him captive?"

He stroked his short pointed beard. "Where all unclean dogs gather to rejoice in their spoil. Where else but Tortuga, the rabid den of *Diablo* himself!"

"Yes . . . so I have heard. A foul place, Senor. But surely! Even dogs will treat your nephew well, seeing as how they expect to be paid a ransom?"

"This pirate *capitan* is the cleverest of the dogs, Senorita. Perhaps. Even so, though Miguel is safely returned, we will not rest until this dog hangs."

Emerald fanned her face briskly and lapsed into silence as Zeddie drove the buggy down the cutoff toward the house. She knew he was listening, too, by the way he kept shifting his hat in nervous gestures. Senor Vasquez might think as he wished, but capturing the pirate captain who had taken the *Don Pedro* and abducted Miguel would not be an easy matter. Did Baret know that Miguel's uncle was here on Foxemoore?

Emerald casually steered the conversation toward Geneva and Porto Bello.

Dr. Ricardo Vasquez turned and looked at her. "You have interest in Porto Bello, Senorita?"

Caution. "Lord Felix wishes me to voyage with my cousin and your niece, but alas, I cannot go. I have my duties here on Foxemoore."

"A disappointment, Senorita Emerald. Your presence, I am certain, would bring even more pleasure to the Vasquez hacienda. It would be a satisfaction to Lady Buckington and my future niece, Carlotta, as well. You must favor us and reconsider."

They drew up in front of the manor house. The lanterns were all glowing, and Yolanda waited on the porch, her turban showing like a lemon in the shades of evening. She came down the steps, her dark face lined and anxious.

61

"Has Minette taken to the worse?" asked Emerald.

"No, Miss Emerald, she's perked up fine, like one of them wilted daisies." She lowered her voice as she stopped in front of Emerald. "It's Ty. He upped and went to Chocolata Hole, lookin' for his cousin Rafael."

"Levasseur?" whispered Emerald so that the doctor wouldn't hear. Her heart lurched at the thought. "Why does he wish to see Rafael? Did he say?"

Yolanda's face glistened with sweat, and her eyes were troubled. "He been saying the reason for long time. You knows how Ty feels, Miss Emerald. He's been looking at the blue water since he was a boy and prayin' he can sail it. It was only 'cause he had to hide in the Blue Mountains that he's not joined the pirates yet. Now he says he's going a-buccaneering with Henry Morgan and the others. He's wanting to sail with Captain Erik Farrow, he says. But says his French blood makes Rafael's bargain sweeter."

Her hands clenched. *Rafael's bargain?* "What bargain?"

Yolanda shook her head. "He's not saying."

"He can't sail with Levasseur," she hissed. "I won't let him."

"You'd be blessed to stop him if you can. When I tole him so, he smiles. 'You behave yourself, Yolanda,' he tells me."

"I'll stop him," she promised grimly. "I'll have Baret stop him for sure." She became aware that Dr. Vasquez watched them whispering. Leaving Yolanda, she walked toward him.

"My cousin is upstairs, Senor Vasquez. This way, please."

"I am at your disposal, Senorita."

Emerald now agreed with Lady Sophie in her doubts about Dr. Ricardo, even though he was indisputably a physician. Knowing how Felix had hired the now dead assassin to destroy Baret, could she trust Geneva and Jette's safety to Miguel's uncle at Porto Bello?

Emerald wondered if she could speak with Carlotta. Perhaps she could learn more about the doctor from her, since the girl appeared in no mood to cooperate in the arranged marriage with his nephew. Since that was true, there should be little reason for Carlotta to betray Baret as the captain of the pirate vessel who had taken the *Don Pedro*. As long as Carlotta was determined to marry Sir Jasper and live in Jamaica, she would wish Baret to hold Miguel prisoner. Her love for Jasper was beneficial after all, thought Emerald wryly.

Yet any hope of speaking alone with Carlotta was slim. The girl had disappeared from view soon after her arrival, and Emerald suspected she was under the watchful eye of both her father and her betrothed's uncle. They would make certain she didn't manage to escape again before the voyage to Porto Bello.

There was a chance that Sir Jasper would try to come for her secretly, but Emerald held little hope for that to occur. Jasper was a paid vassal of Felix and would not risk angering him by running away to Tortuga with his daughter. Evidently Felix had well-laid plans to use Carlotta in his dealings with the Spanish dons, and woe to Jasper if he interfered.

Jasper was not the sort of man to throw his life and riches to the wind in a daring raid to have the woman he wanted. His odious behavior toward Emerald had not been intended to cost him anything. With her father believed dead and Baret away, Jasper had thought he could get by with his actions. Had he known he would end up in a duel with Baret and be shot, Jasper would have avoided her.

The return of Carlotta to the Main was certain, as was her marriage to Miguel, *if* Baret released him. But even if Carlotta had nothing to gain by keeping her secrecy about his involvement, who knew whether the mood of a girl given to fits of temper and jealousy would remain trustworthy? Baret must be told that Carlotta was at Foxemoore in the company of Don Miguel's uncle. Was it even safe for Baret to show up here? He might now be considered the king's agent, and Earl Winston Cunningham of the High Admiralty might be willing to have the charges of piracy and disloyalty to the king dropped, but Baret's many enemies remained, as did her father's.

Several hours after Dr. Vasquez had treated Minette, Emerald stood at the window of her cousin's room. The doctor had assured Emerald that the girl was more exhausted than dying of some treacherous disease. He had ruled out typhoid and cholera and suggested plenty of rest and good food, then left medication to treat the fever.

"The little senorita will be up and waltzing at your betrothal. You have nothing to fear."

The news was heartening after an afternoon when events had left Emerald wondering what else could go wrong. Her return to Foxemoore had turned into a battleground, and it didn't appear to be over yet. There was still the reaction of the Great House to her removal of Mr. Pitt from his position of overseer.

And she wasn't certain what Lady Sophie or Lord Felix would say about Ngozi's being in charge. Overseers were usually Europeans. Emerald was sure she hadn't heard the end of the matter, either from the House or from Mr. Pitt. He was furious enough to complain to Lady Sophie. And the first thing that went wrong among the slaves on Foxemoore would be blamed on the ineptitude of Ngozi to handle the position. Emerald's fears brought second thoughts about her bold decision. Had she acted too hastily?

Fears of all sorts enlarged into threatening shadows that stalked the empty rooms of the manor house. The big yellow moon offered a smile of brightness as it began to set behind the vast cane fields, setting them aglow, but the house grew darker.

She left the window and looked over at the bed. Minette, bathed and wearing the first clean gown she'd seen in months, was resting peacefully, fast asleep from the medication. Emerald could almost imagine a wistful smile on her face as visions of hope and happiness were resurrected from the depth of hopelessness she had known in the slave fields under Mr. Pitt.

Emerald's own smile faded into a look of determination. *Nor will I forget those who have no hope still but who are doomed to live and die in the sunbaked furrows of the fields. And the prisoners at Brideswell...*

She would work a little at a time to ease their burdens and would contact the church about holding a worship service at the prison house. She wouldn't forget the miserable wretches she had met while there. Faith and the others would soon receive clothing and other items to make their existence more bearable.

She sighed as she walked over to Minette. There was so much to do and seemingly so little time to accomplish it all. Surely Felix had not told her the truth about Baret's wishing her to voyage with Geneva and Jette to Porto Bello.

Jette. She remembered that he had overheard. The boy would not rest easy now, thinking he might be sent to the Main. He'd be on pins and needles waiting for the arrival of Baret to beg that something be done so he wouldn't need to be with Felix.

Minette's hair was still damp from the good washing that Yolanda had given her, and it lay in ringlets across the pillow, amber in the moonlight. She was dreaming of Erik Farrow, thought Emerald with a smile. Again she took time to pray and express her thanksgiving to the Lord for having protected them both through their fiery trials and bringing them safely together again to face the future.

Emotionally exhausted and physically tired, Emerald then went down the narrow hall and passed the little gallery her father called the "crow's nest." She descended the steep flight of steps that hugged one side of the wall. Below in the receiving hall, Zeddie dozed and snored in a wicker chair by the door, his pistols on his lap and his feet propped up on a settee. She smiled and walked past quietly.

This was the first moment Emerald had had to herself, and she realized how hungry she was. Some mango and hot tea would be delightful before she tumbled into bed.

As she walked softly toward the back of the house to the cook room, she made plans for tomorrow. There was no choice; she must write a message to Baret, warning him about Miguel's uncle being on Foxemoore. First thing in the morning she would send Zeddie with the letter into Port Royal. The buccaneers' meeting with Henry Morgan as Modyford's admiral was under way, and Baret would be there.

For the first time she considered what Felix had told her in Geneva's bedroom. Was it likely that Baret would tell his uncle he wished her to voyage with Geneva and Jette to Porto Bello? The idea seemed contrary to what she knew of Baret. It didn't seem reasonable that he would want *any* of them on the Main— not when Morgan intended to attack. And if his father was a slave there, would Baret want more of those he cared about at the planter's hacienda? She frowned. There was so much to tell Baret that hinted of new dangers.

She touched the ruby at her throat.

6

THE KING'S HOUSE

While Henry Morgan and his buccaneer captains were preparing to covertly sail against Spanish shipping, dark and dangerous news of another sort arrived at the governor's official residence. Because of that news, Governor Modyford, Captain Morgan, and Baret Buckington—alias Captain Foxworth of the buccaneering vessel the *Regale*—gathered one evening in the parlor of the King's House as the sky darkened with purple hue.

From the time of Morgan's return from successful raids on Villahermosa and Gran Granada, the governor had befriended him, and both Morgan and Baret had become frequent evening visitors at the King's House, coming and going secretly by way of the small walled garden.

Baret stood near a screened door that opened onto the garden. The evening smoldered, matching his mood and the mood of Morgan. A breeze that did little to cool whispered through the thick green foliage of the plantain trees, adding humid fragrance to the smell of tobacco.

Dangerous men, Baret and Morgan were both now restrained in the presence of Gov. Thomas Modyford, who was neither a stranger to buccaneering ways nor a lover of Spain. Tonight he had more reason than ever to secretly support "Harry Morgan's Way," as the pirates spoke of the captain's successful attacks on the Main. Baret had brought Sir Thomas painful news, and Thomas mulled it over with bitterness.

Baret held a Venetian glass of sweetened limeade, and his keen dark eyes sparked with leashed energy. He was armed with a long rapier and a pair of French pistols and was dressed fashionably as Earl Nigel's grandson, who presently was in favor with both the Jamaica Assembly and the Court of King Charles.

Wearing a cool white cotton buccaneer shirt with wide sleeves, dark trousers, and calf-length boots with silver buckles, he stood looking unhurried and thoughtful. His hair, as dark as ebony, was drawn back with a leather cord and, as a royalist, worn in the style of the king's royal-blooded Cavaliers.

"You're confident you can rely on his information?" asked Sir Thomas.

Baret remembered his last productive confrontation with the Spanish *capitan* whom he had abducted from the *Don Pedro*. Miguel Vasquez, son of the don who had bought Baret's father as a slave, had finally broken down and admitted all he knew. He was still a prisoner in the one place Baret was convinced that neither Felix nor his spies would think to search—or dare to: Captain Erik Farrow's ship, the *Warspite*, anchored only a half mile out in the bay, deliberately away from his own vessel, the *Regale*.

"In this instance, Sir Thomas, the informer's words can be vouched," said Baret, restraining a look of pity for Governor Modyford.

Sir Thomas lowered his tall hefty frame into a wicker chair and sighed. His wide thin mouth, which usually bore a twisted smile of perpetual boredom beneath a wide floppy mustache, was now taut. Like many in the tropics, his head was shaved due to the heat, and he wore a clean purple head scarf that went along with his taffetas. Modyford, who had come out to the West Indies as a young man in the days of Cromwell, appeared not so different from the pirates he had previously hanged. His heavy hand, sporting a number of bejeweled silver and gold rings, gripped the ornate knob of his shoulder-high walking stick.

"This isn't pretty news for Lady Modyford," he said of his wife.

"You have my sympathy, Sir Thomas. I could wish it weren't true."

Modyford nodded, preventing his emotions from spilling over. Baret respected him for it. There was no indecision in his wide jaw. Here was a governor who could not be controlled by the Spanish sympathizers either in London or on the Jamaican Assembly. His decisiveness was one reason Baret and Morgan both trusted him. Felix, who worked with Thomas Lynch, the factor of the Royal African Company, had not been able to influence Modyford into a pro-Spanish stance. The governor had the brute strength of a bull, the cunning of a diplomat who was wise to the ways of his opponents in Madrid and London, and he had befriended Henry Morgan, knowing he could use a man of his abilities for the protection of the island from the dons. That gave Baret more confidence.

His brassy complexion was typical of many of the gentry in Jamaica who downed too many rum toddies in the tropical heat. Otherwise, Modyford was an exemplary English governor who had been appointed by King Charles.

But now, Modyford had just learned what had happened to his son.

Four years ago Modyford had sent his eldest boy, Jack, in the frigate *Griffin* to fetch Lady Modyford. The frigate had disappeared somewhere on the Caribbean.

"Thinking of Jack's death has been painful. Lady Modyford and I suspected that the boy was doubtless either murdered or sent into the South Seas by these our cruel neighbors. But the news you bring, if true, Baret, is far, far worse."

Baret's dark eyes were grave. Don Miguel Vasquez had informed him that a Spanish captain, Francisco Martin, told of two English ships that had been wrecked on the Florida coast in August of '64, soon after Modyford became governor. Five men were said to have survived and, after living with the Indians, were later captured by the Spanish. One of those five was a young man with a "very good face and light, somewhat curling hair," who said his name was Jack, or John, and that he was the son of the governor of Jamaica.

Baret understood Modyford's distress. What had happened to his son had also happened to Baret's father, Viscount Royce Buckington. When thinking of loved ones in relation to the Inquisitors, it was preferable to believe them buried at the bottom of the Caribbean rather than chained in dungeons where filth and excrement bred misery and disease.

"He's a prisoner, then," breathed Modyford, dazed, "in Porto Bello."

"It isn't certain whether he's in Porto Bello. He could have been moved to Peru. The informant did not know."

Modyford groaned. The Peruvian silver mines were places of living death.

"However, I've news my father is in Porto Bello," confessed Baret. "And there are prisoners with him. There's a chance—a small one—that your son may be one of them. If not, someone may know where he is."

Modyford was thoughtful. He looked at Captain Morgan. "Whether Jack is a prisoner or dead, anything you attempt on the Caribbean must be deemed of justifiable cause in London. If you go beyond the legal commission I've granted, I'll not be able to save you from His Majesty's ire or the Spanish ambassador's ranting for your head. I can do little more than try to defend you to Albemarle," he added. The duke, Baret knew, was Modyford's cousin, serving Charles in London.

Morgan did not appear unnerved. He looked at his Havana *seegar*, which he had not yet lit, and turned it over as though inspecting and relishing its leaf. Morgan was a sturdy Welshman with hard clever eyes that stared back evenly from beneath the dark brows that slashed across his flat baked-brown forehead. A wide curling mustache and short beard blended into a head of thick brownish hair that fell to an inch or two above his wide shoulders.

He emptied his rum toddy in one gulp. "No need to fret, Sir Thomas. You'll never see Harry Morgan do anything to cause you legal embarrassment. I'll not self-destruct in the clutches of the sweet Spanish sympathizers. The legal commission gives me berth to move, and move I will—but as soft-footed as a cautious fox."

Baret, wearing a thin mustache, looked like the dark and earthy young King Charles, and a faintly sardonic expression hovered on his mouth as he considered Morgan's words. Then he glanced at Modyford to gauge his response.

The governor appeared satisfied and equally cautious. He removed a yellow handkerchief and wiped his heavy brow. He bit the end of his own *seegar* and watched Morgan refill his glass with rum.

There had been other sobering news, which frightened all Jamaican sugar planters and Port Royal merchants. Reports from Cuba had reached the governor and the Assembly that Madrid had ordered the various dons on the Main to assemble a fleet and seize Jamaica.

"The Spanish Council of the Indies has managed at last to get their ships away from Madrid's navy," he warned.

"The *armada de barlovento?*" asked Baret, troubled.

"Aye, and the armada has arrived, I'm told. Six warships. Their upkeep will be charged to the various Spanish provinces.

Two went to Vera Cruz to guard the base of the *flota,* two to Cartagena to protect the galleons, and two are operating from Havana."

Baret looked at Morgan. They knew why the ships had gone to Cuba—to keep the western end of the island free of any buccaneers tempted to attack the plate fleet.

"Do they have an admiral?" breathed Morgan over the *seegar* he'd finally lit.

Modyford leaned toward the carved logwood table and lifted a sheet of paper. "Admiral Alonso del Campo y Espinosa."

Morgan considered the name. "Never heard of 'im." He looked at Baret, who wore a half smile.

He shook his head no. "Spanish warships are no match for the buccaneers, Sir Thomas. The galleons are fit for Spain but not for the Caribbean. They are much too expensive for the provinces to maintain. They are too large, and their keels sit so deep in the water that they can't chase the small and nimble vessels of the buccaneers into the shallow channels."

"He's right. They'll not chase us out of the scores of bays once we've slipped them."

Baret knew that Morgan had already arranged his rendezvous at a particular group of the South Cays of Cuba. The word was out not only in Port Royal, where he was head of the newly formed Port Royal Volunteers, but also in Tortuga, St. Kitts, and Bermuda.

Even now, the buccaneers and pirates interested in joining him for the expedition were preparing to voyage there. One by one the various vessels would come in before the last day of the rendezvous, 28 of March, to receive their commissions from Morgan. They hoped to have some two dozen vessels and seven hundred buccaneers, a mixture of British and the feisty French from Tortuga.

The fact that Morgan had been legally appointed admiral by the governor of Jamaica had already wooed the restless buccaneers to make ready, even though the place of attack was not known. That decision would be finalized at the point of rendezvous. Baret had only one place in mind that he was interested in: Porto Bello.

"I hope you gentlemen appreciate the difficulty facing me as governor." Modyford pushed himself from the chair and began pacing. "His Majesty has ordered the buccaneers to attack the Dutch—" he looked at Baret "—and you refuse and insist on letters to attack Spain."

"Did I not fight the Dutch at Barbados?" Baret asked innocently. "My grandfather is pleased—why not the king?"

"Why not, indeed! With Morgan's own uncle dead at Curacao—"

"Uncle Edward died of a heart attack," interjected Morgan. "And I told him to leave the poor Hollanders be. They've enough trouble with Spain. And you think Baret has a heart to fight 'em when it was the Spanish butchered his fair mother?"

"Yes, yes, I understand, but I'm put in a pretty way. I cannot openly condone your attack on the Spanish Main or issue commissions to such a cause without losing my own head to the king. I must walk a tightrope between angering London, which wishes no open provocation with Madrid, and pleasing the Brotherhood, who do. London demands I 'peacefully pursue' trade in the Indies but offers no means to enforce peaceful cooperation from the dons! And I cannot protect Jamaica and appease the Brotherhood unless I issue commissions to attack Spain."

"There can be no peaceful trade until the back of Madrid is broken," said Baret.

"He's right," Morgan agreed. "Spain does not speak English. They understand one language—seeing their treasure ships gutted and sent to the sharks."

"I need my own frigates," Modyford said to himself, still pacing. "But my request to London is ignored. Yet they warn me to keep the Brotherhood on good behavior. How can I unless I give commissions against Spain?"

"You have our utmost sympathy, Sir Thomas," said Baret gravely.

But the amused glimmer in his eyes brought a frown to the governor's face. "If I only had frigates . . ." he repeated.

For two years Modyford had been trying to persuade the Privy Council to send out frigates so that he wouldn't need to rely on the buccaneers, but to no avail. King Charles insisted he couldn't afford their upkeep.

"The Brotherhood has no heart to attack the Dutch," continued Morgan, leaning back in his chair while Modyford walked to and fro. "It's Spain. No one else. Nothing less."

"And the Dutch have no wealth," added Baret with dry

71

humor. "Will the king pay for our sailing and rigging to attack the poor Dutch colonies?"

His innocent tone suggested otherwise.

Morgan looked at the governor over his *seegar*. "Ye know he's right, Sir Thomas. How else can we protect His Majesty's Jamaica if we cannot collect wages from Spain for our upkeep? And if the Brotherhood has no wages to spend in Port Royal, how will the merchants get rich on pieces of eight? And who will make the Caribbean safe for the planters to haul their sweet sugar to Mother England?"

"Ah, well spoken," Baret said.

Modyford gave a short laugh. "You have me, Harry, and everyone knows you're a smooth talker. When it comes to commanding the buccaneers, that's a valuable asset to me now. Aye, I've no choice but to let you sail against Spain. But remember! If anything goes wrong on this expedition, it's my first duty to denounce you. And that goes for you as well, Baret. Your victory at Barbados will count for little. There's still those, including Felix, who would love to see you hang."

"I'm well aware, Thomas. But freeing my father at Porto Bello, and perhaps even your son, is the answer to a good many unsettled things."

"Then I wish you and Harry Godspeed and happy hunting." Sir Thomas lifted his glass, and the old twisted smile was back.

Morgan stood and bowed. "We have us a gentleman's agreement, Sir Thomas."

Baret parted fellowship with Morgan, who went inside the Red Goose with Jackman and Morris. Arriving on the wharf, he took the worn stone steps down to board the cockboat, where his half-caste waited to row him out a quarter mile to the *Regale*. The moist warm breeze from off the glittering blue water tugged at his hat.

Suddenly a shadow disengaged itself from other shadows and moved toward him.

Baret's hand went toward his pistol.

"Ho! 'Tis only me, Captain Buckington. I bring a message from your lady fair."

Baret recognized the lank frame of Zeddie approaching him.

The man drew near and held out a folded message. "Foul

news, an' she thought you ought to know before you ride into Foxemoore."

Alert, Baret read Emerald's letter. The unexpected arrival of Ricardo Vasquez meant trouble indeed. Was this an unfortunate coincidence or a devious, well-laid plan by Felix?

He knew little about the physician from Madrid. Had he come to Spanish Town seeking the runaway Carlotta to marry his nephew Miguel, or were Carlotta and the medical treatment of Geneva a ruse for a more sinister endeavor to bring Geneva to the don's estate in Porto Bello? Yet, neither Ricardo nor Felix could know that Baret had been involved in taking the *Don Pedro,* or that he held Ricardo's nephew a prisoner. Carlotta knew. But Baret didn't think she would betray him, because she would do anything to stay on Jamaica and marry Jasper.

"Porto Bello," Baret mused.

"Not a friendly spot for curin' what ails a person, I'm thinkin'. Him coming to the hacienda in Spanish Town when he did to find Miss Carlotta smells a whole lot like fish left too long in the sun."

Baret folded the message. Unanticipated events controlled by Felix made him uneasy. A trap was being set, but was it for him or for someone else? Of what benefit to Felix's cause was it to bring Geneva to the estate of Don Miguel Vasquez? Did Felix know that Baret's father had been a slave there? Felix thought Royce Buckington was dead. The old scholar Lucca had been able to deceive Felix in a letter written to Baret from Maracaibo. Lucca, knowing that Felix's spies would intercept the letter, had deliberately given false information as to Royce's death.

But had Felix since discovered the truth? What if Ricardo knew otherwise? Since Miguel knew where Royce was being held, it was likely that his uncle did also. If he did know, he'd mention it to Felix. That meant Baret must make his move to rescue his father before Felix voyaged to Porto Bello or sent a message to the don to have him killed.

"Return to Foxemoore, Zeddie. Tell Emerald nothing will keep me away. I've important matters to take care of here first, but I'll arrive the night of our betrothal."

"I'll tell her, but what of the Spaniard? Might'n all this be a trap set for you? What better place than at the betrothal, when you're unsuspectin' of treachery?"

73

"If it is a trap, I've a few surprises of my own," he said and thought of the physician's nephew, Miguel Vasquez, held a prisoner. He would soon have Miguel moved from Erik's ship and back aboard the *Regale* for the voyage to Porto Bello. Neither Ricardo nor Felix could successfully move against him as long as he held such a noteworthy prisoner. He smiled. Once inside Porto Bello, he intended to use Miguel to lead him to his father.

Zeddie cocked his good eye at him. "Am I right in thinkin' she didn't tell you about Ty?"

Baret remembered the young man who had escaped to the Blue Mountains. The threatened branding of Ty had been the reason Emerald first came aboard the *Regale,* looking for jewels to pay Pitt to not carry out the branding. In the end, Pitt brought Ty to the town pillory and had him branded.

Zeddie straightened his periwig. "She probably wouldn't tell you about Ty since she's protective of him, as well she should be. But I've got some worries, knowin' how that rascally mouthed other cousin of hers is as sharp as a barracuda."

"You mean Rafael Levasseur?" Baret's eyes narrowed. "What about him and Ty?"

"Ty didn't say so, but I'm thinking, if he seeks any pirate ship to sail, it'll be aboard the *Venture.* Ty's as proud of his French blood as any of 'em. He's been planning to escape Foxemoore and run away to Tortuga to join Levasseur since he was twelve. He was going to escape with Jamie Bradford, except Pitt caught him first."

Baret's dark eyes turned hard. "Does Emerald know he plans to join Levasseur?"

"If she's guessed, she ain't said so. I'm thinking she doesn't, since she's had her hands full with the ailing Minette and going up to the Great House for help. There's nothing she can do to stop Ty. An' that's what has me worried. That Levasseur is a cunning fox, and if he can use Ty in any way to get what he wants from Emerald—well, your lordship, you're seein' the direction of my thoughts."

"Quite well, Zeddie. Where is Ty now?"

"I wish I knew. He left Foxemoore this afternoon. He's lookin' for Levasseur."

Baret looked out toward the bay and the various-sized vessels lying at anchor. Although there was a state of war between

England and Holland, and France had sided with the Dutch, it didn't significantly affect the relationship between the various nationalities among the Brotherhood on Tortuga. Morgan confidently expected the French buccaneers to be joining him at the point of rendezvous in the South Cays of Cuba. But Baret hadn't seen Levasseur's *Venture* since his own arrival. Was he even here?

Yes, it was too late to stop Ty, and his unwise association with Rafael would mean trouble. Baret was certain of that.

7

THE SINGING SCHOOL

Emerald didn't know what to expect from the Great House when the news of Pitt's replacement by Ngozi reached the family. She hadn't needed to wait long. Lady Sophie sent the house servant Henry with a terse note: "You've exceeded your authority. I'll not have an African slave as overseer."

Henry averted his eyes as he handed a second note to her. "From Lady Buckington," he said of Geneva.

Emerald, standing on the front porch of the manor house, looked up and saw a familiar gray gelding and rider coming down the road between the cane. *Pitt!*

She read Geneva's message. "Emerald, I fear you've acted rashly by removing Mr. Pitt. This matter must be discussed at length with all members of the family who own shares in Foxemoore. Felix doesn't yet know what you've done, but I'm sure he'll disagree with your action. And you already know how upset Sophie is. Have you forgotten the slave uprising that took the life of Beatrice? Lavender still mourns her mother and is quite frightened of the slaves. She'll not venture to the manor house without a bodyguard. I realize you think well of the slave Ngozi, but we simply can't have an African as overseer!"

Emerald lifted her eyes from the letter to rivet her gaze on Mr. Pitt. So. He was free from the boiling house and back in the position of overseer. He would be sure to vent his cruelty upon the slaves that had bound him. They were not with him today, she noticed.

"I'm sorry, Miss Emerald," whispered old Henry. Turning, he went down the porch steps to where a horse was waiting and rode back up the road to the Great House.

Emerald remained where she was, her face set as Mr. Pitt slowly rode forward. She was less worried about the embarrassment put upon her by having the family overrule her decision than she was of Pitt's regaining his power.

"That jackanapes. For a piece of eight I'd send his innards flyin'. It might be worth my own hangin'."

"He isn't worth it," she said, laying a hand on Zeddie's arm. "We haven't heard the last of this. One thing everyone seems to forget is what Baret will say when he arrives. There's still hope of getting rid of Pitt."

As Zeddie scowled his one good eye and kept his hand on his pistol, Emerald walked to the front step and waited in the glaring sun.

Minette, up and about and recovering from her illness, had come to the bedroom window above the porch and was looking down at Pitt with loathing.

Lord, help me to be wise, Emerald prayed.

He rode up and reined in his horse. Then he swung himself down from his Spanish leather saddle and, removing his wide, dust-soiled panama hat, strode toward the porch. His leathery brow was dotted with sweat, and his grizzled red hair hung limp. The canvas shirt was torn away in places, showing his muscled arms and bare chest.

Pitt's prominent pale eyes held mockery, and his wide mouth spread into a grin. He flicked his prized whip absently against a bronzed hand. Then his smile faded as he looked at Zeddie.

"I come in goodwill, Miss Harwick, but if that one-eyed gooney aims to lift that pistol against me, I'll do what I have to do to save my neck."

Zeddie leaned over the porch rail and spat.

"If you've come to gloat, Mr. Pitt, you best save your celebration," said Emerald. "Your position as overseer will be short-lived. When Baret Buckington gets here, the family may change their mind about Ngozi."

His eyes hardened. "I wouldn't count on it, Missy. There ain't a planter in Jamaica willing to trust a Negro as overseer. Lady Sophie done trusts me, and I've done her well in my job. The sugar's at full production. The slaves ain't caused any more hassle since twenty of the troublemakers were hanged, and I aim his highness the earl hisself votin' to keep me in my proper place."

Emerald feared he might be right, but she was determined to stand her ground and work till the end to have him removed.

"Yes, you've done your job where sugar production is concerned, but you've used your whip to get it done. There'll be no more of that if I have anything to say about it."

"Pardon me sayin' so, Missy, but it just may be you ain't going to have that much to say."

Both Emerald and Zeddie looked at him, alert, catching that his snide voice suggested more than his words. What gave him such confidence?

"I've already explained about Baret Buckington. My betrothal is in two weeks."

"Sure, Miss Harwick." He swept off his hat and grinned. "An' I'll be the first to congratulate you. You and your father were real smart to trap him."

Zeddie straightened from the rail, but Emerald laid a hand on his arm again.

"I'll ask you to leave my presence, Mr. Pitt. From now on, I'll have Captain Buckington give you your orders. In the end it will be he who decides whether you stay on as overseer or Ngozi takes your place. But I'll warn you. If you so much as lay a hand on Ngozi or the other slaves to vent your hatred, I'll beg him to bring you to Brideswell."

Pitt looked like a growling dog forced to keep its distance. "Like I say, Miss Harwick, I come in goodwill. I'm needing my things from Karlton's old room." He gestured his head toward the top floor and, seeing Minette in the open window, glared his animosity.

"Your trash has already been packed!" she called down. "Zeddie threw it out by the smokehouse. You step foot in Uncle Karlton's house again, and I'll shoot you like I did at the lookout house!"

"Minette!" cried Emerald, looking up at her.

"So you admit *you* fired that pistol at me, you little wench!"

"Too bad I didn't aim higher!"

"Minette!" Emerald turned quickly to Zeddie. "Go upstairs and pull her away from the window—"

"I shoulda whipped you to an inch of your life when I had the chance," Mr. Pitt shouted.

"You try it again! You just try it!"

Emerald was afraid to go upstairs to quiet Minette and to leave Zeddie alone with Pitt, but Mr. Pitt seemed to have had enough of Minette, for he turned on his heel and stalked to his gelding.

"That's it, run. Run for your life, Pitt. You just wait till Ty comes back, a pirate! He'll get you good for the evils you did to us."

Pitt mounted and jerked the reins of his horse to ride to the fields. He glared up at her. "It ain't over yet." He rode away, dust rising.

Emerald looked after him. Then she turned and went into the house to scold Minette for worsening matters. She could understand the girl's frustration, but until Baret settled accounts, it seemed that Mr. Pitt remained a prowling mad dog on Foxemoore.

Zeddie closed the door. "I'm thinking he has himself more cockiness than he would if he didn't know somethin' that we don't, or think he does."

"He has most of the family on his side," Emerald complained. "That's what gives him confidence. Was Minette right? Did you move his things to the smokehouse?"

"Aye, m'gal, 'twas the first thing I did. The idea of him having things in Sir Karlton's room was loathsome. Looks like the trunk was broken into and his desk drawer searched by a hungry rat. But I wouldn't know if anything's missing."

"Nor would I." She sighed and looked up the steps. It was time to see what she could discover or learn what Pitt had destroyed.

"Yolanda? Get Minette back to bed, will you?"

"She's behavin' herself now, Miss Emerald. I done hauled her away from the window and paddled her good!"

A phony yowl went up from Minette. Emerald smiled. She had the feeling that Yolanda had been with her all along, enjoying the upbraiding Minette had given Mr. Pitt.

Her father's room looked as though Pitt had torn it apart, even as he had her own. As Zeddie said, the trunk had been broken into and papers and maps were lying about in disarray. But surprisingly, Pitt had not seemed to have been interested in destroying them or searching through them. They were strewn into a pile on the floor, apparently untouched.

Then she'd been right. It *had* been the jewels of her cousin Rafael that Pitt had foolishly thought might be hidden in the house. Had he bypassed the box her father had shown her as a child, the one supposedly containing a deed to a portion of Fox-emoore? That seemed too much to hope for. The box had been ornate and would immediately draw Pitt's attention as a place to stash jewels.

She saw it then. The box was sitting on the old scarred desk, the lock broken open and its contents dumped out. Emerald's anger arose as she picked up several old letters, one of them from her mother's family in Tortuga. There was a broken locket, too, and a braided dark brown tuft of her mother's hair. Gently she put them back, along with the cameo showing her mother at sixteen, full of life and hope. Then, to her utter amazement, she picked up a paper signed by old Earl Killigrew Buckington, awarding Karlton Harwick shares in Foxemoore sugar. The Lord had protected the deed—Pitt could have destroyed it!

So. Her father had told the truth all along. She felt a surge of pride and a longing to see him again. Tears wet her eyes as she ran her fingers along the deed. He was alive, and Baret would find him. Surely, in the midst of all her trials and sorrows, the Lord Jesus had overshadowed her with His grace. He had good plans for her, and He would see them fulfilled in His time and in His way.

Later that evening, Ngozi showed up at the back door of the cook room to assure Emerald he was doing well and that Pitt hadn't taken revenge against him or the others.

"Not that he don't dream about it, but he cannot. He is walking like a butterfly on a fragile blossom, Miss Emerald. He don't say so, but the man is afraid of Captain Buckington."

As the days passed, Minette grew healthier, and the two of them talked incessantly of the upcoming betrothal in the Great House. Emerald had heard that Lavender was back, as well as Sir Cecil Chaderton, Baret's old tutor from his days in London and France. Geneva, too, was feeling better and, though often con-fined to bed, had seen to it that Lady Sophie sent out invitations for the betrothal. The servants were under orders to prepare a great feast as they had at Geneva's wedding. And Earl Nigel sent his valet down to the manor house with a written message:

Is Minette's illness an excuse to hide in the manor house? I expect the betrothed of my grandson to behave like a future countess,

80

which includes looking elegant in the dining room of the Great House. I will expect you to take up residence tomorrow.

Emerald frowned over the imposing stationery signed by the earl of Buckington. She and Minette were seated in the cook room, where Yolanda, for the noon meal, had fried a chicken that Zeddie claimed he had stumbled across while out hunting. Emerald had the notion the hen had come from Lady Sophie's personal reserve, penned behind the Great House.

"Not bad news again?" Minette groaned, seeing Emerald's frown.

"Earl Nigel expects me to move into the Great House tomorrow. Next week's the betrothal, and the family is getting things ready." She looked across the table at Minette. "You're coming with me. I'll insist."

Both Minette and Zeddie looked up from their chicken legs.

"You too, Zeddie," said Emerald firmly. "You'll have a room in the back of the house with old Henry and the others."

"Now, m'gal, I'd rather sleep here in your father's house. I'm taking no pleasure in the fancy ways of nobility."

Emerald smiled sweetly. "Zeddie, I want you near. If I needed you for some reason, it would take too long to send for you. Anyway, I don't trust you here alone where Pitt can reach you."

"I'll go, but I'm not thinkin' I like the notion none. But Captain Buckington would expect me to stay nigh at hand."

Minette's eyes shone with excitement. "You mean you really want me with you in the Great House?"

Emerald laughed. "I wouldn't stay without you. And just wait until you see the dress I have for you to wear to the betrothal ball." She looked at Zeddie munching his chicken. "We've got to find Captain Farrow and invite him."

Minette scrambled to her feet, wringing her hands. "Ty will know where he is." She looked at Zeddie. "Ty's got to be in Port Royal. You've got to find 'em both. Oh, what a grand event!"

Zeddie cocked his eye from Minette to Emerald and cleared his throat. "I'm thinkin' Ty's made a beeline for Tortuga."

Yolanda turned from the big woodstove. "No, he ain't. He's in Port Royal. Him and Captain Levasseur both. They was seen by ol' Henry at the Red Goose. They's all making big plans to sail with Morgan."

Emerald didn't like the sound of it.

"Then Captain Farrow must be in Port Royal too," said Minette. "Emerald, you'll write the invitation so Zeddie can deliver it tonight?"

"Yes, of course," Emerald said absently, now thinking of Levasseur. The fact that he was in Port Royal might mean trouble. And what of Ty? He was still considered a runaway slave by the family. Could Baret do anything?

The next day, while preparing for the move to the Great House, Emerald was surprised to hear a horse and buggy pull up in front, carrying the dignified and friendly Sir Cecil Chaderton, Baret's friend and staunch Puritan tutor. He had come, so he told her, to escort her home in the style Baret would wish, even if he had to do so himself.

Sight of the godly Cambridge scholar with his sharp, sanctified gaze brought new confidence to Emerald. Here at last was one friend in the house, who not only thought well of her but who would see to Minette's care.

Despite the heat, he was impeccably dressed in a black frock coat and a wide-brimmed scholar's hat absent the plume of the king's dashing Cavaliers. His jaw-length silver hair was neatly paged against a lean, hawklike face, toughened and browned by the Jamaican sun, and he wore a well-groomed, short, pointed Sir Walter Raleigh beard.

"Well, my dear Emerald, I congratulate you. You have Lady Sophie up in arms about the removal of Mr. Pitt. I assume, that upon Baret's arrival, the justice of your decision will be determined."

"I hope you're right, Sir Cecil, unless Mr. Pitt alters his ways considerably, but I think he's hopelessly bound and cannot change."

"You're right. The man is an odious creature. Quite in danger of losing his soul to the devil. I am profoundly amazed that the refined gentry in the house could stubbornly attest to his usefulness.

"I'd like you to know I've taken a great interest in Mathias's first work in establishing a singing school. And if you wouldn't mind my involvement, I would like to stand with you in getting it

82

built and functioning on Foxemoore. Jette tells me it was wondrous indeed. So have those two rascals of his, Timothy and Titus, who have been boasting of it since I arrived."

Emerald's surprise turned into a smile of joy. "Would I *mind* if you were involved? Sir Cecil! Your attentions would be received as an answer to my prayers—and those of Mathias before he died. I couldn't think of anyone more qualified."

"I'm pleased you feel that way, my dear. And I thought we might take a buggy ride out to the old spot where it was burned down in the slave uprising and rededicate the ground to His work."

The day was fresh with promise as they drove toward the burned-out bungalow that had once doubled as Great-uncle Mathias Harwick's singing school and living quarters.

Emerald remembered back with affection to her first meeting with Mathias. She'd been a child when he had come to Jamaica to start his missionary work among the indentured servants of various races on the plantations. They had first met on a Saturday morning at the manor house, when he came to tell Karlton that Emerald must be brought to his Sunday gathering. Hearing Mathias arrive, Emerald had come running down the steps—wearing pirate's drawers.

Uncle Mathias Harwick had turned pale. "An abomination," he breathed to her father.

Emerald had not known what an "abomination" might be, but she learned soon enough while attending her uncle's Sunday gatherings. The Puritan code of ethics condemned the wearing of anything masculine by women, and men's wearing feminine clothing. "It's all there in the Scriptures," he had told her. "In Leviticus and Deuteronomy."

As they drove on, Sir Cecil leaned back in the buggy seat and told her of his interest in renewing the singing school work.

From the time she had told him about translating the slave chants into the message of Christianity, making it more understandable for the slaves brought from their tribes in West Africa, he had been touched by the Spirit of God to become involved. Because he was a lover of languages, the translation work appealed to him. And once he had firsthand knowledge of the miserable, destitute life of slaves, he felt called to spend his years on

Foxemoore seeing that they heard about the grace and love of the Savior of the world.

"I've already mentioned it to Baret. He heartily approves. It will mean, however, that I'll not be able to go with Jette to attend his schooling in London as I first intended. Yet, I feel it's more important to work with these people who have no hope at all. Jette, of course, is already favored. I am sure Nigel and Baret both will see that the boy receives the best tutorage available in London."

She wondered if he knew yet that Geneva and Felix hoped to take Jette with them to Porto Bello. She didn't think he would approve any more than Baret would when he found out. She hadn't told Baret in the letter she'd sent him through Zeddie, thinking it best to explain when she saw him on Foxemoore.

"I have all of Uncle's notes," she told Sir Cecil. "It's been my hope these months to one day have the time to continue his work, but there's been one closed door after another. But now my heart has been made light. I know that your scholarly efforts will be far better than anything I could do."

"We will both strive to get the work done." He took her arm and walked her to the scarred ground that still bore marks of the burned rubble. "Tell me more about Mathias," he said. "I feel I should know this saint better before I deign to pick up his fallen mantle."

As the tropic wind blew warm and soft, Emerald poured out her heart about the elderly man who had first taught her to trust in the Scriptures as the infallible Word of God. Mathias had led her in prayer to receive the Savior. He had taught her to bring all her worries to Him and, later, to worship Him not for what God could give her but because of His incomparable goodness and greatness.

Prior to coming to Jamaica, she told him, Mathias had often preached repentance to the pirates in London before they were hanged on Execution Dock.

"He was in no way a cold and hard man who bore a scowl for wretches, but he was a worthy representative of Christ, kindly showing forth the compassion of God and proving his concern for the buccaneers by his fair deeds.

"Sometimes his days consisted of twelve-hour vigils in which he treated sick slaves and indentured servants on many sugar and cocoa plantations here on Jamaica, receiving no remuneration from the planters and little encouragement from the families. Now and then, certain slaves would bring him gifts of lemons or plantain bread, trying to show their appreciation."

She paused, and Sir Cecil looked toward the plot where Mathias was buried.

"He used to say his labors were trifles in comparison to the bounty of blessings the Lord had bestowed upon him," Emerald continued. "He would as readily treat the leper in Christ's name as any sick of gout or dysentery, and he used to bemoan the fact that he couldn't gain the approval of the governor-general. A leper colony on Jamaica is forbidden, and so is teaching the slaves to read and write."

"Yes, so Baret told me. We need planters elected to the Council who will rewrite the laws," he said. "Who knows? One day Baret himself may settle on Jamaica and stand for the Council himself."

She told him about another building Mathias had developed, a rambling structure made of palm trees near Chocolata Hole, the pirates' "sweetest cove," as they called it. Mathias had managed to hold some teaching services there without incurring the wrath of the planters, but there were many Sundays when he'd preached to only one or two. Once, only Hob, the retired pirate who sold turtles to the buccaneers in Port Royal, showed himself. And even his motives were suspect, for he always brought a turtle or two to sell to her uncle. Hob didn't know it, but Uncle Mathias would return the turtles to the beach.

But though ministry to the Brotherhood went ignored, the singing school for indentured servants and slaves did not. Teaching Christian music and trying to form a choir was considered unusual and on the borderline of apostasy, because at this time hymns were not sung in the churches. Mathias's unusual music ministry eventually kindled the wrath of the inland planters.

"They told him he was piling up wood for the fires of insurrection. They complained to the governor-general and the Council, several of whom were planters themselves. Uncle Mathias's music was swiftly condemned. They accused him of learning voodoo music and said that if he persisted in his meddling they could arrange for a public whipping for witchcraft.

"Geneva used her influence to protect him, but the matter

was far from ended. The turmoil persisted, and a few from inland rode to confront him, threatening to put him in Brideswell. They relented as long as he kept his work confined to Foxemoore.

"Geneva was willing to wait and see if the conduct of the slaves improved, and at one time she was considering building a brick structure to replace his thatch church—'a terrible eyesore,' so said Lady Sophie. But it wasn't any worse than the slave huts."

"What happened to the work at Chocolata Hole?"

"It must have ended when he died, but I can't really be sure, since at that time I went aboard the *Regale*."

"Ah, yes . . . how we both remember that sprightly adventure." The corner of his thin mouth turned down with wry amusement. "Since pirates are considered scum of the earth, no one is likely to care about the church out there. Maybe I'll look into that as well."

Emerald turned to him, her eyes bright, thinking of the time she had been at Brideswell. She told him about her vow to have a minister come at least once a month to hold a meeting there.

"We'll certainly do something about it," he said.

Sir Cecil told her that Mathias's work was truly original. "I suppose you know that Protestant missionary work in the West Indies is unheard of. Before the buccaneers came, it was forbidden by Spain's Jesuits. These men first brought Christianity to the Main, but unfortunately they disbursed it with cruelty toward the Caribs and Africans. Mathias was a rare individual," he continued. "He has left us good footprints to follow, but it is a very lonely path he trod—there has never been a Protestant missionary in Jamaica."

She looked at the energetic old scholar as the breeze touched his silver hair and saw in him a man equal to Mathias in many ways. Emerald smiled and looped her arm through his.

"Baret thinks a good deal of you. Now I know why."

Sir Cecil reached into his frock coat and brought out a King James Bible. As they stood on the spot where the singing school had been born, he opened the worn pages and read from Luke about the Lord Jesus beginning His ministry:

> "The Spirit of the Lord is upon me, because he hath anointed me to preach the gospel to the poor; he hath sent

me to heal the brokenhearted, to preach deliverance to the captives, and recovering of sight to the blind, to set at liberty them that are bruised, to preach the acceptable year of the Lord."

Afterwards they prayed, dedicating the new singing school to bringing the redeeming message of God's love and forgiveness to those bound by the iron chains of slavery.

Thank You, Father, for sending Cecil Chaderton to take the place of Uncle Mathias, she prayed silently. *Thank You for what You are going to do in the future in the lives of these people on Foxemoore.*

Then Sir Cecil put his arm about Emerald and prayed aloud for her and Baret, thanking God for bringing them together and asking that He use them both to further His kingdom. "In Jesus' Name. Amen."

Emerald looked up at him, her eyes moist. Then they both looked off toward the place where the earthly remains of Mathias rested until the promised day of resurrection. A moment later they walked back toward the buggy.

"I'll begin at once," he said as they drove toward the Great House. "The first rascals who'll be rounded up for a class of three will be Jette Buckington and Timothy and Titus."

Emerald laughed. "You'll have your hands full, Sir Cecil. They're as rowdy as a class of ten!"

"So I've already discovered."

8

JETTE'S
IMPORTANT SECRET

Lady Sophie had retired to her room by the time Sir Cecil arrived, escorting Emerald and followed by Minette and Zeddie. Emerald had seen to it that Minette was dressed like a little princess, her amber ringlets arranged in a profusion of French curls. Even Zeddie had on a new frock coat, a new hat and boots, and a new eye patch—made by Minette.

"That old frayed thing makes you look worse than that pirate Lex Thorpe."

Surprisingly, Earl Nigel was there to welcome Emerald. He was as forbiddingly royal as she had remembered him at their first meeting in Port Royal when he had come up with a scheme to keep Baret from marrying Lavender. That scheme had been to pretend a betrothal to his grandson. Was he still pretending?

The earl's wealth of silvery hair was drawn back from a tanned face, making a striking contrast with his dark eyes, as cool and hard as gems. At first he made no response and stood looking at her, a commanding presence who, despite tropical heat, was immaculately garbed in an olive green satin doublet, thigh-length jacket, and black leggings.

Under his regal stare she felt herself wilting and wanting to turn and flee like a frightened rabbit. He stood taking her in, as though deciding whether or not she passed the test. Emerald struggled to keep from flushing.

Sir Cecil cleared his throat, and Nigel's dark gaze was diverted to the scholar. Nigel's brow lifted, making him look too much like Baret.

"You know Baret's soon-to-be betrothed, of course?"

The earl gave a laugh. "I do indeed, Cecil. But I hardly recognize her. You have done yourself well," he told her. "Baret will be enchanted. And so will the king," he added wryly. "We best keep you far afield of Charles."

"Your lordship," she said and gave a curtsy, wondering that her practiced manner turned out so well and that her voice didn't shake.

There was the flash of sapphire ring, and lace spilled from his cuff as he stepped forward, caught her hand, and bowed over it. "Lady Harwick."

Emerald kept her eyes lowered, afraid she would reveal her tears. The earl of Buckington had deigned to call *her* Lady Harwick!

Cecil was smiling, evidently pleased that she had neither fainted nor broken out into a Gin Lane dialect.

"Ah!" came a voice from the stairs. "So my new niece has arrived, looking every bit a soon-to-be countess."

Felix Buckington walked up, greeted his father and Sir Cecil, and then, following Nigel's display, bent over her hand. His dark eyes danced maliciously. "Sophie tells me you've sent our overseer to the boiling house and elevated a slave to the position. I must say, my dear Emerald, Baret has indeed chosen himself a bride to keep the gossips in London overworked."

"I acted too hastily perhaps—my order has been revoked. But the man is odious and doesn't deserve the position on so fine a plantation as Foxemoore."

Nigel looked at Felix and gave a laugh. "She seems to know how to answer you, Felix."

"Assuredly so. I agree Pitt is a disgusting fellow, but he gets the job done. And after all, that is what Foxemoore is about— sugar production, not the coddling of Africans. They're born sullen, and one must lay the beam to their backs to get them to do anything."

Sir Cecil cleared his throat again. "I doubt this is the moment to discuss the evils of slavery. Baret's betrothed has just stepped through the front threshold. Shall we not allow her a few minutes of peace? I think," he said, "that Baret would expect it."

"He's quite right, Felix. There is no need to discuss the overseer now," said Nigel. "We best wait until Baret arrives. Don't forget that, between him and Emerald, they will have as much voice in how Foxemoore is run as you and Geneva. And I shall cast the deciding vote."

Felix's face hardened, but he was the essence of charm. He smiled at Emerald. "Yes, I didn't mean to upset you, my dear.

Your sprightliness is most refreshing after Lavender's indifference. You'll come by and say hello to Geneva? She's waiting to welcome you. I can't say the same for Sophie."

"Yes, of course," murmured Emerald and deliberately turned toward the door. "Come along, Cousin Minette. Tonight you'll share my room. I'm sure a room of your own will be arranged tomorrow."

Minette had hung back in the doorway and now came forward with a flush on her cheeks as though she expected Earl Nigel and Lord Felix to speak disparagingly of her.

Neither man welcomed her but turned away to speak of Foxemoore.

It wasn't that they were deliberately being offensive, thought Emerald. It was just that the pride of blooded nobility afforded them a natural environment for arrogance. To them Minette was like a servant disguised in ribbons and lace. But because she was pretty and young, they were more merciful than to order her out of the house, as Lady Sophie might have done.

Emerald smiled at Minette bravely, looped her arm through hers, and together they walked toward the magnificent stairway, followed by Sir Cecil. Zeddie had gone to the back of the house to take up his residence with the serving men. Since he knew old Henry well, they were probably already sharing a secret glass of Madeira wine.

As Emerald walked with Minette to the stair, she looked up to see Lavender standing above on the landing. Automatically, Minette paused, and Emerald felt her stiffen and try to draw back. But Emerald tightened her hold on her arm.

"Don't you dare cower as though you are less than she. You're a daughter of the King, remember?"

The words must have bolstered Minette, for she went forward again, her silk skirts rustling softly.

Emerald had often thought that Lavender was the embodiment of the British view of beauty: fair complexion, golden hair arranged in lustrous waves and coquettish curls, and graced with outward poise. Having expected her blue eyes to show icy scorn for her and Minette, she wondered that Lavender smiled and came down the stairs, hands held out in sisterly welcome.

"Cousin Emerald and Cousin Minette, how glad I am you've come." A moment later her cool lips brushed Emerald's cheek, then Minette's. "How sweet you look, Minette. We'll definitely need to find a young gentlemen for you at the ball. And Emerald —you *do* look so like a countess. How anxious Baret must be to sweep you away!"

What's gotten into her?

"Hello, Lavender," said Emerald.

Lavender stepped between her and Minette. Then, taking their arms, she led them up the stairs, chattering as though they were the best of friends.

Minette's eyes were wide, but she fell into step and carried herself well.

"I would have come to see you days ago, but I don't like to even look at the slaves," Lavender said with a grimace. "It brings back the uprising and the death of Mother. Shall we say hello to Geneva before I show you both to your rooms? Oh, yes, Minette has her own. We know how you'd want that. And after all—" she smiled sweetly at Minette "—she's one of us now."

Later that afternoon, the sunlight filtered in through the bedroom curtains as Emerald, alone, fell across the lush four-poster bed and stared blankly at the ceiling, dazed. She had made it through the horrendous ordeal of walking into the Great House and meeting the family on equal terms. She was emotionally exhausted. She wanted to laugh and cry at the same time, especially when she thought of Minette, two bedrooms down the hall in a room as grand as her own with satin coverlet, lace curtains, and a wardrobe that would soon be brimming with pretty frocks and slippers! Who would ever have thought Emerald Levasseur Harwick and Minette Levasseur would be living here like the Buckingtons?

One week before the betrothal! She closed her eyes and smiled as the image of Baret came to life within her heart. *He's mine.* She touched the ruby pendant with her fingers, then looked at her left hand and laughed. Soon now she would be wearing the Buckington family ring . . .

"Psst! Emerald! You awake?"

She sat up, startled by a child's whisper coming from beneath her big bed. She stood and lifted the edge of the coverlet. "Jette! What are you doing under there?"

He crawled out on all fours and looked up at her with luminous gray green eyes showing from under a shock of dark hair.

Emerald, forcing a frown she didn't feel, pulled him to his feet. "Why are you sneaking about? And don't think I didn't see you in Geneva's room the other day. It was only my kindness that allowed you to keep hiding."

The boy, small for his age because of a year's illness upon his first arrival at Foxemoore, didn't blanch at the scolding but smiled, and her heart contracted. He looked so much like Baret.

Jette knew he was blooded royalty and that there wasn't much anyone would do to him without Earl Nigel's approval. "Sorry, Emerald, but I had to talk to you alone."

She folded her arms. "And what excuse do you have for hiding beneath *Geneva's* bed?"

He shrugged his small shoulders and glanced cautiously toward the door. "I wanted to hear what that old Spaniard had to tell her about Porto Bello."

"What old Spaniard—oh, you mean Dr. Vasquez."

"He's still here, you know, though nobody sees him much. I don't like him any more than I do Uncle Felix."

"Jette, you mustn't say things like that about your uncle."

"I know, but it's true. He doesn't like me much either. I know, because Timothy and Titus heard him say so to Carlotta."

Timothy and Titus were orphan twins that Jette had saved from being sold to another plantation by buying them himself. The idea was outlandish to Emerald, but it often happened in the Caribbean. Jette, the twins, and a spotted hound were seen together often.

She lifted a brow. "I suppose the twins were snooping about the house as well?"

"Yes, and it's a good thing they did, too. 'Cause Cousin Carlotta found 'em. Then she told them to find me and bring me to see her before they locked her in her room for good." His eyes brightened like polished green stones. He stepped closer and whispered, "Carlotta's my friend. She trusts me and my brother with anything. She gave me something to hide. Something for Baret when he comes. When's Baret coming, Emerald?"

Her mind halted. Something for Baret? She knelt until they were eye level, and she held his shoulders.

"What did Carlotta give you?"

His eyes gleamed. "She told me not to tell anyone but Baret. Not even Sir Cecil."

"But you just told me about it. So you might as well tell me what you have. You can trust me, can't you?"

He nodded, then looked away, as though he wanted to tell her.

"Did she tell you not to inform me?"

"No-o-o . . ."

"There, you see? Jette, what did she give you? What did you do with it? Maybe you should give it to me. I'll keep it in a safe place—"

He cast his eyes downward. "I can't tell you yet. Maybe I'll tell you tomorrow. Or the day when you get engaged to Baret." His smile widened. "I'm glad you're going to be my sister instead of Lavender." Then he went on, "Me and the twins hid it so no one can ever find it unless we get it. It's like buried treasure. And we're the buccaneers."

She sighed. "Where is Carlotta now?"

"Locked in her room. Uncle Felix and Dr. Vasquez won't let her out until the night of the betrothal. They're afraid she'll run away again. The doctor keeps the key. His room's next to hers. But Timothy and Titus and me, we got in before they locked her inside. She knew they would lock her in, so she was smart. She gave me a box to hide for Baret."

Emerald cast about in her mind, trying to come up with what might be in the box. The jewels of Levasseur? But why would Carlotta have had *them*? Unless Baret had given them to her to keep safely. But no, somehow the idea didn't seem quite right. Then, what?

"Jette," she began—

"Are you going to help Sir Cecil with my tutoring?" His eyes pleaded silently.

"Both Baret and Sir Cecil have requested my help, so it looks like I will."

"And Sir Cecil said he's going to rebuild the singing school. Timothy and Titus have a song they thought up. Wanna hear it?" He drew in a breath and stood tall and straight.

"The Lord built—"

93

"That ain't how it goes, Jette. You cain't sing like we's can sing."

Emerald eyes closed as the voice of one of the twins sounded from beneath the bed. So they were all there.

"Is the hound under there, too?"

"He goes where we goes, Miss Emerald, but he don't bark. He's a good hound."

Two pairs of eyes peered up from beneath the coverlet, and the hound's tail flapped hard against the floor.

"You sing it for Emerald, then." Jette ordered them.

They crawled out, two small thin boys dressed as richly as Jette, because they were wearing his hand-me-downs. The spotted hound lay with his head on his front paws, his tail whipping from one side to the other. In a moment Timothy and Titus were crooning.

"Der once was a man named Paul," said Timothy.

"He once had de name of Saul," Titus chimed in.

"An' he found two boys in de boilin' house, an' he tells 'em their names is Timothy and Titus—"

"That doesn't even rhyme!" scoffed Jette. "You changed it. A song has to rhyme."

Timothy gave Jette a sullen look. "No, it don't. Sir Cecil say it don't."

Jette's mouth tightened. "If it doesn't rhyme, it sounds wrong."

"No'm, it don't," said Titus. "Uh-uh, no sir. Jesus loves us, ain't it right, Timothy? We was found in the boilin' house when Mama died there. Not everybody's lucky enough to be found in a boilin' house. Sir Cecil said so. Takes lots of blessing to be discovered in a boilin' house. That's why *we* has black skin. Jesus had black skin."

"No, He didn't," Jette said stubbornly. "He had brown skin."

"No matter. You don't got either kind. You only has white skin, and the Lord likes us a whole lot more'n He likes white skin."

Jette frowned. "My skin's tanned—look, it ain't white."

"You can't say ain't," scolded Timothy. "You has to speak like Sir Cecil."

"But *we* can say ain't anytime we wants to," said Titus and gave a stout nod of his head for affirmation. He looked at his twin.

"Sure we can, but Jette can't. There's lots o' things we can do that Jette can't do."

"I can do anything I want—even say ain't."

"No, you cain't. Even de hound can do more things than you can. Hound can roll over and bark three times."

"Because I taught him!"

"Stop!" Emerald ordered, covering a laugh. "All three of you! Sit down! *Now!*"

They did so, looking up at her with guilty eyes.

Emerald looked from one to the other. "All right, I want to know what you did with the box Miss Carlotta gave you."

The three of them looked at each other. They locked arms and pretended to button their lips. The hound whined in agreement.

"I don't think there is any box," whispered Emerald. "I think you made it up."

Timothy started to speak, but Jette elbowed him.

Emerald folded her arms. "You're not going to share your secret with me?"

Their eyes dropped.

Jette unbuttoned his lips. "I'll tell you when the big dinner and the ball come. All three of us will tell you—and Baret. We'll bring you to the buried treasure."

She might threaten them, but she believed that would do more harm than good. "I'm disappointed you won't tell me now, but maybe you'll change your mind."

"Maybe, Emerald."

"Remember, you mustn't tell anyone else first. It's a secret for Baret."

Jette nodded gravely. "A present for his betrothal." Then he turned to the twins, and they went through their ritual. Timothy placed his small hand over the mouth of Titus, who did the same to Timothy. Jette crawled over to the hound, placing his palm over the hound's wet snout. He whispered: "Our secret is bound to death in the ground."

They walked to the door in single file and peeked out, then slipped away silently.

Emerald stood thinking. Perhaps it was Carlotta's own jewels she wanted kept safely away from Dr. Vasquez or even her father, Felix? But why give them to Baret?

On the evening of the betrothal, the pillared veranda encircling the lower level of the Great House was thronged with guests. Upstairs in her bedroom, Emerald and Minette practiced waltzing and curtsying, as Lavender sat glumly watching.

"No, m'lord," said Minette silkily, fluttering her white lace fan toward Emerald. She drew it back with a tilt of her head. "Yes, m'lord Buckington. How kind of you to say so, m'lord!"

Lavender moaned her boredom. She was seated on the cane daybed, while her chin rested in her hand. "Minette, you're not playing Shakespeare."

Minette cast her a doleful look but brightened as she gazed at her image in the mirror. She whirled, her skirts flaring like yellow butterfly wings. "Anything you say, m'lord!"

Emerald was busy pretending she was drawing near to Baret to accept the ring.

Again Lavender groaned. "It just isn't fair. There's no romance in my life at all. And I'm going to be a duchess!"

"You have Lord Grayford," said Minette. "How can you say there's no romance?"

Lavender wrinkled her nose and primped in front of the gilded hand mirror she held. "I always did think Sir Erik Farrow was an exciting man."

Emerald paused and looked at Minette. The girl did her best to cover her alarm as she turned away and walked to the bed.

Lavender glanced at her, satisfied.

She's jealous of how pretty Minette has become, thought Emerald. *And she's determined to try and ruin things by flirting with Captain Farrow at the ball.*

"I'm tired now," said Minette, sinking to the bed. She tossed aside her fan dejectedly. "I'll never learn how to do things like a lady."

It was the wrong thing for Minette to say, and her surrender to Lavender's dominance made Emerald angry. The girl had to believe in herself and try, instead of being afraid to compete. She might never win Erik Farrow, but if she didn't, it would be Erik's fault. If he could be trapped again by Lavender, he deserved getting hurt all over again.

"Don't be silly, Minette. You'll be as fancy as any girl at the ball."

Lavender made no comment as she got up from the daybed and went out onto the terrace. "Yasmin, bring me another glass of limeade." She leaned over the rail. "The guests are all arriving, Emerald. You best get ready."

Emerald forgot Minette and turned with excitement as Zunsia came through the dressing room door, smiling, carrying her gown with its yards of pale blue satin and cream lace.

Minette for a time forgot her fears and rushed to help Emerald into the dress, careful to not muss her elaborate hairdo of French curls. She clasped her hands together. "Ooh, Emerald! Wait till Baret sees you!"

Lavender glanced resentfully over her pale shoulder, her blue eyes cold. Jealousy had turned her normally pretty face into harsh lines.

Emerald looked at herself in the mirror, and her heart fluttered with nervous excitement. She wouldn't say it. She wouldn't even think it. She turned away from her lovely image, her cheeks flushed, and smiled at Minette, who had tears in her eyes.

"I wish Uncle Karlton was here to see you now."

"That's odd," Lavender murmured as she took the limeade from Yasmin and looked down the palm-lined road.

"What is, Miss Lavender?"

"Those men. I've never seen them before. Have you?"

Yasmin shaded her eyes with her hand. "No, Miss. Must be folks from Saint Jago. They've come from all over Jamaica."

"I suppose you're right. Has Lord Grayford arrived?"

"Yes, Miss. He's downstairs in the library, talkin' to Lord Felix."

Lavender sighed. "And the viscount?"

"I expect he's here, Miss, in the earl's chambers. I think he arrived an hour ago with that Sir Farrow."

Lavender's eyes gleamed as she sipped her limeade and glanced back to the strangers on the road. "I want you to deliver a message to Sir Farrow for me."

"Yes, Miss Lavender."

9

THE GRAND
BETROTHAL

Twilight set in with a mixture of inky shadows and soft shades of rose. Baret swung from the large pepper tree branch and caught hold of the railing. A moment later he hauled himself over the side onto the veranda as easily as climbing the rope ladder to board his ship.

The sleek-muscled frame of Erik Farrow came behind. "You have fifteen minutes, your lordship," he said too calmly. As usual his chiseled face showed no emotion. "A word of caution—do not permit the woman you expect to marry to know you nearly forgot to keep your hour of betrothal. You will never hear the end of the matter."

Baret laughed and came swiftly into Earl Nigel's elaborate bedchamber, tossing aside his hat and baldric and unbuttoning his shirt.

Erik remained by the rail, looking below into the back side of the little used garden. He glanced toward the next room above, where golden light spilled over the veranda trellis and a familiar female voice laughed merrily like chimes. Minette.

"Bristol!" Baret called.

His grandfather's serving man rushed in from a dressing room and, seeing Baret, threw up his hands with relief. "There you are, m'lord. I was so afraid—"

"What! You, too, thought I'd forget? What ill thoughts you and Farrow have of me!"

Bristol hesitated, looking at him.

Baret smiled. "Tonight the buccaneer is a viscount. Where are my suitable garments?"

The old man scrambled to the walk-in wardrobe and with great flourish brought out a stylish dark velvet jacket and a ruffled white silk shirt, which he laid on the large bed as though offering a display of the Buckington jewels.

"Your bathwater, my lord Viscount, waits. Er—would you like a smidgen of rosewater, m'lord? A bit of oil perhaps?"

"Put that in the bath, and I'll dunk you in it. Where's my grandfather?"

"He waits in the parlor, m'lord, as does Lord Felix and the rest of the family. Lady Emerald will not be escorted down until your presence is—er—accounted for."

"You have the ring?"

"Right here, m'lord, waiting." He produced from his own jacket pocket a tiny silver box bearing the insignia of the house of Buckington. "Earl Nigel gave it to me only minutes ago."

As Baret quickly finished drying, Bristol handed him the white silk shirt. He snatched it and put it on while Bristol proceeded to the task of getting on Baret's polished black boots.

Baret saw Erik leaning against the terrace rail, arms folded, looking up to the next terrace.

"I should have abducted Emerald and married her aboard the *Regale*." He fumbled with the buttons on the shirt, unhappy with it. He didn't like silk. "I loathe this formality." He gave up on the black ribbon cravat and tossed it on the bed. "How much more exciting to marry her beneath the stars on the Caribbean."

"She may not think a captain's cabin is as fine a place as you do," Erik said.

Baret's dark eyes squinted. "Nevertheless, I have finer memories of that cabin. And maybe I'll abduct her yet."

Erik laughed. "And hang—by request of your grandfather."

"Here, m'lord, allow me," said Bristol and tied the cravat with the expertise he used daily on the earl.

"I suppose Emerald and Minette have had the entire day to dress."

"It's like a woman, m'lord," said Erik. "They have everything prepared a week in advance. Men, especially viscounts, wait until five minutes before the ball."

Baret cast him an irritated look, slipped on the impeccable jacket, and buttoned the cuffs. He stomped his feet in the leather boots, helping out the flustered Bristol, who was struggling and sweating.

"I always thought a man's betrothal should be a leisurely affair," continued Erik, strolling about the red velvet and dark mahogany furnishings of the grand chamber.

All the while, Baret's dark glittering gaze followed him. A sardonic smile was on his mouth. "There's nothing stopping you from getting yourself betrothed to Minette tonight. You look leisurely enough. And there's always a stray bit of jewelry about the chamber to lend you for the amorous occasion."

Erik looked at him with a lifted golden brow.

Baret smiled, satisfied to see his moment of fear. "Cheer up, Erik. The black hour will come when you, too, are doomed." He looked down at Bristol, who was giving a final whisk of his cloth to the boots. "Enough, Bristol."

Baret placed the ring in his jacket pocket, then added the finishing touches to his handsome appearance, smoothing his thick dark hair and stuffing his pistol in his belt before buttoning the jacket. Even tonight, he trusted not his enemies.

Bristol poured refreshment and brought it to Baret and Erik. "You have five minutes, m'lord."

"A leisurely amount of time. To Porto Bello, Erik."

Erik returned the toast. "At long last."

Bristol disappeared, leaving them alone.

Erik sank into a plush red velvet chair, and Baret walked to the edge of the large bed and stood gazing at a painting of Royce Buckington on the ivory wall. It wouldn't be too many weeks before he expected to rescue his father from his Spanish captors —or die trying. He knew Morgan was already sailing to the South Cays for the rendezvous, as were many of the other buccaneers.

The room was muggy, for a tropical storm was beginning to blow in, snapping the drapes near the open veranda. Outside there were many voices and the sound of laughter. Baret was thoughtful.

"There's something I should tell you," said Erik quietly.

Baret turned and looked down at him with a steady gaze. He wasn't surprised. Erik had been behaving oddly since he'd shown up at Port Royal to accompany him here to Foxemoore.

"Tell me anything, Erik, but do not tell me Miguel has escaped your ship."

Erik watched him over interlaced fingers. "You can be sure the Spaniard is locked safely in the hold of the *Warspite*. No, it is ill news of another sort, affecting Emerald."

Baret's mood altered to gravity. He wasn't sure he wanted to hear it. "Say on. There's little time."

"Jackman told me he has trustworthy news. The Dutch slave ship with Sir Karlton aboard was attacked recently and sunk."

How would he tell Emerald that dark news? Especially tonight.

"Who was it, does the Brotherhood know?"

"No one appears to know anything."

As Baret contemplated, the door opened, and Bristol stood in the outer hall. "M'lord, the earl has asked for you."

The doors to the spacious parlor opened, and Emerald and Lady Sophie entered with Geneva. The two older women were perfectly gowned and carried an aura of nobility. Lady Sophie had donned her best jewels—"in honor of Baret, of course," and carried the family Bible. This she ceremoniously presented to Sir Cecil Chaderton, who was overseeing the betrothal ceremony at Baret's request. Geneva looked almost well again, though she had risen from her bed for the occasion. Her red-gold hair shone regally, and her gray eyes appeared to glow with well wishes for Emerald.

Behind them, Minette carried a basket of white roses on her arm, and her amber curls glinted with interwoven pink rosebuds on a gold netting.

Only the immediate family was in attendance at the ceremony in the parlor. The myriad of guests loitered outdoors, dining on roast capon and nibbling on plates of fresh bite-sized fruits, or they waited in the ballroom for Emerald and Baret's first waltz after the ceremony.

Minette had cast her amber eyes down the hall where other guests stood watching as Emerald and the small family procession entered the parlor. Minette looked to see if Captain Farrow was nearby. He was.

Emerald entered through the parlor doors, where woven garlands of white roses sweetened the air. She thought that if her heart beat much faster her stays would cut off her breathing. The flames of hundreds of tapered candles welcomed her in flickering silence like the smiling eyes of hovering angels, and she felt a catch in her throat. *This can't be happening. I am dreaming.*

Music drifted in from the terrace but not the kind she had expected. Her eyes turned toward the sound. She could hardly believe it! Who had arranged for this?

101

On the open terrace, with the darkening sky as a backdrop, a handful of African humsters formed a dignified line, their dark faces grave and their eyes cast upward toward heaven. Robed in white tunics, they were humming from the soul the only slave chant that Great-uncle Mathias had managed to arrange with a Christian High Church musical slant. The sound was African Christian and pulled at the heart as though each note were wept before the feet of Jesus.

Tears filled Emerald's eyes when she saw all her dearest friends among the slaves—Yolanda, Ngozi, Jitana, even Yasmin, Lavender's maid, and Zunsia.

Lady Sophie in seeing this display—never before witnessed in all her seventy-two years—gasped and swayed in her white silk slippers. Felix caught her arm, hauled her across the parlor to a velvet chair, and gestured for the twins.

Timothy and Titus emerged from behind the potted palms. Each gathered up a great palmetto leaf, stood on either side of her wingback chair, and swished his fan in time to the humming. Then they began to join in, loudly, and Sophie groaned.

Jette, standing in green velvet beside his grandfather Earl Nigel, tried to get their attention to be quiet until the earl laid his jeweled hand on his head.

Emerald parted with Geneva as planned and walked forward alone to the middle of the room. There she waited, just as she had practiced at least fifty times with Minette in the bedchamber.

The warm honey-colored light from the candles spilled down upon her gown and its yards of pale blue satin and ribbons of velvet embroidered with gold. A two-inch trim of cream lace fluttered at the edge of her bell sleeves. Her dark hair shone in countless French curls, and her cinnamon brown eyes looked expectantly at the male assemblage for just one particular man.

She saw Baret, and her heart raced. There had been a last minute avalanche of whispered gossip that he wouldn't come, that he had set sail with Morgan, having changed his mind about "Harwick's daughter."

But he *had* come for her, just as he had promised. His vow in the garden of the governor's residence had been true and faithful. She waited, her eyes on him expectantly, and he came forward without hesitation.

It was all so formal. Almost as though they were strangers, he bowed, then reached for her left hand. But there was nothing in his touch that carried the thought of their being strangers. It made her heart leap, and the warmth in his dark eyes wrapped about her in an embrace as real as though he had swept her into his arms.

A faint flush of color rose into her pale cheeks, and her eyes clung to his as he slipped the Buckington ring onto her third finger. It was, of course, too large, for it was a man's ring and meant only to announce that this man had chosen her to eventually become his bride. But to Emerald it was as precious as though the ring had been brought from heaven by a messenger of joy.

Soon, she thought, perhaps next year at this time, Baret would put a wedding ring on that same finger, and after that she would be his forever. She almost thought that she should have agreed to marry him now and just ignore the ugly gossip that might attend. An engagement was a serious matter, but how much more wonderful this moment would be if Sir Cecil were stepping forward to pronounce the vows rather than offer a prayer for the blessing of God upon their future union.

Emerald smiled down at the ring. Who but her father would ever have dared to think that she would become the betrothed of a viscount?

Baret enclosed her small hand in his, and then, because it was not deemed proper to kiss her in public, he brought the hand to his lips and kissed her palm. His eyes, however, promised more, and her warm gaze responded.

Sir Cecil held out the Bible. Baret laid her hand on it, covered by his own, and the Cambridge divine prayed for God's blessing, protection, and guidance.

A moment later the mild congratulations followed, and even Lady Sophie recovered enough to plant a dutiful kiss on her cheek while Jette waited to congratulate the couple.

"I am honored you're going to marry my brother," he said with a rehearsed tone. Then he blurted out honestly, "Like Grandfather, I'm glad it wasn't Lavender."

"Jette!" Lady Sophie groaned, and a hand went to her forehead.

Baret laughed and swooped him up in his arms. "So am I. Now give her a kiss."

Jette shyly leaned over and planted a kiss on Emerald's cheek and whispered in her ear, "I got the box for Baret. Me and the twins will be in the garden by the stone lion."

Earl Nigel came up and bent over her hand. "Congratulations, Emerald. I can see why you've stolen Baret's heart. You are charming, indeed."

He turned to Baret, and a look passed between them that brought a stilted moment.

Emerald's hand closed over the ring as she glanced from the earl to the viscount.

"Remember our agreement, Baret."

"How could I forget?"

The earl excused himself and walked from the parlor to the ballroom as did the others, and Jette was ushered off by Zunsia.

Emerald felt her throat tighten. There had been much more to that exchange, and she thought she knew what it was. The earl was reminding Baret that the betrothal was as far as the ruse was ever to go, but surely—surely Baret wouldn't—

They were alone. She turned toward him, and if her insecurities bade her fear otherwise, the look he gave her swept them away with one torrid glance.

"You'll make a beautiful countess."

She laughed nervously.

His arm slid about her waist, and he drew her into his arms, the other hand lifting her chin; and Emerald met his kiss, her arms holding him.

"I must be a fool to have agreed to wait a year. There are advantages to being a reckless buccaneer, you know. One of them is having the prerogative to ignore rules and marry you tonight. Tell me, Emerald, is there any of the pirate's daughter from Tortuga left in you? Why don't you tell me you feel reckless, too? Tell me to marry you now!"

She could easily have blurted out yes! She struggled to safeguard the emotions of both of them by pulling away a little and saying lightly, "You mean I've been practicing my curtsies for nothing? And I thought I pleased you tonight with all my manners."

"Your manners please me very well. And so do your lips."

"Oh, dear" . . . She spoiled everything by giggling, but she couldn't help herself. "I didn't think you wanted a pirate's brat from Tortuga," she said, lowering her eyes and running her fingers along the ruffle of his shirt.

"I want *you*."

"I think you're a tempter. Just where is that Cambridge divinity student?"

"He's here, too. And he agrees."

"And what if I said yes!"

His hold tightened. "Do you?"

She laughed.

He glanced toward the door. The music had begun in the ballroom. The guests were waiting for their entry to lead the first waltz to quiet applause.

"I have other ideas. A ship waits—a yellow moon, and the wind—"

He swung her up into his arms and turned toward the terrace.

She gasped. "Baret! You're not serious—"

"You have a few things to learn about how serious I can be."

He carried her toward the steps, and she almost believed he meant it. He was only teasing, of course. He had to be. Her heart was throbbing with love because it cried *yes! yes!*

"Stop!" she said, laughing. "We can't!" She whispered a warning, thinking it might sober him. "What will Earl Nigel say?"

"Going somewhere?"

They stopped.

It wasn't the earl but Sir Cecil who stood on the terrace steps. A wry half smile showed on his thin mouth, but his sharp eyes danced. "So there is more of the scoundrel in you than viscount!"

"My dear Cecil, I didn't realize there was that much difference between the two."

"Maybe you're right, but Emerald has the final say in this. Don't you, my dear?"

Baret didn't look the least embarrassed, but Emerald flushed and elbowed Baret to put her down. He continued to hold her.

"You're just in time," Baret said. "I was about to run off with my betrothed." He looked at Emerald. "On the other hand, it looks as though heaven has intervened and we must wait. A disappointment." He set her gently on her feet and bowed toward

105

Cecil. "I do believe the guests are waiting for us to lead the first waltz. That's the third time the music has returned to the beginning. If you will pardon us . . ." And taking Emerald's arm, he turned her about and led her toward the ballroom as Emerald covered her laughter.

"He knows you well."

"Too well."

As they entered the ballroom, Baret bowed sedately to the guests, and Emerald curtsied. Then they were on the wide, polished floor, waltzing. She had unobtrusively slipped the ring inside her bodice for safekeeping, afraid she would lose it. After several times about the floor, they were joined by others until the floor was filled and they were no longer the object of every eye.

Lavender had not come to the betrothal ceremony, but she appeared now. Lord Grayford led her in from a side door. Neither of them looked especially happy. Lavender refused to look at Baret, though Grayford spoke as they waltzed by, offering his congratulations.

The hour was all that Emerald had ever hoped for, and not until they had danced to at least a dozen waltzes and Baret had escorted her to the table for refreshments did she remember Jette.

"Oh, dear, I'd forgotten. He'll be so disappointed."

"Forgot who? Rafael?"

She ignored the little jest and explained about the box and Carlotta.

Emerald glanced about. And just where *were* Carlotta and Dr. Ricardo Vasquez? They hadn't been at the betrothal either, but she'd been so occupied that she hadn't noticed their absence until now. Had Felix decided he couldn't trust his daughter even at the ball?

The news that Carlotta had entrusted something important to Jette had sobered Baret. He glanced toward Felix. But his uncle was with Geneva and Earl Nigel, and he appeared unconcerned about Baret.

Baret led her toward the cooler terrace, where he handed her a glass of sweetened limeade. "I'll see to Jette and find out what's on Carlotta's mind." He looked back toward the ballroom, glittering with a rainbow of color and jewels. "I don't see Erik, or I'd have him attend you."

106

"I don't see Minette either . . ." Emerald scanned the dance floor. "I'd prefer just to sit in the cool and gather my wits. You go find Jette and the twins."

Baret placed a hand behind her neck and drew her face toward his, kissing her. Then he was gone.

Emerald leaned against the railing, holding the tall glass with its fresh mint leaf. She reached into her bodice, removed the ring, and held it up to the moonlight. She smiled and kissed it.

Minette felt like crying until her eyes were red and puffy, but she tried not to. Then Emerald would be disappointed in her, and Lavender would be smug and pleased that she'd been able to hurt her.

The ball had been going well for Minette. She'd even had enough courage to enter the room when the music began, believing that Emerald and the viscount would arrive for the first waltz. But they hadn't come immediately, and Minette stood alone, afraid and anxious until Erik Farrow seemed to emerge from nowhere and very politely bowed.

"Good evening."

She became tongue-tied and hated herself for it. This is what she'd been planning for, praying for, and now the wonderful moment was here, waiting with expectation for her to speak profoundly—"Good evening, m'lord"—and maybe even give a little curtsy as her skirts shimmered.

And what did she do?

Nothing. She looked at him but could not speak.

The handsome face looked back at her blankly, but there'd been stifled amusement in his eyes—she was sure of it.

"You look lovely tonight, Miss Levasseur," he commented, and she still said nothing. She tried to swish her fan but dropped it with a foolish clatter. And when she bent to pick it up, so did he, and she bumped into him clumsily.

And then she turned red when he handed it to her with a brief smile, and instead of saying, "Why, you're very kind, m'lord," she stood there like a goose.

Then Lavender had come as the essence of everything a lady is. She'd asked Erik where he'd been all these dreadfully long months and said she was so pleased to see him again and

107

would he mind awfully if he would walk her to the terrace for a breath of air?

And then she turned to Minette and said, "Minette, can you go help Zunsia find Jette? And then run along to the kitchen and bring out more Madeira for the guests."

And she'd walked off with him.

That was all of ten minutes ago, and Minette's throat hurt, and she was terribly thirsty and miserable. She ought to run upstairs to her room and lock the door and cry all she wanted. Who would care? Who would even miss her? Oh, she could see their glances her way. "That's Emerald's half-caste cousin," they were saying. "She used to be a slave, and look at her now—acting like one of us."

One of *us*.

She threw down her fan with a sob. "I *am* one of them!"

"Are you?"

Minette whirled, and Erik stood in the anteroom doorway, leaning there, sipping from a glass.

"I don't think either of us is," he commented. "I'm learning I do not much care whether I am or not. I'm a buccaneer and will always be so. I've decided I wouldn't trade my ship for any number of titles in London. Maybe if you were smart you wouldn't try to make those old cats in there accept you. What do you care what they think?"

She shrugged her shoulders and sank weakly onto the flowered muslin of a settee. "Everyone wants to be treated with respect."

"Lavender will never treat you so. Her heart is too small to share it with anyone but herself. Her world is no larger than her gilded mirror. So I would not worry about her—or the Buckingtons and Harwicks. And there's little else in London except more of them. Rather boring, isn't it? Now, St. Kitts! That's another matter. You would like it there, I think."

She smiled for the first time. "Maybe you're right. I used to dream of London a lot, of getting away from Jamaica, but now . . . well, maybe I belong here."

"Then we may have more of the same interests than I first thought." He smiled and watched her over his glass.

Minette knew she flushed. She reached down and picked up her fan and swished it. She glanced toward the door.

108

"I best be gettin' back."

"Why?"

The simple question completely undid her.

"You can't use the excuse about 'gossip.'"

She laughed wearily. "No, I guess not." Her eyes came to his. He was so handsome in fine hunter green velvet and a Holland shirt with a wide collar. She saw he carried his weapons. She realized he was a dangerous man in more ways than one and that he was watching her with a keen interest he had never shown before. A warning bell went off in her mind. It was as if she could hear the voice of Great-uncle Mathias calling from a distance. She was naive, and she was a half-caste, and her infatuation with such a man as Captain Farrow, a buccaneer, could leave her in great trouble.

"So you didn't go to the Blue Mountains to find Ty?"

"Blue Mountains? Ty's not there. He's in Port Royal. He expects to sail with Morgan."

"I was told you ran away to the Blue Mountains to find him."

Startled, she wondered aloud, "Why did you think that?"

"Sempala told me. I went to the fields looking for you, but you weren't there."

Dumbfounded, she stared at him, then she slowly stood. *He had come looking for her.*

"I didn't go to the Blue Mountains, but I would've escaped if I could have. I didn't know what had happened to Emerald in Brideswell, and we were told Uncle Karlton was dead."

She saw a flicker of gravity in his eyes at the mention of Emerald's father, but it was still amazing to Minette that Erik would have cared enough to come to the fields to look for her. She hadn't thought a man such as he would even remember her, even though he had rescued her from aboard the *San Pedro.* But what did this confession mean—that he had come to the field?

"I—I was kept from escaping by Sempala and Mr. Pitt."

He watched her calmly, but she suspected he was interested to know what had happened. She blushed. Did he think—

"Sempala had you?"

She nodded, averting her eyes and playing with the fan. Erik wouldn't believe that the Lord had protected her, even if she told him so. It was an awful fact that half-castes, Africans, and

Caribs were considered mere concubines. No one worried about them. No one cared about their purity but God.

"If I had known that, I would have taken you away from him. Maybe he will still die for lying to me."

Her amber eyes rushed to his, and the anger she saw stunned her. *But—but why would he care?*

Her heart began to beat like a rabbit's. She remembered how he had briefly kissed her aboard the *San Pedro*. She had never forgotten that kiss, but she had thought he didn't even remember, that he must have kissed a hundred women. Was she wrong? Was there more to this buccaneer than she thought? After all, he *was* a close friend of the viscount, and the viscount didn't have evil men for friends, but rather men of gallantry and honor, even though buccaneers.

He set down his empty glass and looked toward the door as though something was on his mind. He still looked angry but as cool as a viper ready to strike.

"Better get back to your Cousin Emerald. I have some business to see to."

"Wait, Sir Farrow, please!"

He looked at her with detachment, but she had begun to recognize that look. It could mean determination.

He smiled briefly. "I'll be back."

There was so much in those words. She sank back to the settee, feeling weak.

He began to walk away, and then Minette found her voice. "But Sempala didn't touch me. Nobody did, because I prayed every day and every night and asked the Lord to help me. And Jesus did help me. He sent Ngozi to father me. And even Sempala became kinder and left me alone. So—so you don't need to be angry at anyone for hurting me."

He paused and looked at her for a long moment, and Minette turned warm, then cold, all over. She recognized that look. She had seen Baret Buckington look at Emerald that way.

She bit her lip and tried to blink back the tears.

Slowly he walked back to her and gazed down. "You're telling me the truth?"

She nodded and swallowed. "The whole truth."

A circle of silence enclosed them, until nothing became

real to Minette but his presence, his face, his eyes. Then his hand took hers, and he lifted her gently from the settee.

"I could love you," he said.

Tears spilled from her eyes and down her cheeks.

"When I get back from Morgan's raid, I'll come to see you often. That is, if you grant your permission, Miss Levasseur."

She smiled. "You have my permission, Sir Farrow."

He began to draw her into his arms, then apparently changed his mind. He held her from him and gently kissed her. "Would you waltz with me?"

She nodded, smiling. "I was hopin' you'd ask me."

"I've been anxiously waiting for the right moment."

10

A MESSAGE
FROM SIR KARLTON

Emerald waited for Baret, but the box that Jette had wanted to give him must have offered more interesting prospects than the ball, for he hadn't returned. She watched Minette and Captain Farrow on the ballroom floor and smiled, knowing how happy Minette must be to have captured his attention at last. A glance toward Lavender showed that she was not as pleased, but she seemed to have resigned herself to holding onto the devotion of Lord Grayford. Lavender now favored him with her full attention, and Emerald thought he looked rather surprised and pleased.

Then there was an unexpected roll of drums and an announcement by Lord Felix.

"On this night of my nephew's betrothal to Lady Emerald Harwick, we as a family rejoice to announce more fair news regarding our own Lady Lavender Thaxton. The marriage of Lavender to Lord Grayford will be held before he sails to Curacao."

There were attending smiles and light applause and bows toward Lavender and Grayford, and then the music began again —the same Strauss waltz that had played for Emerald and Baret. Everyone stepped back to give Lavender and Lord Grayford the floor. Lavender gazed up at him as they circled the ballroom.

Maybe she means it this time, thought Emerald. *She's lost two men by her shallow ways. Maybe she's smart enough now to know she might lose Grayford too, if she doesn't treat him as well as he deserves.*

She hoped so. Despite Cousin Lavender's spoiled ways, Emerald did care about her and wanted her life to turn out well. Watching them waltz, she began to think it would.

Soon other couples were joining them, and Emerald looked toward the garden door. What was keeping Baret?

Henry, the main serving man, came toward her.

"Someone's here about your cousin, Ty, Miss Emerald."

She stood at once. "Ty?"

"Says it's important or he wouldn't have bothered you now."

"Where is he?"

"He's waiting in the garden just outside the parlor. He wouldn't come in."

"Thank you, Henry."

She slipped away from the ballroom. A moment later she entered the parlor, closing the doors softly for privacy against the muffled strains of the music.

The candles had been extinguished, and the lamps were all lit. The warmth of the evening reached out to her, causing the sweet aroma of the white roses to permeate the room. A mild breeze blew pleasantly through the garden doors as she paused there to look about the flower garden.

"Lady Harwick?"

Her head turned toward the raspy voice, and she saw a stranger, hat in hand, come forward. He looked to be a priest, but he wore no cross, just an ankle-length tan garment that might have been stitched together from a few yards of discarded sailcloth. His hair was gray, in contrast to a tanned face. He lowered his eyes and bowed decorously.

"Yes?" she asked curiously.

He bowed again, hat at heart. "*Pardone,* Mademoiselle Harwick, but, you see, I bring ze sad news of your cousin, Ty. I bring him in ze wagon from Port Royal as he ask me. He was shot in a duel at Red Goose. Most disturbing, Mademoiselle!"

"Shot! Oh, no!" She came down the steps, clutching her skirts.

"In ze leg," and he gave a slap to his right thigh. "By ze evil pirate no less, ze wicked Captain Rafael."

Rafael, that rakish fiend!

"Ty asks you make speed and say nothing. Monsieur Pitt searches for him. Zeddie is with horse and carriage waiting. Ty, he is in ze manor house, asking you come at once."

"I'll come. But what happened? Why would Rafael shoot his own cousin?"

"Ah, I do not know. Ty in too much pain for talking."

He led the way down the garden walk toward the back gate.

One good thing might come of Ty's injury, she thought as she hurried after him. *He would know better than to trust a gaggle of pirates . . .*

Emerald's breath caught, and her eyes narrowed suspiciously as she took a closer look at the man she followed.

Gaggle of pirates—

She turned to flee, but the man whirled and sprang as nimbly as a cat, clamping his hand over her mouth before she could scream. In the struggle his gray periwig toppled from his head, revealing long black locks.

"Now, now, Mademoiselle," he breathed, "do not make for trouble. We are gallant gentlemen, all! You will come peaceably with us, yes?"

She bit his hand and tried to kick him.

He cursed but held tight. "Pierre!" he called toward the trees.

A second man, adorned in blue satin, rushed forward. He ripped off his jacket. "Ze cat!" And forcing Emerald's arms behind her, he held her while the first pirate stuffed a handkerchief into her mouth.

Emerald fought and struggled, landing a solid kick to the pirate's knee.

He snarled and wrapped the jacket around her head. One of the men swung her up and across his shoulder. Hissing something in French, they took off, footsteps pounding the earth.

Emerald struggled to free herself. Each jarring step jostled her and cut off her breath. His shoulder dug painfully into her ribs.

"Into ze wagon!"

She kicked again and let out a muffled cry as a heavy smelly blanket landed on top of her, sealing her into suffocating tomb-like darkness.

"Lie still, Mademoiselle!"

The wagon jostled along for unnumbered minutes until they picked up speed. Soon the horse was running along the road, and she heard the two pirates conversing in French and laughing.

Levasseur! This revolting deed had to be his foul work! Was Ty really shot? Or had it been a lie to trick her into following the man away from the house?

What a fool I was!

A short time later, they came to a halt, and one of the men

pulled the blanket from her and removed the wadded cloth from her mouth. She gasped in the night air, feeling the wind cooling the sweat on her face and throat, and saw that they were in front of the manor house.

"You fiend!" she choked. "Take your hand from me. Baret Buckington will see you hang for this!"

She saw several French pirates loitering in the shadows of the porch, all armed and dangerous looking and drinking rum. They walked forward and took turns bowing elaborately as Emerald was hauled down and set upon her feet. A chorus of appreciative *ahs* greeted her until the front door opened and Captain Rafael Levasseur stepped out.

"You sound like English dogs! Bring Demoiselle in here!"

So it was *Rafael!* she thought angrily, yet with growing fear. What would cause him to take such a bold risk as to come to Foxemoore on the very eve of her betrothal to Baret? And with Baret at the Great House!

The French pirates stepped aside as Emerald, not daring to show Rafael how afraid she was, evoked the old feisty manner she knew he expected. She flounced toward him, hands on hips.

"You French dog!"

Rafael was tall and vigorous. His handsome swarthy face wore a haughty and dangerous smile. His shoulder-length black periwig was waved meticulously beneath a plumed purple hat, which he did not remove as he raked her with his gaze.

"So, *mon petite* cousin, you have betrayed me, your own blood, to marry Foxworth. Ah, so you think, *mon cherie*. But it will not be." He walked toward her, his black eyes snapping. "You and I have much to discuss." His wiry hand latched hold of her arm and yanked her toward him.

Emerald's other hand darted like an adder and slapped his smirking face.

"You dare touch *me?*"

His lip twitched. He snatched her against him in a crushing embrace, and his lips took hers possessively.

She twisted her head away. "No, Rafael, let go!"

"Ah, yes, Demoiselle, but only for a time."

He released her abruptly and did not smile. His eyes were slits beneath his dark brows. "Do not mock me again. Do not tell me no. Do not make me angry."

"You are spoiled and arrogant. And by kissing me thus you have written your own doom. Captain Foxworth is a very jealous man. And while he behaves the viscount tonight, do not forget his manner on Tortuga. The Brotherhood knows well what he can do."

He laughed merrily. "Yes, so you admit the viscount is a pirate."

"I admit nothing."

"He and I are not so different, Mademoiselle. It is only that Foxworth can hide behind a title. And I? I flaunt my daring rapier in the name of the king of France."

He swept back his hat and looked down at her with a bold challenge. "And you, my cousin, are of my blood, not his." His restless black eyes darted over her. "I've heard how you took the vow tonight, but you will toss it to the wind. Vows mean nothing to me. You are a Levasseur. You have my blood, and, as I have told you before, you are destined to be mine."

Emerald's gaze narrowed. "I never told you I cared for you. I never even thought—"

"Thought? It does not matter what you thought. It is what *I* think. Always I have said you would be mine. And our fate has not changed. Do you think you shall be received by English dogs in London as a countess? They shall mock you at every bow, scorn you with every wink of the eye! You are a fool to marry a Buckington! You will not be happy." His thin lips tightened.

"I love Baret, and I will marry him after he returns from sailing with Morgan."

"*Mon petite,* do not goad. I am in no mood for patience."

"So! That's why you come like a villain, abducting me from my own betrothal, daring to treat me with scorn. You feel you must insult my betrothal. Very well, you have done so with your ill-bred manners and your tongue you use so well. Now, go! Leave me forever!"

He lifted a hand dripping with silver lace and rings to his ruffled chest. "Ah, *cherie,* how you pain poor Rafael's loving heart. No, no, Mademoiselle! You will come with me—of your own free will you will come."

"Of my own *will?*" She forced a careless laugh, hoping to unsteady his confidence. Anything to drag out the time, in hope that Baret would learn she was missing. "Never. I have vowed to Baret tonight before God. There it stays, till death do us part."

"Do not tempt me. How easy to put a rapier through his heart."

"Easy? Was it easy at Tortuga?"

"Tortuga was no fair duel, my cousin. I was ill with fever, and no one knew it. My pride would not relent, and my gallantry forced me to fight him. I was not at my best, but, ah, I am now ready. I have practiced for months. I now know all the ways of the Spaniards and the English dogs."

So. This was not the quick, rash decision for which he was known. He had been planning this action for some time.

"Rafael, be sensible. There are many women who love you. We shall part friends. As cousins. I cannot go with you. I will not go of my own will."

His teeth showed beneath his narrow mustache. "We shall see, Demoiselle."

What did he mean? She backed away. "Where is Ty? Have you done anything to him?"

"Ty? My French cousin? Would I betray a brother who wishes to sail with me?"

"Sail with *you?* He wouldn't!"

"Ah, but he is safe aboard the *Venture* now, where he wishes to be. And you will come with us to Margarita."

Margarita—the island of pearls, the island where the treasure of the *Prince Philip* was said to be hidden.

"So that's it," she scoffed, almost relieved that his motivation was merely the rebirth of greed. "You think I know where the treasure of the *Prince Philip* is hidden. You think Captain Buckington told me?"

"*Oui,* he told you. And Uncle Karlton knows where it is, too. He will not talk, and so I shall have you there to make sure he tells me all."

She sobered. He knew where her father was?

"You're wrong. I wouldn't betray Baret and tell you, if I knew. That treasure is needed to bring to His Majesty—to prove the innocence of his father."

"There is more waiting near Margarita, *mon cherie,* much more. And if you wish to see your father alive, you will cooperate. There will be no more squabbling like a squawking hen. As I say, you will come willingly."

She watched him, cautious now. "What about my father?"

117

He smiled and, sweeping off his hat, bowed. "I have him a prisoner, Mademoiselle Emerald. A cunning, sweet move on my part, yes?"

Rafael couldn't have him. It was another lie like the one Lord Felix had flung at her at the hacienda in Spanish Town, telling her Baret had been taken to Cadiz as a religious prisoner for the Inquisitors.

"Do you think I'm foolish enough to believe you?"

"No, I shall prove I have him at my mercy. He was betrayed by Jasper and Felix to the captain of the Dutch slave ship bound for Cartagena. I was privy to it all, Mademoiselle. Ah, yes, I admit it. And I intercepted that ship, outsmarting your Monsieur Foxworth. I lay in wait for the vessel and attacked with grand skill. I sank her to the bottom of the Caribbean. The slaves I took as booty and sold them on St. Kitts. And your father? Ah! My sweet, he is my prisoner—even as Don Miguel Vasquez is Foxworth's prisoner. Am I not clever, Mademoiselle?"

He laughed. "And what do I ask in return for his release?" His eyes flashed, and he took firm hold of her arm and escorted her into the manor. "From you I demand a renunciation of your betrothal to Foxworth. You will sit down tonight and write him. You will tell him your godly conscience burns with regret that you lied to him but that you lie no longer. You love *me*, Rafael Levasseur, yes! And with the letter you will leave here the Buckington ring for Cousin Minette to find and bring sadly to him."

"You beast!"

He gave an airy gesture and a mock sigh. "My regrets, Mademoiselle, but alas, what can I do when you are so foolish as to think you will choose him?"

Then his eyes glittered like hard stones. "And from Foxworth there is one thing more I wish. I care nothing for the dog who is king of England. The treasure of the *Prince Philip* is to be divided as we signed articles aboard his ship. Remember, Mademoiselle? You were there, yes? Remember how he willingly signed the articles with me and with Monsieur Farrow? Those articles are in my possession now. Foxworth will come to the South Cays of Cuba to rendezvous with Morgan. He will keep his bargain with me there, or he will live to regret his black treachery."

Emerald sank weakly into a chair, gripping its arms, staring up into his determined face. He meant it. Every word of it.

He reached inside his jacket and pulled out a letter.

"From Monsieur Karlton to you. Proof, *mon petite,* that I do not lie. Proof that you will leave with me tonight—willingly. You will tell Monsieur Foxworth that Rafael Levasseur does not abduct you. You walk freely beside me to my ship."

Emerald's shaking hand grasped the letter. Yes, the handwriting on the envelope belonged to her father.

Rafael smiled.

She opened it with shaking fingers and read. As she did, her heart died slowly.

Dear Daughter Emerald,

Rafael took the Dutch slave ship with great loss of life to those aboard. I am now his prisoner. He will not let me write more except to tell you he will leave me for the Spaniards unless you sail with him aboard the *Venture.*

Your loving father,
Karlton Harwick

Emerald's hand lowered to her lap. She stared defeatedly at the letter.

"*Mon cherie,* do not grieve. He will live. And you will live. You see, I have the command this time. And what is your decision? Will you come with me?"

She knew Rafael would think little of leaving her father to the *guarda costa* if she refused him. There was only one hope, as she saw it. She would cooperate now in order to insure her father's safety. After that, she would hope and pray that Baret would not believe her letter and would confront Levasseur at Morgan's rendezvous.

But would he? He had vowed his love tonight, but what if his pride was so injured that he refused to rescue her? What if he believed her letter?

She shuddered, thinking of Sir Jasper at the hacienda and how for a time that Baret had suspected her of wrong. He believed in her now, but if she hurt him again—if again he thought she had betrayed him . . . and he had already been suspicious of something's being between her and Rafael.

Her trembling fingers touched the ruby pendant, and she

119

bit back the tears. How could anything so vile as this happen to her on the very night of her betrothal?

"Well, Cousin Emerald? Do you write the letter to Monsieur Foxworth, or will you see your father abandoned to the *guarda costa*?"

"I will write it," she choked bitterly, "but you will pay for this despicable deed, Rafael."

He indicated a table where a sheet of parchment, pen, and inkwell waited.

"A wise decision. I will tell you what to write." He strode to the table and quickly gestured for her to come.

She stood and slowly walked to the table and sat down.

"Good, my sweet. Quickly, quickly."

After agonizing minutes, Emerald signed her name to the letter, then let the pen fall to the table. Head in hand, she sat there as a teardrop splotched the paper.

"No matter now, *mon petite.* You will soon love me when you are my bride. Up!"

She stood wearily, and he snatched the letter, laughed with satisfaction as he read it, then folded it. "The Buckington ring." He held out his hand.

She turned her back, retrieved it, and then hesitated.

"The ring. Come, come." And he made a clucking sound for her to hurry.

Angrily she slapped it onto his palm.

He held it up for inspection. *"C'etait magnifique!* If it were not better to leave it for him to see, I would take it as my own. Alas."

With regret, he dropped the ring inside the envelope.

"Where is Zeddie? What have you done with him?"

"Pierre has him safely. He will come with us. Do you think I want him running to Foxworth before I reach the rendezvous?"

At least Zeddie was safe for the present, she thought, and there was some consolation in knowing he would be aboard the pirate ship with her, though she doubted she would be able to see him.

Then Emerald remembered something, and her breath paused. She gave Rafael a side glance, but he was busy. She touched the ruby pendant. Rafael did not know that Baret had given it to her. She thought of its meaning. Since she was not

120

returning the pendant, would Baret then know that the letter was insincere? Her hopes spiraled upward like incense. Yes, he would know! And he would come for her. Her beloved would come!

Rafael sealed the letter with wax and propped it against a book on the table to be readily seen by Minette when she came to look for Emerald.

"Never mind your things," he said happily. "There is all you will need aboard the *Venture*. I have made careful and ample provision for this time."

"I will never marry you."

He arched his black brows. "No? You had best pray we do, Mademoiselle, for you will be mine." He caught her arm and strode with her toward the front door. "We leave now. Our horses are in back. Philippe! Pierre!" he shouted out the door. "Quickly!"

Unable to locate Jette in the garden, Baret climbed the wall and entered Carlotta's room to discover that she was gone. He made a quick survey of her possessions and gathered what he'd expected all along—that she'd managed to escape, was on her way to rendezvous with Jasper, and Felix was unaware. But Carlotta, at the moment, was the least of his concerns. Where was Jette?

He returned to the terrace. Emerald was not where he had left her. At first thinking she might be waltzing with his grandfather or one of the other gentlemen, he scanned the floor with its dancing couples until it became obvious she was not among the guests. He checked her room. She was not there.

Back in the ballroom, Baret casually glanced about to see if Felix looked suspicious. But he was conversing with Governor Modyford, still undoubtedly trying to get him to change his mind about giving the buccaneers commissions against Spain's shipping.

Baret ignored the curious gaze of Lavender, who was waltzing with Grayford.

Minette had not seen Emerald since the ceremony.

"Could she have gone to her room?" Erik asked.

"No, I went there."

Minette frowned. "Maybe she found out Jette wasn't in the garden. Him and the twins like to go to the manor house and play hide and seek, and maybe she went looking for him. Shall I go see, m'lord?"

Baret had already considered that. He wasn't satisfied. Something was amiss.

"She wouldn't have walked," he said. "Her buggy is parked in the carriageway. And Zeddie isn't there. No one has seen him all evening."

Erik's alert gaze met his as he followed Baret's line of thinking. "Carlotta hasn't shown up tonight."

Baret's wordless glance was enough to warn Erik to silence. He was to do nothing to cause Minette to display alarm to any who might be watching, especially Felix.

Erik seemed to know what to do. He took Minette's arm. "We'll make another search through the garden," he told Baret and led her away as though casually interested in little more than visiting the refreshment table, followed by a stroll for a breath of evening air.

Baret was turning to leave when Lavender walked up, smiling sweetly. Grayford wasn't with her. She laid her fan on his arm.

"I should at least have one waltz with the viscount on the eve of his betrothal."

He was on the verge of refusing, anxious to search for Emerald and Jette when her low voice said, "Are you looking for Emerald?"

His eyes searched hers and saw no resentment there, only a flicker of strange curiosity.

He obliged her with the waltz, noting that Felix turned to look toward them. Then his gaze left them abruptly. Had he sensed something was wrong?

As they waltzed, Lavender pretended to smile and chat, but her words were anything but casual.

"I saw her leave soon after Henry delivered her a message. She looked concerned."

"Which way did she go?"

"Through the parlor. Then the garden, I think. And Baret—before the betrothal, I saw someone arrive by way of the back garden. There were four or five men I've never seen before. They certainly weren't planters or friends of the governor. They looked French, with rather foppish and arrogant behavior—"

"Frenchmen?"

"Yes, I—"

Baret took firm hold of her elbow and propelled her across

the floor as though they were walking in agreement toward the parlor.

"What is it?" she whispered.

He drew her into the outer hall and, once alone, turned her loose but held her gaze steadily. "Do me well this once, for what we meant to each other?"

Her eyes misted. "Baret, I—"

"No, Lavender. I'm in love with Emerald. There can never be anyone else. I need you to do something for me. Will you?"

She lowered her gaze with resignation and slowly nodded. "Yes, of course, I will."

"Waltz with Felix. Keep him busy for the next hour. Don't breathe a word of what you told me to anyone until this night is over."

Anxiously she searched his eyes, then nodded. "All right. I promise."

He gave her a look of silent affection, as he might give a sister, then was gone out onto the terrace and down the steps.

Lavender stood looking after him, her heart swelling with pain. But unlike so many other times in her life when loss prompted her to manipulate to regain what had slipped through her fingers, she could see that none of her schemes would touch him—Baret had made up his mind.

Two weeks ago at the governor's residence he had told her to treat Grayford well, that she would not likely find another man who loved her as genuinely.

Tonight she had told Grayford she would marry him before he sailed. Henceforth she would strive to make the most of her relationship with him. Several doors had closed on the pathway of life, but her future as a duchess in England with Lord Grayford remained open. She would enter that door, lest she end up with nothing but ashes.

"God save me from myself and all my folly," she whispered, then turned with head erect and walked back into the ballroom to divert Uncle Felix. Somehow she must also stop Geneva from sailing with him to Porto Bello. There was something odd about the medication Dr. Vasquez was giving her. She was beginning to think Sophie's concerns had substance to them. She would mention all this to Earl Nigel—and to Sir Cecil Chaderton too.

123

11

IN SEARCH
OF EMERALD

Baret slipped his baldric over his head and strode quickly down the garden walk toward the manor house. There was little doubt remaining in his mind that the men Lavender had seen arrive earlier were Capt. Rafael Levasseur and several of his French buccaneers.

I was a fool to be so lax, he thought. *Coming here tonight at this dramatic hour is the sort of theatrical deed in which Levasseur prides himself.*

His jaw set. "He'll pay handsomely for this. If he has harmed Emerald, I'll run him through."

As he made his way through the garden, three children darted from the trees near the back walk. One recognized Baret, gave out a cry, and ran up, grabbing him, his luminous eyes wide with terror. It was Jette.

"That French pirate stole Emerald away! We were hiding inside the manor house and heard the whole thing!"

Baret stooped and drew him into his arms. The boy was shaking and trying not to cry.

"All right, Jette, steady. Tell me everything. Which French pirate? Captain Levasseur?"

"Yes. We were afraid, because that Dr. Vasquez was in the garden when we came to wait for you. We went to the manor house, and a few minutes later the French buccaneers came inside. Levasseur sent two men to bring her, but by then we was hiding in Uncle Karlton's crow's nest and couldn't sneak down to warn her. The men came back with Emerald, and Levasseur grabbed her and tried to kiss her—she didn't like it neither. She got mad, and she hit him hard!"

"We done heard the blow, didn't we, Titus?" whispered Timothy.

Baret showed no emotion, but his anger rose, cold and

deadly. His hand closed firmly on his baldric. "Where are Emerald and Levasseur now?"

"He took her away—to his ship."

So! He would need to confront Levasseur at the rendezvous. No doubt that was what Rafael wanted.

"The box Carlotta gave you—where is it?"

Jette quickly turned and gave a low whistle. The spotted hound came from the bushes, panting and wagging his wiry tail. A gunnysack was tied to his back.

"That be my idea," boasted Timothy, jutting out his chin at his brother.

"If that Spaniard or Uncle Felix caught us, we were going to tell the hound to run," Jette whispered.

"Smart boys," said Baret, using his knife to cut the rope and free the bag.

"There ain't nobody can catch de hound once he runs," Timothy said.

"He runs like lightning," added Titus with a grin.

"You've done well, indeed. Now, quickly—what did you hear Captain Levasseur tell Emerald?"

Jette's childish explanation was somewhat lacking, but Baret was able to understand enough to know that Levasseur claimed to have sunk the Dutch slave ship and held Karlton as a prisoner. He was leveraging Karlton to convince Emerald to write Baret a letter that she had changed her mind and was in love with Rafael.

There had been a time when Baret would have been suspicious, but he had held Emerald in his arms, and her kiss had left no doubt as to her love. And she would never willingly leave Minette behind.

Baret's anger burned toward Levasseur.

"Where is the letter? You left it on the table?"

"No, we put it with the box."

"Good. Now listen carefully to what I want you to do next. Go back to the house and wait in your room until Grandfather Nigel comes to tell you good night."

"He always comes. We have cocoa together."

"You will tell him everything that's happened. Is that clear?" Jette nodded.

"Then tell him I've gone to rendezvous with Morgan. That

our plans will be carried through to the end. If all goes well, we will see him in London in the court of His Majesty. Is that all clear?"

Jette's eyes shone like pools beneath the stars. "What about Emerald?" he whispered. "Will you get her back from the buccaneer?"

Baret hugged him tightly. "One way or the other. And now, do you think you can get back inside the house and up to your room without anyone seeing you?"

"We have a secret way. Not even Grandfather will see us till we have cocoa with him."

"The three of you will have cocoa with Grandfather, understood? Then you'll tell him what I said."

Timothy elbowed Titus with a grin. "We gets cocoa, too. An' I'm havin' a second cup, or a third."

"The hound gets some, 'cause he helped us."

"Sure he did," Jette said. "And we'll get Zunsia to get us a big bowl to pour his cocoa in. He won't drink it if it's hot—"

"Jette, say nothing of this to *any*one else, not even Aunt Sophie or Geneva."

"And especially Uncle Felix," Jette whispered gravely.

So he knew about his uncle.

Baret tousled the boy's hair, then stood, snatching up the gunnysack. "Away with you, now. Don't let anyone see you."

Baret waited until the boys had slipped away, then went off to locate Erik.

Minette and Erik were in the front garden near the palm trees. Minette saw him and came running. "Did you find her, m'lord?"

His expression must have alerted her, for a look of fear showed on her face. "Mr. Pitt!"

"No, Captain Levasseur."

He explained, and Minette sank to a rattan chair and covered her face with her palms.

"He'll find her again," Erik told her confidently.

"We must leave now, Minette," Baret told her. "We're sailing with Morgan. It may be that I can overtake the *Venture* before we rendezvous."

She jumped to her feet, stricken. "Oh, sirs! But I cannot stay here without Emerald!"

Erik frowned. "I cannot take you with me now. It is too dangerous aboard ship."

"But it's dangerous for me here! You don't know Mr. Pitt—"

"I do know him," said Baret flatly. "And I have already made arrangements for Pitt—and for you, Minette. Sir Cecil is in charge of all my possessions on Foxemoore. He has orders to watch Pitt with an eagle eye and to begin training Ngozi to take his position. He'll be teaching Ngozi to read and write. There's also a Jewish family that Emerald told me about whose land was taken by Jasper and Pitt. It's to be returned. You are now under the guardianship of Sir Cecil."

Minette, despite her agony over Emerald's abduction, managed a brief smile. "M'lord, you are very kind."

"And now, Erik and I must leave. There's a chance I may yet overtake the *Venture* before the rendezvous with Morgan . . ." He looked at Erik. "I'll meet you with the horses."

Baret left them to their final good-byes and slipped through the palm trees to where his horse was tied and waiting.

Emerald, he thought, *I will find you again.*

It was easier than it might have been for Henry Morgan to round up the buccaneers for the expedition to Cuba, because the French were now at peace with England but at war with Spain. The War of Devolution had begun the previous May to the delight of the French buccaneers at Tortuga. Some of the first men to volunteer to sail with Morgan were his old friends John Morris, Jackman, and Capt. Edward Collier. Soon Morgan's flotilla consisted of more than five hundred buccaneers with various-sized ships and barques.

"Others still on the Caribbean are coming in to the rendezvous," said Yorke, Baret's lieutenant. "Including the French at Tortuga. Ye'll be seein' Levasseur is my guess."

Morgan had arranged to rendezvous among the hundreds of tiny islands on the south side of Cuba, the so-called South Cays, because they provided a good lee for vessels at anchor. The reefs and islands to seaward kept out the swells, whose sudden snatch at an anchor cable was more likely to part it than was the steady strain of a strong wind. Another danger for the anchored vessels was no wind at all. In the tropical bays and anchorages, an otherwise good sandy bottom had a scattering of coral heads that reared up like large cauliflowers, often six feet high and many feet across. The danger was that if the wind died, the anchor rope got caught on coral heads. At the first breeze, the strain on the rope would cause it to be sawed by the sharp coral, and a ship would find herself adrift.

Though Morgan now held a commission from Modyford appointing him admiral over the expedition to Cuba, the written commission had little effect upon the authenticity of the voyage. More important, now that Mansfield was dead, was that the Brethren of the Coast accepted Morgan as their leader. "The governor of Jamaica may say ol' Morgan is admiral of the Port Royal privateers, but he's leader of the Brotherhood because we trust him" was the word among the pirates.

And so the *Regale* and the *Warspite* set sail for the South Cays.

12

CONFLICT ON THE CARIBBEAN

Dawn found the *Venture* far at sea on the Caribbean. Emerald, who had slept little during the tense prayerful night, was already up and pacing when she heard a discreet knock on the cabin door. It sounded too gentle to be Rafael. He had locked her in his cabin before departing Port Royal, and she had not seen him since.

"Emerald? It's Ty."

She rushed to the door. "I can't let you in. I don't have the key."

"I have it."

The key rattled, and the door swung open. Ty entered, and she was dismayed to see him looking as devastatingly dangerous as Rafael. He was dressed in white-and-black satin, wore a baldric with long pistols, and carried a full complement of wicked things.

He saw her dismay, and his dark eyes twinkled proudly. "I am a *boucanier* now, and I'll be captain of my own ship one day."

"A mistake. You shouldn't have come."

"I suppose being a slave on Foxemoore or hidin' in the Blue Mountains is better? What else is there for me? At least I'm free."

"Free? With Cousin Rafael? You'll always be in danger of capture by some island governor, trying to hang you for piracy."

His lips thinned. "They won't catch me. Have they caught Rafael? Or Foxworth?"

She moved uneasily. "Never mind Baret. Anyway, his name is Buckington, as you know quite well. Where's that scoundrel Rafael?"

He sank moodily into the small chair. "Asleep. Don't worry. He's got the treasure on his mind."

She wondered. "And my father?"

He frowned. "He's somewhere near Margarita. Rafael left

him with Lex Thorpe. Don't worry," he repeated. "I'll try to get him out of this somehow."

"You're no match for that vile Lex Thorpe! He's a fiend! Baret left him marooned months ago, and you can be certain he won't forget. I thought he was dead by now. He's vicious and diabolical." She turned away, head in hands.

Ty stood, looking guilty, and laid a hand on her shoulder. "I'm sorry, Emerald. I didn't know Cousin Rafael was gonna abduct you. Or Uncle Karlton, either. I didn't want any part of it. All I wanted was to join the *Venture*. I didn't even know about Uncle or about Rafael's plans until we was at sea." His dark eyes boiled. "He won't hurt you. I won't let him."

"He expects to marry me." She told him about the letter he'd forced her to write to Baret.

"Rafael has always wanted to marry you. I remember him comin' to Uncle Karlton when you was only fifteen. What do you think the viscount will do?"

She turned away, fingering the ruby pendant. "I don't know. If he believes the letter, he'll do nothing."

"I can't say, 'cause I ain't never met him. But some of the buccaneers aboard are saying that Rafael went too far. That Captain Foxworth will hunt the *Venture* down and make him pay for his folly, and they ain't happy about you bein' aboard. All they wanted was the treasure of the *Prince Philip*." His eyes shone with fervor. "I'll be gettin' enough to get my own ship. I'm gonna learn how to sail, Emerald. I'm goin' to be the best buccaneer on the Caribbean."

She sighed and sank back into the chair. "Better that Baret would sink the *Venture* and all of us aboard. Oh, this is the worst thing that could have happened. And poor Father is left to that vile Thorpe."

"Cease your moaning, Demoiselle," said Rafael from the doorway. "Uncle Karlton will live. Without him, we do not know where the treasure is. Even Lex has enough brains to treat the golden goose gently." He proceeded to bow, balancing a cup of coffee. "Good morning, *mon cherie,* and why so wan?" He entered with a bold smile. "Today I may wish it to be my wedding day!"

She jumped to her feet. "Don't be absurd, Rafael. I will not marry you, least of all aboard a pirate vessel."

His black brows shot up. "Then you will marry me at Margarita? The friar will come to pronounce his blessing upon us in the chapel, *oui?*"

She turned away.

He chuckled, setting the cup down firmly and spilling coffee. "Cheers, *mon petite.* I am a patient man but not overly patient, so do not test me by pouting in grief over Foxworth. I will marry you aboard my ship."

Her eyes swerved to his. He meant it. Anger churned in their black depths.

"And who will perform the vows? Your gunner? Though you are captain, you cannot officiate at your own wedding. It wouldn't be valid."

"Then we will find a captain at Morgan's rendezvous."

"And who will that be," she scoffed. "L'Ollonais?" she asked of the most notoriously evil French pirate on the Caribbean.

"It matters not to me, but a marriage we shall have, Mademoiselle, and why not buccaneer style? Were you not born on Tortuga?" He leered.

"You will never forget that, will you?"

"It is where we both belong."

"Baret will meet us at the South Cays. Do you think he will allow it? You cannot avoid him—your greed will force you to confront him over the treasure."

"You mock, but you will cease your amusement when you are mine at last."

Ty attempted to intervene, but Rafael turned on him sharply. "Silence, Ty. I am captain of this ship! You are blessed I took you aboard."

"You see now what he is truly like," said Emerald to Ty. "It is a curse being aboard his ship."

"I know you are captain," said Ty. "Perhaps the best on the Caribbean. But Emerald is our cousin, and while you want her for your own, you needn't bully her. We had too much of that from Pitt."

"Ah? The little cousin tells *me, Levasseur,* what to do!" He laughed. Then he looked back to Emerald and ran a finger along her cheek. "*Mon petite* has a temper is all. She will learn soon to smile and treat me pleasantly. You and I will have breakfast together—in my cabin, *oui?*"

He turned to Ty, who was frowning. "You may be a cousin,

131

mon ami, but aboard this ship you will not question the captain."

"I am not hungry now, Rafael," Emerald said. "And I wish to be left alone until brought to my father."

His laugh was unpleasant as he drew her into his arms. "What you wish is of little consequence."

Ty grabbed Rafael's arm. "Let go of her, Cousin. She doesn't want you—"

Rafael struck him across the mouth, and Ty staggered back, his lips bleeding from the rings on Rafael's fingers.

Emerald suppressed a cry.

Ty stared at him, apparently stunned as he reconsidered his estimation of the daring French buccaneer.

Rafael did not look apologetic. "I will not take your lectures, my cousin. You will learn that what I say aboard the *Venture* is law! Now leave the captain's cabin before I have you confined to the hold!" He strode to the door and flung it open. "Out!" he demanded, pointing. His black eyes snapped.

Emerald tensed when she saw a look of defiance on Ty's face.

"Have I run away from Jamaica to become a slave to you?"

"Ty—" Emerald began, knowing what Rafael might do to him at sea.

Rafael appeared to consider, then gave a harsh laugh. "Enough, you young cockerel. Come! We will both leave Demoiselle to her contemplations—" he looked at her with mocking challenge "—for now."

Her sails filled with wind, the *Regale* slipped gracefully through the Caribbean on a steady course in pursuit of the *Venture.* In his cabin, stripped to a pair of leather breeches and pistol belt, Baret studied his father's historic journal as Hob poured his coffee. The blue parrot, King Charlie, stretched one leg, then the other, and continued gorging on an overripe mango.

Hob grinned as he looked at Baret. "His lordship's journal be a better prize than all the gold on the mule train from Porto Bello, says I. Ye be owin' Miss Carlotta."

To Baret's amazement, when he had opened the box that Carlotta had entrusted to Jette, he'd found the long-sought journal of his father, who had been commissioned by Cromwell to establish a British colony in the West Indies and to harass Spanish shipping. The account of the taking of the *Prince Philip,* which had first opened fire on the *Royale,* was precise, and further information had been added by his father's secretary, Lucca, that was dated and signed. There was mention of the storm, the need to cast some of the booty and heavy goods to the sea. And then the account broke off abruptly—only to begin again on shore, where a hasty entry had been written in by his father of the approach of a Spanish war vessel. The treasure was stored securely, but there was no mention of where.

Baret's gaze darkened as he meditated over the information. Had there been mention of Margarita, Felix would have narrowed his search long ago. Now, of course, they all knew it was stored on that isle, but only he and Karlton knew the precise location. Levasseur would have done his worst to get Karlton to talk, but Baret had no qualms about his soon-to-be father-in-law's secrecy. He would say nothing, whatever the cost, knowing that once Lex Thorpe or Levasseur knew where it was, his life would no longer be considered useful. And Emerald might no longer be safeguarded by Rafael.

Baret had one consolation—Levasseur knew that if he harmed her in any way, he would never see the treasure. He must still think he could bargain with Baret, or he wouldn't have sailed for the South Cays, knowing there would surely be a confrontation there. Had Levasseur merely wanted Emerald, he would have sailed away to Tortuga or even St. Kitts.

Baret had not at first realized that Rafael's scheme was to use Emerald and Karlton to gain the treasure. But soon after Baret had set sail from Port Royal, he decided that since Levasseur was destined for Morgan's rendezvous, it was the treasure of the *Prince Philip* that Levasseur's lovesick heart pined over, not just Emerald. Realizing that, he had been able to relax a little and turn his mind to the journal.

"This journal, dear Hob, will see us dining with His Majesty within a year. If things go as planned, my father will be vindicated of the piracy charges, and we'll all be back in the good graces of Charles and the High Admiralty."

"*Har,* ye already be acclaimed by that Earl Cunningham. An agent of the king, he calls ye. That be a sticker in the throat of Lord Felix. An' what'll he do when he learns Miss Carlotta ran away with that Sir Jasper?"

Felix would be furious, since he had plans to use his daughter in Porto Bello to bridge his friendship with the Spanish government in Madrid. It was all set forth in the letter Carlotta had written to Baret and placed with the journal in the box.

Carlotta had written of how her father as a leader in the Royal African Company intended to gain the favor of the dons on the Main in order to have a market for West African slaves. To establish this rich trade, Felix was spying for Madrid in the High Admiralty Court and the king's court in London through his contacts with the Spanish Peace Party. Information had been passing through Felix to the Spanish ambassador. And after coming to Jamaica, Felix had held secret meetings in Cartagena over smuggling by Jasper and others in Spanish Town.

Baret had known most of this. But to have it in writing from Felix's daughter, with Jasper also willing to confess, was added support for his father's innocence.

Baret had one more asset in hand—or perhaps "in ship"; he had the son of an important ruling don in Porto Bello. *Capitan* Miguel Vasquez was under guard in a cabin and was the crucial bait to be used in negotiating with the governor of Porto Bello for the release of Baret's father and other prisoners.

Then the big frame of his lieutenant, Yorke, shadowed the open doorway.

"Cap'n? Jeremy's sighted a ship!"

Baret swiftly locked the journal in his sea chest and, snatching his shirt, strode out the door onto the deck, as Hob came behind with Yorke.

His boatswain, Jeremy, had been in the crow's nest since before dawn with high hopes. The captain of the *Regale* had promised that the first man to spy the ship that turned out to be the *Venture* would be given an extra half share from the pickings at Porto Bello.

Jeremy was swinging from the ratlines, the wind in his fair hair. He called down, "Can't tell yet, Cap'n, but me instincts tells me it's the *Venture*."

Baret's boots sounded firmly on the quarterdeck as he walked to the rail and took hold with both strong brown hands. He looked toward the sea, his dark eyes squinting against the tropical sunlight. The wind ruffled the jade waters and warmly

134

touched his face and hair, billowing the sleeves of his tunic, still open at the front.

Then he climbed the main shrouds and braced himself, holding the brassbound telescope steady as the ship cut through the water beneath a stone-blue sky. He smiled.

Aboard the *Venture*, the tall Frenchman Pierre, his lean swarthy face grave, approached Captain Levasseur.

Rafael was coming up the quarterdeck steps with Emerald, on the way to dine on deck. "What is it, Pierre?" he asked impatiently.

"Monsieur *le Capitaine*, the storm you worry about last night does not come, but the crew, we think a storm of another kind is coming. A ship follows. We think it is the *Regale*."

Emerald's heart swelled with a rush of joy. *Baret*. She smiled jubilantly toward Ty, standing by the rail.

Rafael said something between his teeth and brushed past Pierre, shouting for his telescope.

Emerald joined Ty at the rail, hoping for a glimpse of the grand sight she had spent most of the night praying for.

"It's Captain Foxworth, all right," he whispered.

"How do you know?" she whispered back, keeping a cautious eye on Rafael.

"Pierre and I spotted the ship an hour ago. We watched her until she got in close enough."

She shaded her eyes and looked astern, hearing the Frenchmen murmuring among themselves.

"And now what, Monsieur *Capitaine?*" growled Pierre. "Did we not say, do not take to sea with the betrothed of Foxworth? Nay, Monsieur, let us make a parley with him. Send the demoiselle to him by longboat! For you may bring his wrath upon us. It is the treasure we want. Did we not say there would be wrath to pay? Then you did so on the very night of the vow—"

"Silence, you cowardly dog! Foxworth will not dare fire on us with Mademoiselle Emerald and her cousin on board. And he does not know that Karlton is not also aboard. He will not risk a fight with us but will trail us like a spy!"

"Eh! And where do we lead him, my *capitaine?*"

Levasseur's lips twisted into a sardonic smile. "Where else, Monsieur, but to Morgan's rendezvous? We will settle things there."

Emerald threw her arms around Ty. "We will both be free, you'll see."

"Do not rejoice, Mademoiselle," snapped Rafael, looking over at her. "It may be that I have wished to trap Foxworth in the South Cays. Do you think I fear his rapier? I shall cut him to pieces and feed him to the sharks."

Emerald looked out toward the *Regale*, following in their wake. Baret hadn't believed the letter—he knew that her love for him was unwavering.

For the remainder of that day, Rafael's thoughts must have been diverted from his plans for marriage. He remained on deck, his eyes upon the *Regale*. Then toward late afternoon, as they were sailing the waters south of Cuba, Pierre came with a warning.

"How will we take refuge at the South Cays? And what will Foxworth say when you need to deal with him? You saw how he disdained you at Tortuga over the demoiselle."

"It will be as I expect," said Levasseur with a thin smile. "He will wish to duel me, of course. And I will accept."

Pierre gave him a dark look. It was clear that, after his previous defeat, not all his men believed him to be the better swordsman.

"Do not forget, Pierre, I have Emerald. And he cannot lightly take her away unless he wishes to board and fight. He will not."

"You are so sure?"

"*Oui, mon foi*. Foxworth will think well before he opens fire. He will not try to kill me. No, not as long as he knows I am in control of Emerald and her father."

"And what do you intend next? You cannot force the mademoiselle to marry you. And if you have her without marriage, he will deliver you to the Spaniards himself. Or skin you alive."

Levasseur smiled unpleasantly. "*Mon ami*, am I a beast? Mademoiselle is safe. To have all the treasure at Margarita, that is now my consolation. What else? All that Foxworth has he will give for the precious life of Mademoiselle Emerald and Monsieur Karlton. He will yet disclose the hiding place of the treasure. And when he has done so—if my plans go well—I shall have the treasure and Demoiselle too."

Pierre did not look altogether convinced, but his mood cheered somewhat, and he smiled. "You expect to kill him?"

"Thorpe has pleaded for satisfaction. While he duels Fox-

136

worth, we shall make off with the treasure and Mademoiselle. And perhaps I shall leave both Foxworth and Thorpe—or whoever survives the duel—to the Spaniards on Margarita." He laughed confidently. "I tell you, Pierre, I know what I am doing. I have planned long and well these months since he defamed me at Tortuga. I am not one to forget a slap in the face before the Brotherhood."

They were just off the coast of the South Cays, sailing beneath an aquamarine sky. Baret could see other ships belonging to the Brotherhood already at the rendezvous point and anchored closer to shore. By now, Henry Morgan and his *Golden Future* would be there too.

Baret balanced himself as he leaned into the shrouds, holding his telescope fixed upon the *Venture* as she made for the Cays. The *Regale* followed, steadily gaining.

"*Har!* Me lordship, ye owes me twenty pieces o' eight," a gloating Hob called up. "I tells ye it were the ship o' that cuckoldy jackanapes."

His heart leaped. The eighteen-gun ship was moving slowly and deeply through the water, her canvas billowing, the fleur de lis streaming gallantly.

Jeremy, the bosun, clung to the ratlines, swaying in the wind. Cupping a hand to his mouth, he called down to the crew, "'Tis the *Venture!*" and a resounding cheer went up.

As the *Regale* continued to overtake Rafael's vessel, Baret lowered the telescope with restrained satisfaction.

"Levasseur's an indolent fellow for not careening his ship," he murmured contemptuously.

"Why do you say so, Cap'n?"

"Look how it bellies deep in the water. His speed has been reduced."

"Aye. Ye could easily overtake him, Cap'n!" the bosun urged breathlessly.

"And blow him to the sharks if it were my intent."

"I should like to see it, Cap'n!"

"You have a greedy appetite, Jeremy. You forget the delicate prize he carries."

"Aye, Cap'n, but not for long. The drawing ye did of her comes swiftly to mind."

"Cap'n!" called up Yorke. "The captain of the *Venture* refuses to dip her colors!"

"So I see, Yorke."

The audacity of the dawcock! He heard Yorke climbing up, and a moment later the man's broad Scottish face, blue eyes sparkling maliciously, grinned at him.

"What d'ye say, Cap'n?" he wheedled. "Just a very wee lesson to teach the Frenchie to obey the common courtesies of the Brotherhood."

Baret lifted his telescope again, focusing on the flag. "I'm thinking about it, Yorke. It's a sore temptation. The man lacks manners on land and sea."

"Shall I order Jonstone to run out the guns? Slip a volley or two over his bow?"

Baret considered, while the wind tugged at his hair. "We'll dip his colors for him—prepare to take out his topsail."

Yorke's eyes flared with a moment's surprise, then he laughed deeply. "Aye, Cap'n!"

Jonstone, the burly master gunner, came up from the waist and stood looking upward, his square hands on the hips of trousers cut off above the knee. His blue head kerchief whipped in the wind. "What's the word, Yorke?"

"Ready the gun crew!" shouted Yorke. "Use only the best gunners—Cap'n says we'll just take out her topsail and colors!"

Baret called to unfurl the topgallants. The buccaneers sprang to the ratlines. Others swarmed over the decks to their duties. Again, Baret lifted his glass and focused. The *Venture* was altering her course to face the *Regale*.

There were rumblings as the *Regale*'s guns were run out.

Baret came sliding down the backstay. He lifted his glass to focus again.

"Cap'n!" Jeremy cried, swinging from the crow's nest, disappointment in his voice. "They're curtsying 'er colors!"

"Only after seeing our guns. Proceed as planned," ordered Baret from the quarterdeck.

A shout of glee went up. "Aye, Cap'n!"

A short time later the master gunner stood halfway up the companionway, looking toward Baret and prepared to give the final signal to his crew. "All's ready, sir!"

On the quarterdeck, Baret looked toward the *Venture*, but

his jaw flexed with irritation. Now a third ship loomed, coming out of the heat haze near the Cays with canvas billowing and colors flying.

Baret frowned.

"Sail ho! It's Cap'n Farrow's *Warspite!*" called Jeremy from the crow's nest.

"No," stated Baret and gave a short laugh. "It's Henry Morgan."

"Morgan!"

The news rippled like a wavelet among the crew.

Morgan's *Golden Future* was making straight for the *Regale* and the *Venture.*

As Morgan came closer, Yorke shouted, "Cap'n! The *Golden Future*'s running out a twenty pounder!"

Baret saw that Morgan was signaling both him and Levasseur to desist all hostile intentions. Baret knew why. The *Venture* carried eighteen guns, and French buccaneers were noted for tenacity. Although Morgan held no love for Rafael, he needed every ship and buccaneer he could muster for the expedition on the Main.

Infighting among the Brotherhood was dealt with fast and furiously, and Morgan obviously intended to stop Baret from firing on Rafael. Baret had only meant to harass Rafael's pride, and he half smiled as he focused the glass on the *Golden Future.* He could see Morgan standing, hands on hips, the yellow plume in his hat snapping cockily. Morgan raised his own telescope and fixed it on Baret.

But Baret's smile vanished when the *Golden Future* let go a volley that landed in the sea between the *Regale* and the *Venture,* parting the water with a splash that reached the *Regale* before it rode the swell. Another volley landed, this one much too close! The water splashed over the *Regale* and rained down on Baret. His dark eyes snapped as he felt the brine wet his face.

The Welsh shark!

Hob chuckled.

Baret, wet and irritated, was nevertheless disciplined enough to consider that the Lord had used Morgan unwittingly to stop him from an act that he might regret when of a cooler disposition.

Morgan dipped his colors, and Baret wryly looked at Yorke,

then gestured to respond in kind. The colors of the *Regale* curt-sied, as Jeremy liked to put it, and Baret ordered a welcoming shot to be fired in honor of the arrival of their admiral.

"What are you grinning at?" he asked Hob, who returned with a towel in one hand and a mug of coffee in the other. He well knew how to soothe his captain's temper.

"I be thinkin' ye'd have sooner sent that welcoming shot into Morgan's hide."

"You're right." And he smiled. "But it wouldn't do, old spy. We need Morgan's good graces to attack Porto Bello."

"Aye, me lordship, but ol' Morgan be cantankerous to wet ye like that, says I, an' more worried about your temper than Levasseur's, I'm thinkin'."

Baret snatched the towel and dried himself as Yorke walked up, equally grumpy and wet.

"Morgan's signaling for a parley. Can't say I'd blame ye if ye didn't go, Cap'n."

Baret laughed.

The *Golden Future* dropped anchor and lowered two long-boats. One was rowing toward the *Regale,* the other toward the *Venture.*

Baret handed the towel back to Hob, watching the longboat as he drank the black coffee and deliberated.

"Prepare my regalia, Hob. It's time for doffing hats. It may be we can settle Rafael's treachery another way."

"Aye, but I'm a mite disappointed, seeing as how I was hoping to see Levasseur's topgallants singed and smoking."

"So was I," muttered Yorke. "That fancy French dawcock has himself a lickin' coming one day. And when it comes to it, Cap'n, I'm hoping I'll be there to see it."

Yorke turned to Jeremy. "Prepare to lower the cap'n to the longboat. We'll be boarding the *Golden Future* for a parley."

13

ABOARD THE
GOLDEN FUTURE

Baret sat in the longboat as Morgan's crew rowed him across the jade green swells toward the *Golden Future*. Levasseur had arrived some ten minutes before him, and through his spyglass Baret watched him climb the rope ladder, bringing three of his crew with him. Baret came with Yorke. Capt. Erik Farrow, who had boarded a pinnace and rowed out to join the meeting, was waiting in the small boat near the ship.

The tropical sun was blazing, and Baret lowered his wide-brimmed hat to divert the glare that reflected off the water like a school of silvery fish. The briny tang of the damp sea breeze did little to cool him.

Morgan's crewmen rowed alongside the rope-boarding ladder and grabbed it to steady the boat against the side while Erik went up first with his lieutenant, a large African with a silver ring in his ear.

Capt. Baret Foxworth climbed up next and swung his muscled frame over the side, stepping onto the deck at the ship's waist. He stood looking as dangerous and gaudy in black velvet and cream lace as was expected of him for a buccaneers' meeting.

His flashing dark eyes scanned the waiting group. The first man he saw was Morgan, standing on the quarterdeck steps. The wind caught the admiral's burgundy jacket with its silver lace worn over a rough tunic and gave it a jaunty snap.

Baret, thinking of the volley of shot that had been fired against him, allowed a wry smile when he saw the subdued humor in Morgan's eyes. Then he doffed his hat, one with a white ostrich feather curling about it, in buccaneer salutation. "A fine afternoon, Colonel Morgan."

"It was, so I thought."

Baret remained beside the ship's rail until his alert gaze spotted Capt. Rafael Levasseur and his three sullen and dangerous Frenchmen on the other side. They were all likewise donned in their best taffetas and with crimson plumes in their hats. As though on cue, they swept them off in unison and bowed toward him, but their black eyes sparkled with anger. The fact that he would have fired on the *Venture* clearly had infuriated them, just as he'd known it would.

He smiled at them unpleasantly. "Ah, *bon jour*, my *gallante* brothers!" and he bowed deeply, leaving his hand on his baldric where his dueling pistols were displayed. Then his mocking gaze met Levasseur's, and irony turned into cold anger.

Rafael smirked and stepped out briskly, hand on the hilt of his rapier. The warm breeze blew between them. "You have insulted the *Venture*, Monsieur Foxworth!"

"Have I, my captain?"

"Oui!"

"Ah, but it was nothing such as you shall yet have. Of that I vow. You have so much to answer for, Captain Levasseur, that the hour must wait. For Morgan's sake, your heart remains beating for another day."

Levasseur's black eyes were malevolent, but he gave a smirk. "No, Monsieur Captain, it will not be, I solemnly assure you!" He flipped a hand toward him, showing an inch of silvery lace. "It is well that you did not dare open fire, else I would have sunk your fine ship!"

With a cool smile Baret suggested, "Easy, my captain, lest I lose all restraint and beg you to try." He replaced his hat too carefully.

Morgan glowered, hands on hips. "Cease this verbal swordplay at once, you fancy rapscallions! Baret, what is this all about? Is it not enough you shall have a commission to attack the Spaniards? Are you so impatient that you must threaten sinking a ship of the Brotherhood?"

"He has tested me sorely. He's blessed I have godly restraint, else he would be swimming by now."

Levasseur's brow grew dark with temper. "But what words! He attacks without provocation!"

Erik Farrow stepped forward, the essence of coolness. "I think, Captain Morgan, I am the one to explain, having been at Foxemoore when the abduction of Lady Harwick took place by these French dogs."

Henry Morgan turned to Levasseur with a scowl. "What is this? You have abducted Karlton's daughter?"

"Mind your tongue, Monsieur Farrow!" said Rafael. "Thus far we have had no quarrel, but that is not to say it shall remain so."

"Dare I hope, Rafael?" Erik said.

"Stay out of this, Erik," Baret warned. "When the moment comes, he is mine to take."

Morgan strode to the center of his deck, his snapping eyes circling the captains as though he himself might draw cutlass against all three.

"Any more threats and I vow, though I need your ships to skin the Spaniards, I will tear up your legal commissions now and I'll seize the three of you as pirates!"

The men looked at him, startled, then Levasseur laughed disdainfully. "Pirates!" He turned to his three officers, who smiled. "Monsieur Morgan, I am most repentant!" said Rafael and bowed. "But I did not know the English governor of Jamaica has hired you to arrest the Brotherhood."

"I'll carpse ye and dry ye for salted meat on the yardarm if ye don't watch your tongue," Morgan growled, stepping toward him with hand on his cutlass.

"Pardieu, my *capitaine!"*

"Yes—so you had best say," breathed Morgan.

A moment of silence blew by with a ghostly wind, then Morgan gestured his big head of wavy dark brown hair toward Baret.

"Speak first, Baret. 'Twas you who would have fired on the *Venture.* You owe explanation—if not to Rafael, then to me as Modyford's appointed colonel of this expedition. And you keep silent, Erik. Baret can speak for himself." He then added with blunt good humor, "Any viscount who can speak French and Castilian can find witty tongue enough to explain himself in English."

Erik stepped back, with a lift of golden brow, to lean against the bulkhead. He kept an eye on the three French pirates, who watched him with similar mistrust.

Levasseur was staring at Baret angrily.

Baret remained where he was, allowing himself space to maneuver if it came to a duel in spite of Morgan's intervention.

"An explanation you will have," he told Morgan. "And when

143

I have finished, I expect action. This fellow buccaneer—this Levasseur, who claims to bear the honor of the king of France—has committed a low crime for which he will heartily pay. On the eve of Lady Harwick's betrothal to me, he has dared to abduct her. He has her a prisoner aboard his ship. He will either send for her now, or I will fetch her myself, at whatever the cost to his ship and mine."

Morgan's blunt gaze swerved to Levasseur. "Is this despicable deed so? You have Miss Harwick on board the *Venture?*"

"Foxworth lies to protect his vanity. Mademoiselle Emerald Levasseur—my cousin—has reconsidered her rash vow of betrothal and has come with me of her own free will. Because her action has shone scorn upon his honor, he seeks a cause to fight me, a *gallante!*"

Morgan rubbed his chin and looked curiously at Baret.

"I suggest we call for her and let her speak for herself," Baret said.

"What need?" protested Levasseur. "She has already written Monsieur Morgan a message." And he drew out a folded parchment from under his jacket and handed it to Morgan.

"He forced her to write it. Levasseur also holds Sir Karlton a prisoner."

"Lies. I do not have him."

Morgan looked at Baret. "You have proof Rafael has Harwick?"

"He has no proof," Rafael said disdainfully.

"Lady Harwick can bear witness whether I speak truthfully or—as Rafael claims—that I seek an occasion against him because of pride."

"Foxworth's right." Morgan gestured to his own crew, standing about and growing impatient with the situation. "You heard him. Send for Miss Harwick."

Levasseur spun around to glare at Morgan. "I have told you, Monsieur Colonel. What need? You have the message she writes. There is argument between me and Foxworth only!"

"You did not wish it so cozy when the guns of the *Regale* were pointed at your gizzard. Is this then your wish, you French peacock? To be left to Captain Foxworth?"

Baret walked forward. "This whole incident can be settled quickly enough. Call for her. Or shall I fetch her?"

"Eh, no, no, Monsieur," came the menacing warning. "One step aboard the *Venture*, and I will order your head to be taken!"

"You can try that now, Monsieur," Baret said.

Morgan stepped between them. "Listen to me, you young cockerels. The rules of the Brotherhood are laid down and clear enough for us all. Since ye'll both look me in the face and deny the other's words, there'll be a meeting on the beach to decide, with all the captains. We'll settle this according to the rules of Tortuga!"

Levasseur grew livid, but Baret was satisfied, since it meant Emerald would be present to speak her mind. He was confident she would heartily denounce Rafael, as would Zeddie and Ty, whom he'd learned were also aboard the *Venture*.

"It is well spoken," he said, knowing the captains would remember Tortuga and how he had already dueled Rafael for Emerald.

Levasseur must have been thinking the same, for his eyes smoldered. "She will not agree to denounce me," he insisted.

"Why so? Because you have Karlton with a knife to his throat?"

"My uncle?" Levasseur mocked.

Baret turned to Morgan. "We'll gather on the beach tomorrow. But until then she does not stay aboard the *Venture*."

"And who do you suppose shall keep her if not I? You, Monsieur?" Levasseur taunted.

"No . . . there is time enough for that. Colonel Morgan shall hold her aboard the *Golden Future*."

Morgan raised his bushy brows, and Levasseur stared at him, livid.

"Ah, no! No! Not so," Levasseur cried.

"Yes, yes," mocked Baret. "On board Morgan's ship, and on one condition." And he looked at Morgan, whose brows inched even higher.

"Conditions, he says!"

Baret's eyes narrowed with grim calm, and he offered a slight bow. "Conditions, my captain, yes."

"And? What are they?" growled Morgan. "That you camp on one side of her door, I suppose? And Rafael on the other side?"

"No, that her friend and guardian, Zeddie, come with her, as well as her cousin, Ty Levasseur."

"Ah, no! Not that. It will not be!" came Levasseur's furious response.

Morgan looked at Rafael with growing distrust. "So you have one-eyed Zeddie and her cousin also, do you?"

Levasseur swept off his hat, looking defensive and uneasy, as though the wind had turned against him.

"They are aboard of their own will."

"You are a much-beloved captain, Rafael," Morgan said. "You seem to attract many to your ship. If they are aboard willingly, then there should be no cause not to send them along as her guards."

Morgan turned to one of his captains and with a curt wave gestured toward the *Venture*. "This drags on and worries me. Jackman! Send men to the *Venture* to bring Miss Harwick to my ship. Bring Zeddie and Ty Levasseur as well. If anyone tries to argue, arrest him in the name of the governor of Jamaica!"

Levasseur sauntered to the other side of the deck, and the French pirates gathered to his side. They cast sullen glances toward Baret as they prepared to go over the side to enter their longboat.

"Monsieur Levasseur! You will stay aboard," Baret ordered, touching his pistol. "Do you think I'm unwise enough to let you leave for the *Venture* before Emerald is brought here?"

Startled, Levasseur and his officers turned and looked at him.

"Captain Foxworth speaks fairly," said Morgan. "You will stay aboard."

Levasseur offered a mocking bow and turned away to the other side of the deck, where he lounged against the rail as Baret watched him.

"Now, look here, Baret," whispered Morgan through his teeth. "I'm not pleased with any of this, as you can see. A woman among the buccaneers means trouble. An' I've close to over a dozen vessels at the South Cays and six hundred buccaneers. If she chooses you tomorrow, she's to go aboard your ship and stay there out of sight. Is that clear? Elsewise, ye best go home."

"I intended to leave her at Port Royal—until Levasseur abducted her. But to return there now is out of the question. Miguel Vasquez is aboard the *Regale,* and he's related to the governor of Porto Bello. I've planned carefully—I'm getting my father out of the dungeon in Porto Bello, and I'll either sail under your flag or I'll go it alone. And Farrow and a few others, like Pierre LaMonte, will join me."

Morgan scowled and gnawed his lip because the buccaneers who would go with Baret were some of the best among the Brotherhood.

"It'll do neither of us fair if you break off with Farrow and LaMonte and leave me with the rebellious curmudgeons. Truth is, I *need* you and your ships. And the truth is, I'm in no bickering mood, but if the girl breeds unrest—"

"She won't."

"And how do you expect to see she doesn't?"

Baret's mouth showed a brief smile. "By marrying her before we sail."

Captain Farrow walked up and handed Baret his telescope. He looked toward the sea. "That ship is about three miles away. Looks like trouble. What do you make of her?"

Rafael had also noticed it. He straightened abruptly from the rail and raised his spyglass.

The ship was apparently on its way to the rendezvous.

Baret tensed, his dark eyes narrowing, and he said nothing even when Morgan inquired if he recognized the vessel. He set his elbows on the rail for steadiness and leveled the glass once more, taking a long minute to inspect her before speaking. He scanned the tall gray hull, the carved dragon, the masthead with its chipped red paint and yellow crest. He counted the gun ports visible on one side and looked at the billowing canvas—all sails unfurled. And above—no flag of any country.

Baret's jaw tightened. He lowered the glass and looked at Morgan and Erik.

"If my guess is as good as Levasseur's, it's the *Black Dragon*."

"So I thought, m'lord," said Erik in a low voice.

"Thorpe means trouble," said Morgan, casting an uneasy glance to sea as Baret passed him the glass.

"I left Thorpe on the coast of Venezuela swarming with Spaniards," said Baret. "Either the blackguard has uncanny luck or Levasseur returned for him."

"Thorpe and Levasseur together mean trouble," said Morgan. "But they'll either follow me, or I'll not issue them commissions."

"Levasseur does not look pleased to see his old sailing partner," said Baret thoughtfully, tapping his chin. "My question is, why?"

Erik pursed his lips thoughtfully. "Maybe he was telling the truth about not holding Sir Karlton aboard the *Venture.*"

"So I'm thinking. Which means Karlton may be a prisoner of Thorpe. No wonder he's not pleased to see the *Black Dragon.* He's not only losing Emerald to Morgan's ship, but if Karlton *is* aboard the *Black Dragon,* Levasseur is in a very weakened position since we must make sure Karlton is set free before the meeting tomorrow."

The *Black Dragon.* Baret remembered Capt. Lex Thorpe's promise to find him again and kill him.

"You're in a pretty pickle, your lordship," Erik said. "You've two of the most dangerous pirates on the Caribbean here, both sworn to have you dangling from their mastheads."

14

PIRATES RAFAEL LEVASSEUR AND LEX THORPE

Rafael was infuriated. Lex Thorpe's ill-timed arrival at the rendezvous could jeopardize his plans for Margarita. And now he intended that the uncouth Englishman understand just how inept and accursed his presence was.

As purple ebbed into blackness in the night sky and the surf washed ashore, Rafael stood on the beach some hundred feet from the enclosure made of old sailcloth that sheltered Lex. The man was inside, drinking rum and gambling with a handful of his men.

Rafael's three officers were gathered about him, trying to soothe his temper and urging him to ignore the matter and proceed with their plans.

Philippe was the first to point out the disadvantages of riling Thorpe. "Is he not an ill-tempered English mongrel?" he asked. "If he turns on you, what then?"

"I will manage his just end. Are you so unwise as to think I can be defeated by this jackal?"

"But my *capitaine,* is it not so that Thorpe has Harwick aboard the *Black Dragon*?"

Rafael groaned at his own folly, wishing now he had made arrangements to hold Karlton aboard one of the other French ships.

"And what will you do if he becomes angry and sails away on his own?" continued his lieutenant. "He would torture Harwick and learn where the treasure is. And if so, what will befall Mademoiselle? Your hold on her depends on your control of her father's fate."

Rafael was grim. "Wait here. I will speak with him alone. If you come with me, he will seek a quarrel. The quarrel must wait until after Margarita. Then I will deal with Lex as he deserves to be dealt with."

He brushed his way past his three French fellows, leaving them to watch the shelter, and walked purposefully toward the confrontation.

Capt. Lex Thorpe was sprawled before a table with four of his men seated around him playing cards when Rafael announced himself and sauntered in, in the style of Louis XIV. He tossed back the lace at his wrists and flecked the dust from his burgundy velvet jacket.

Thorpe looked up, took him in over his urn of rum, and leered a wicked smile.

"*Och,* now, I be deceivin' meself, gents. D'ye suppose the cuckoldy king of France durst enter me abode?" And he stood and gestured to his men to stand and bow.

But Levasseur did not take their humor for anything less than mockery. His swarthy countenance remained sardonic, and his eyes smoldered.

"So, Monsieur. You did not listen to me. You have disregarded our plans! You have foolishly come to flaunt the *Black Dragon* before Monsieur Foxworth, knowing Harwick is aboard?"

Thorpe's men cast dark glances toward their captain to see how he would take the verbal assault. Captain Thorpe flung aside his cards, made from the leaves of a signature tree, and with impatience cursed the French and their ways. He gestured for his men to leave them alone.

Rafael watched them go, careful to not turn his back on Lex. He reminded himself that signing articles with a man he could not trust was like putting a dagger to his own heart.

Thorpe stood angrily gaping at him, reeking of old sweat and rum. He was broad of shoulder and chest and wore a sweat-stained cotton shirt open from neck to waist. He was breeched in leather, and a tangle of red brown curls clustered about his thick neck where veins protruded. His quick-darting eyes sized up Levasseur, and a flash of teeth bared beneath a rat-tailed mustache. His leather *bandero* lay within easy reach. It housed six pistols.

"So the wench has her shark teeth in your bleating gizzard, has she?"

"It is so that you have risked our plans by coming here with Monsieur Karlton. Were we not to rendezvous at Margarita once I had Mademoiselle Emerald? Her presence would have forced Karlton to talk. Now you have blundered! What if Foxworth knows Karlton is aboard the *Black Dragon*? What if Demoiselle finds out? She will not come with me but will turn to Foxworth! Then I must duel him."

Lex sat down again, obviously wobbly on his feet from rum, and sprawled backward, fixing Levasseur with a cold eye. He raised his silver goblet, taken from a Spaniard when he sailed with L'Ollonais, and emptied it.

"Ye is as squawky as a nervous hen. I's able to make me own choices, and who's to say I's to follow the likes of you?"

"It was I, Monsieur, who saved your neck from the *guarda costa* on the Venezuelan coast."

"So I owes you, does I? Mebbe, but can I trust ye now, eh?"

"Now you speak as a fool speaks, Monsieur."

"Mebbe, mebbe not. While I was waitin', Rafael, ye was takin' a mite long time coming to the rendezvous. What's to keep ye from runnin' off with the wench *and* the treasure?"

"The treasure, you sodden cockerel, is not within reach of either of us until Karlton or Foxworth tells us where it's hidden!"

"So it's by your leave I's free to move me ship when I wants to heave to—is that what you're saying, Rafael?"

"We had our plans."

"Aye, and mebbe I'm thinkin' it weren't so good for me. The devil take ye, Levasseur. It's a wonder I don't pistol ye now! I figure ye had plans to run off with the wench *and* the treasure."

"You're out of your mind, Monsieur. We need Karlton. And if you think to call me a liar, you shall die for your foolish tongue. There is not a man who can outshoot me, least of all you, as rummed as you are." He leaned over the table, his hands resting on either side. "Now, Lex, breathe a cool whiff of the Caribbean and calm your fettered soul. You and I are at league. We've signed the articles, Monsieur. So why, then, are you here? Why have you put to risk our plans?"

"Bah! I've ruined nothing. I's not afraid of ye, Rafael, nor of Foxworth. The devil take ye both, if it comes to it. But I has me a wee matter to settle with Foxworth, and settle I will," he promised in a dry, harsh voice. "Before—or after—the treasure be divvied up. I's here 'cause I don't trust ye any more than I trusts him. Now, sit down. Cool your gizzard with this—" He shoved the rum across the table, then slouched back and looked at Rafael through slitted eyes. "No one knows Harwick be aboard, leastwise Morgan or Foxworth. Our plans be as safe as they be. We'll soon have us Foxworth and the wench both. Now drink up. Ye always was as taut as a prowling cat."

Levasseur considered. Then, as his emotions began to cool, he reminded himself that he needed Lex to accomplish his purpose on Margarita. As Philippe had said, it was Thorpe who had Karlton. Because he did, he must appease Lex—for now.

Rafael raised his mug and drank, beginning to understand how badly he had erred in transferring Karlton from the *Venture* to the *Black Dragon* after sinking the Dutch ship. At the time it had seemed wise. But he had expected Lex to keep his ship away from Morgan's rendezvous.

Levasseur sat on a barrel and rested his elbows on the table, chin in hand, his dark eyes brooding over Lex Thorpe.

"If you have plans to even yourself on Foxworth, it'll need wait until Margarita. He's no fool. He's slippery and dangerous. Try anything now, Monsieur, and he will turn on you."

Lex poured his rum. "I've plenty o' patience. I's biding me time for the sweet moment." He looked across the table with cold, compelling menace. "An' when it comes, Rafael, ye need remember it's mine."

Rafael fingered his prized thin mustache. His black eyes were sullen and bored. "The shares in the treasure and Emerald will suffice me."

Lex gave him a wicked smile. "Ye'll have her. Ye needs be patient too. Until the treasure is under our hatches, we'll both need to shackle our fancies. Just make sure the lovesick notions ye have for the wench don't sink our chances on Margarita."

"If anything sinks our fortunes, Monsieur, I suggest it is your arrival with Karlton."

"Sink your cuckoldy ways, Rafael. Like I says, there's naught to concern ye in this. 'Ow long will ye make weary me bones? Tomorrow the wench will be brought from Morgan's ship. She'll behave herself, knowin' her father's gizzard will get plucked if she don't do as ye want. After that, we gets us Foxworth—like a rat caught in a trap. Soon as he hears her squeal, he'll come runnin'. An' when he does, we has him, and we sails to Margarita."

He pushed the rum back to Levasseur.

Rafael was not pleased, but there was little he could do about things now. He told himself he'd been a fool to trust an

Englishman. He should have signed articles with his cousin Ives, he thought, until he remembered why he had not done so: Lex was privy to the treasure's being hidden on Margarita.

With the silken tongue of the French, Levasseur stood and toasted Capt. Lex Thorpe. Though Lex didn't understand the language, he gave a sly grin and drank heartily to the smoothly flowing words.

15

THE *BLACK DRAGON*

Morgan's pirate crews were drinking rum and gorging themselves on roast pig, which they had confiscated from the Spaniards, as they boasted of plans to attack the Spanish towns. Many were remembering the booty taken at Gran Granada, and they were eager to make another raid soon.

The location had not yet been decided, for Morgan had not yet held the captains' meeting aboard his vessel. Baret knew Morgan to be a man who kept the final destination to himself until nearing the prize, for even among the Brotherhood there were some who would slip away to warn the Spaniards for a bribe.

The orange glow of the moon cast a luminous color onto the midnight sky. The Caribbean stirred softly, and its water rippled silver on the quiet section of the beach where Baret stood with a dozen fellow buccaneers. He looked out across the waters toward the *Black Dragon* at anchor. A few lanterns glowed, and her masts were stark and white against the darkness.

Back on the darkened beach, campfires gleamed like small candles with yellow flames. Someone was coming from that direction. Baret could hear boots sinking into the sand. But Lieutenant Yorke was on lookout, and the big redheaded Scot, carrying machete and broad-blade cutlass, wouldn't be caught off guard.

"It's Captain Farrow and Hob," he called.

Baret walked along the edge of the beach, where the wavelets bubbled softly before seeping into the sand.

The broad outline of Erik's hat stood silhouetted against the moon's glow. Hob came behind with something dark slung over his shoulder.

"You were successful?" asked Baret.

"Your scheme worked. Levasseur's on his way to confront Lex Thorpe even now," Erik said.

Baret smiled unpleasantly. "It is too much to hope for that

both enemies could put an end to themselves for us, but they should be occupied by their tempers for a time. How long do we have?"

"Perhaps three hours."

That would be time enough to execute his plan to board the *Black Dragon*.

Baret had sent Hob among the pirates to sell turtles and learn what he could about the alliance of Lex Thorpe and Levasseur. Hob had lived in Port Royal for years, where he had owned a weather-beaten boat that was permanently anchored in Chocolata Hole. There he had lived and harvested turtles to sell to the buccaneers and was occasionally a valuable source of information.

"Learn anything, old spy?" Baret asked.

Hob dropped his gunnysack of turtles. His baggy cotton drawers were still wet and sandy. His crafty blue eyes were alert, and he lowered his voice. "Aye, me lordship, aplenty. Some are sayin' the *Black Dragon* were to stay near Margarita, holdin' Sir Karlton till Levasseur made his showin' with Emerald—and you."

"With *me?*"

"Levasseur 'spected to use 'em both as ransom. Ye'd have no choice 'cept to cooperate and spill what ye know about where the treasure be hidden. He's snarlin' at Thorpe for blunderin'."

It was as Baret had hoped. Levasseur's displeasure at seeing the arrival of the *Black Dragon* had to do with Karlton. And if Emerald should learn that her father had been freed, Levasseur would lose his hold over her.

"Then we need to make certain Karlton is at the buccaneer meeting tomorrow as a free man," said Baret. He looked at Erik. "You saw Lex on the beach, you're sure?"

"I made sure. He was throwing dice with the worst sharks— L'Ollonais and the Dutchman—and sopping up rum as fast as his sodden crew could pour it."

"Fortunately his debauchery plays quite well into our hands. And Rafael?"

"As I said, on his way to confront Thorpe. There should be trouble soon."

Baret was encouraged. With Thorpe off the *Black Dragon*, lounging under sailcloth and dried palm shelters, there was a slim opportunity to get aboard and locate Karlton.

Someone came striding toward them. Jeb, the lieutenant of

Captain Farrow, a giant African sporting a gold ring in his left ear, stopped on the beach.

"We's taken a prisoner, Captain Foxworth. A crewman from the *Black Dragon*. Says he's the cook."

"*Har,* I be knowin' who he is," said Hob. "He'll talk, your lordship. Just threaten to send him to Don de Guzman!"

Baret followed Jeb to a cluster of palm trees farther back from the water. Jeb had caught the pirate unaware, while the *Black Dragon's* crew was gambling.

"They's all so rum-sodden they don't notice he's not with 'em."

Flanked on either side by a scowling Jeb and a coldly indifferent Captain Farrow, the prisoner sat tied to a tree trunk, looking up warily at Baret. Seeing Baret's determined expression, the man cringed.

"It wasn't me who took Harwick, Cap'n Foxworth. It were Lex. He hates ye with good cause, so he says. You left him marooned for the Spaniards."

"A mistake, I agree," said Baret with mock repentance. "I should have used him for shark bait. So! Levasseur returned to get him off the island? I suppose you informed him that Lex was justly marooned?"

"Weren't me but the others." He looked over at Hob for help. "Tell your captain I be an old turtler comrade, Hob."

Hob, sitting on a rock, pushed his floppy hat back from his shaggy gray locks and leaned on his stick. He spat in the sand. "An' cheated me out of me boat, says I. Time for reapin' the sowin', Tom." He pointed up to a signature tree. "*Har,* me lordship. There be a strong branch to leave him for the crows."

The man's face twisted with fear. "I'll be tellin' ye anything your sweet heart desires, Cap'n Foxworth. I ain't never been a pirate. I be a cook. Make better turtle soup and mendicant oil than even ol' Hob."

"Bah," said Hob and poked his stick at him. "Ye stole my recipe, ye thievin' barracuda."

"All right, Tom," said Baret. "You've a chance to come clean. If you're not a pirate like your foul Captain Thorpe, then what are you doing back on the *Black Dragon*? Did I not allow you to board the *Warspite* with Captain Farrow?"

The man darted an apprehensive glance toward Erik and then looked down at the sand.

Erik folded his arms. "He couldn't be trusted. Nor the others. I turned them ashore in a boat a mile from Tortuga. Evidently they met up again with Rafael and signed on with him."

"Is that so?" Baret asked the cook.

"Aye, Rafael went there on Tortuga all right. Some of the brethren told 'im what happened to Lex. So Rafael swears he'll rescue his ol' friend. We all went with 'im. The Spaniards didn't find the *Black Dragon,* and it were waitin' nice and pretty-like for us in the cove just as though nothin' happened. It was then Lex and Rafael signed new articles together. Levasseur knew about Harwick from Lord Felix Buckington. So we sailed to attack the Dutch ship and took Harwick prisoner. Rafael and Lex wanted him for ransom, him and his daughter, so you'd bring 'em to the treasure."

Baret gave him a measured look but believed he was telling what he knew. "How much do they know about the treasure of the *Prince Philip?*"

"That it's hidden on Margarita. We all knows that, but none knows where, 'cept ye and Harwick."

Baret's face revealed nothing. Emerald also knew where the treasure was. He wondered at his lack of discernment for having told her. The knowledge placed her in grave danger. If Rafael or Lex learned that she knew, they wouldn't waste time on either himself or Karlton. Had she been wise enough to keep the matter to herself? She must have. If not, Levasseur wouldn't be bothering with Lex right now but would be trying to get Emerald from Morgan's ship to make off with her for Margarita . . . unless he had some scheme he thought would avail him at tomorrow's meeting.

It was imperative to rescue Karlton tonight.

The cook must have taken his scowl for displeasure, for he begged, "Now, Captain, the others may be forgetting your kindness in the past, but I'm rememberin' well. I be telling ye the truth. I can tell ye where to find Harwick aboard ship, who's on duty, and how many."

Baret left Hob to guard the old cook.

"If we return safely with Karlton, you can untie him and let him return to his foul captain. If it's proven he's led us into a trap, send him to Havana!"

"*Har,* your lordship, with smilin' pleasure."

There were not more than a dozen of Thorpe's crew left on board the *Black Dragon*, so totally engrossed were they in their pleasure-seeking on the beach. While Lex Thorpe and his officers feasted and drank themselves into a stupor, the bosun and his crew lolled on the quarterdeck with rum and roast pig sent to them from shore.

From a distance, Baret saw several pirates keeping vigil on the gun deck. They too carried jugs of liquor and must have supposed the seeming security surrounding them would last indefinitely. They were among the Brotherhood, with hundreds of like-minded crewmen on shore, and there was no fear of the Spaniards from Havana or Santo Domingo coming upon them because the Spanish ships couldn't maneuver the narrow cays.

As the longboat approached, gliding almost silently under cover of late-night darkness, Baret gestured to Yorke to lower the anchor. Armed only with cutlass and machete, Baret, Erik, and the best swimmers of their company removed their shirts and slipped quietly into the warm water. They swam below the surface toward the *Black Dragon* and came up under its aft quarter and waited.

The longboat glided forward with no pretense, her oarlocks squeaking their need of grease.

As Baret had hoped, the sentry on guard in the stern came to the rail to confront the approaching longboat.

"Who is it?" he called down with a tongue heavy with rum. Undoubtedly he thought some of his fellows were returning from shore.

The rope-boarding ladder on which Lex and his crew had descended earlier still hung against the hull. While the sentry's attention was on the longboat, Jeb deliberately began speaking to him in Swahili, further distracting him. Baret and Eric went quickly up the ship's side.

The sentry must have heard them come over the rail, however, for he turned with surprise and saw Baret approaching, dripping wet. Before the man could speak, Baret covered his mouth and tossed him over the side with a splash.

The second of Lex Thorpe's drunken sentries had been standing under the great lantern at the *Black Dragon*'s prow, but he appeared to be the less alert of the two.

Within a few minutes, Yorke, Jeb, Jeremy, and the others were aboard and crouching on deck.

Yorke handed Baret his rapier and his brace of pistols, which he quickly belted on.

Baret gestured for Jeb to remain as lookout and then led the others down the companionway steps. From below, the voices of the remainder of Thorpe's crew floated up from the gun deck. There was drunken laughter, and someone was mocking a Spanish ballad and praising Henry Morgan.

Erik remained in charge of the others while Baret crept forward alone, his muscled frame moving as lithely as that of a prowling leopard. He ascended the steps, crouching, his bare feet making no sound. He reached the quarterdeck.

There the sentry stood looking toward the beach where the campfires dotted the shore like bloated fireflies. As Baret moved toward him, the man must have sensed someone's presence for he turned quickly and saw him, making a startled sound as his breath sucked in.

A brief struggle ensued and ended swiftly as the pirate sank to his knees. A second splash broke the silence as he struck the water, joining his comrade.

While Baret rejoined the others in the waist, the revelry below continued, in the apparent belief there was complete security. Baret signaled. In a moment his men surged upon the unsuspecting crew and surrounded them with drawn cutlasses.

The half-drunken laughter was abruptly halted. The gloating over what they would do when Thorpe led them into the Spanish town perished on their tongues. Bewildered at first, staring at the cutlasses gleaming, they froze like sunbaked statues garbed in gaping cotton shirts and calico drawers, scarves tied about their heads.

Baret stepped forward and mocked a bow. "Good evening." And his eyes glinted with malicious humor. "Your two comrades are keeping permanent company with the squid. You will surely spare yourself such like fate by surrendering your weapons. Yorke, Jeremy—if you please," he ordered, and the two men proceeded to gather them while the numb crew gaped at Baret and Erik Farrow as though they were ghosts come up from the depths of the sea.

159

"And now," said Baret, "on your feet! Make one untoward move, and you will die."

They obeyed like dazed goats, with no trouble other than the need for the warning tap of a cutlass against a bare chest when some hesitated. All tramped in file down the companion-way steps to be placed in the hold.

"All except you, Hacket," he told the bosun.

The hatchet-faced giant with pale eyes and a dirty head scarf stopped and measured Baret uneasily.

"Why me, Foxworth? It's Lex ye want to settle things with. I got nothin' to do with the quarrel between ye and him."

"Perhaps not, but I spared your miserable life back on the Venezuelan Main, and what have you given to me in return?"

"I knows it, but a man has to sail with whatever cap'n brings in the purchase."

"You will have the devil to pay since you chose to serve Thorpe in spite of his evil ways. You killed that Dutch crew and sold many into slavery, a fate you know to be worse than death. You also betrayed Karlton Harwick and would have sold him too, except that he was worth more to Lex. And you'd do the same to me now without the blink of an eye if you could. In fact, it's Lex's plan to betray me, is that not true?"

"Lex wanted it that way. Karlton and the pretty wench was to force ye to talk once we had ye aboard, sailin' for Margarita. Lex, he knows how to make a man talk. An' he was going to use the wench to trouble ye."

"Yes, of that I'm sure. In trouble he excels. In honor, his soul is as barren as the salt ponds of Virgen Magra! His plans, however, will die in his teeth."

"It were the treasure he and Levasseur wanted. The goods o' the *Prince Philip* tempts the devil hisself, ye've got to admit it."

"I would prefer the treasure to satisfy the greed of His Majesty and not the captain and crew of the *Black Dragon*. Now! What has Lex done with Captain Harwick?"

He gestured with his big head. "He's below."

"Bring me to him. Any trouble, Hacket, and this time I'll not hesitate to use this cutlass."

Baret followed him down the steps and into the hold. The hull creaked, and dirty lanterns radiated yellowish light onto the beams as the hull lolled at anchor. Baret glanced about, almost afraid that something had happened to Karlton.

Then a familiar voice boomed out jubilantly. "Aye, but ye're a clever and bold blackguard, Baret Buckington, and I'll go to me grave remembering it and thanking you!"

And Sir Karlton, limping on his right leg, but otherwise in one mendable piece, came up and grabbed his forearms Roman style.

His pointed beard, auburn in color and curling upward, had grown an inch or two in captivity. His once fine shirt was tattered and his leather breeches soiled. His straight wide brows slashed across a roughened face that showed the marks of hunger, and his piercing eyes were sharp with intensity.

"Better to break your chains here on the coast of Cuba than have to search for you all the way to Madrid," said Baret with a laugh. "Convincing His Most Excellent Catholic Majesty King Philip to free you might be a bit harder than releasing you from Lex Thorpe. Well, you're looking fair enough, considering you've been a galley slave for the Dutch and then a prisoner of Lex for weeks."

Karlton's smile turned lean and hard. He pulled aside his tattered tunic and showed the marks of a whip across his chest and back.

Baret made no response, but his anger churned when he also saw the deep bruises caused by chains around his wrists and ankles.

"Who did this? Lex, or the slave ship?"

Karlton's eyes reflected the depth of his troubling thoughts. "When a man is treated as naught but a work ox, it matters not whether the Dutch own him or the Spaniards. It all comes out the same brew. It happened as a galley slave. And I've Felix to thank for my abduction that night in Port Royal. Him and Jasper both—" His eyes turned to gray stone. "And Pitt. Wait till I wring the man's neck!"

Baret was concerned over what Karlton would do when he learned the worst of Pitt's deviltry, which had resulted in Emerald's incarceration in Brideswell. Now did not seem the time to add fuel to his fiery rage.

"Don't worry about Pitt. I've left him to Sir Cecil until we

161

return. Pitt will get his due reward in time. First we've got to get you out of here."

"Where's Emerald?"

"Aboard Morgan's ship."

"Morgan!"

Baret smiled. "Guarded by both Ty and Zeddie and being escorted tomorrow to a meeting on the beach. Calm yourself, Karlton. The public betrothal to me has already taken place. I've every intention of marrying your daughter—and the sooner the better. Now that you're here, I don't see any reason to wait, do you?"

Baret masked his amusement as he watched Karlton's concern turn to surprise, then satisfaction.

"Aye, my goodly lad, so it's come to it at last, has it? Well, now! And who is to say a wedding among the Brethren of the Coast is to be scorned when the merry groom is a viscount?"

Baret felt anything but a merry groom. "There's Levasseur to deal with first, and Lex. We'd better get off this foul ship. Any other poor prisoners aboard?"

"Bah, who'd survive long under Lex? Nay, nary a one, but I can't say the same for the Dutch ship. There were plenty who went to the bottom of the Caribbean, thanks to Lex and Rafael. I tell you, Baret, being a slave meself for a time turns the light on the whole matter of slavery. I've some deep changes to work on Foxemoore when I get back."

"Emerald will give you all the encouragement you need."

A voice spoke from the dark confines of the hold. "Ye've forgotten one man, Harwick—that wretch I picked up floatin' on a piece of the Dutch ship."

They both turned toward Hacket. Baret had almost forgotten he loitered in the shadows and wondered that he'd bother to mention a prisoner. Would Hacket be a thorn in the side, or was he a kinder man after all? If so, he ought to get away from the *Black Dragon* before all his sensibilities were warped beyond repair.

"Aye, I forgot about him," agreed Karlton thoughtfully and looked toward the stern.

"What prisoner?" Baret looked to Karlton for explanation.

He shook his head. "I've never spoken to him—on the Dutch ship or here. I only saw him hauled down here soon after the ship was sunk."

"He's in poor shape," Hacket said. "We was soon to throw him overboard as feed him. Says he was a prisoner in Havana and escaped. Then the Dutch picked him up."

Any man who had once been a prisoner in Havana was an excellent source of information.

"Bring him," Baret ordered.

16

ENCOUNTER
ON THE BEACH

After arriving at the rendezvous with his ships from Port
Royal, Morgan waited for the Tortuga buccaneers to arrive, ship
by ship. The moment a vessel was sighted, his buccaneers would
prepare for battle, never certain if it was a Spanish galleon from
Havana that had unwittingly come upon them or merely one of
the Brotherhood of the Coast. But the sails spotted almost in-
evitably belonged to another privateer coming in to rendezvous
with Morgan and receive a legal commission from Governor
Modyford.

By the appointed date in March, a dangerous group of
some seven hundred buccaneers had arrived at the rendezvous.

The *Regale* and *Warspite* were the largest ships, then Levasseur's *Venture*, Sir Karlton Harwick's *Madeleine*, now captained
by his friend Hannibal, and Pierre LaMonte's *Bonaventure*. Morgan's old friend Capt. John Morris had the *Dolphin*.

Baret knew that, for the most part, the pirates preferred the
smaller vessels so that they could maneuver easily among cays
where the cumbersome galleons from Madrid could not follow.
The large open boats were fitted with a single mast and a swivel
gun in the bow, similar to the vessel that he, Erik, and Pierre had
used to surprise the *San Pedro*. These smaller vessels were decked
over forward to provide shelter for the crews in the frequent
rainstorms and a somewhat dry place to store provisions. The distance they could sail was often governed by the amount of liquid
they could carry for drinking and by how long the men could
stand being soaking wet—as they were bound to be in a stiff
breeze.

The pirates manning them were not seamen in Baret's
thinking, because he had graduated from the Royal Naval Acade-
my. The pirates rarely would attack a Spanish vessel. They
instead preferred to anchor in some cay or other shallow near a

Spanish town such as Villahermosa, then march secretly many miles overland to attack the town as marauding soldiers. This strategy was Morgan's way, as Baret well knew, since he had voyaged with him to Gran Granada.

Many of these men, like Morgan, had not been seamen until coming to the West Indies but had served as soldiers in the land wars of Europe. They reasoned in terms of overcoming a town's militia rather than of taking Spanish ships.

Baret and Erik Farrow preferred ship-to-ship fighting, but now—sailing with Morgan—they were prepared to march inland to assault the Spanish garrisons.

The *Golden Future* was anchored as close to shore as the coral reefs would allow. The midday sun was scorching, and while the vessels waited at anchor, men rigged awnings of canvas and fished, hoping to lure a big grouper or snapper. Others were gambling, using playing cards made from leaves of the signature tree, which could be carved and dried until they were durable like thin pieces of leather.

A longboat had been lowered to bring Emerald to the beach where Morgan was convening his meeting between Baret and Rafael.

She waited on deck, in silence looking out at the sea and the ships, feeling the wind and smelling the salty air. She was still wearing her betrothal gown. Its yards of pale blue satin and ribbons of velvet embroidered with gold were now torn and soiled. The ripped two-inch trim of cream lace fluttered at the edge of her bell sleeves. Her dark hair, once meticulously arranged in countless French curls was partially undone, though she had tried to rearrange it upon learning to her joy that Baret would be at the buccaneers' meeting.

Then she was taken to shore in the company of Zeddie and her cousin Ty Levasseur. Two of Morgan's crewmen dragged the longboat up onto the beach, and Emerald stepped out onto the wet sand, trying to prevent a wavelet from frothing over her ankles.

Quickly her anxious gaze scanned the meeting place up from the beach, but she did not see Baret. Could something have gone wrong?

She sent up a urgent prayer, pleading for the Lord's intervention, yet her storm-tossed faith was troubled as the ordeal was prolonged and she began to reason how impossible it was that the Lord could work out her circumstances for good. Matters were too dark. How was it possible to escape the snares? Her beautiful and sentimental betrothal ceremony had been ruined, just as her dress was ruined. All her wonderful plans for serving the Lord at Foxemoore had come unraveled like the lace on her sleeves, and here she was among hundreds of pirates in the South Cays of Cuba with Henry Morgan!

"Could anything more go wrong?" she murmured, lifting the hem of her dress as she ascended the wet sandy shore under the broiling tropical sun.

"Ain't all sulphuric news, m'gal," Zeddie said cheerfully as he strode along beside her. His leather sling with pistols had been returned to him by Morgan's crew, and except for a new bruise on the back of his head, acquired at the manor house when he had spied Levasseur and gone there to see what he was up to, he seemed in robust health.

"Captain Foxworth's here, to be sure. He's a rare man to reckon with, and the infamous blackguards all know it. If Levasseur was cocklebur enough to abduct ye like this, it's because he expects ye to side with him to save Sir Karlton. But ye heard what Ty told ye this morning, and I'm thinkin' he's right. Your father's here is my guess. See that ship? What else could it mean? 'Twill be a snowy day in Jamaica when I don't recognize Lex Thorpe's pirate vessel. See yonder?"

Emerald shaded her eyes and looked with a shudder at the *Black Dragon*. She grimaced as old memories came flooding in. Zeddie had pointed out the ship to her when they were still aboard Morgan's vessel, and she had experienced again the past horror of having confronted Captain Thorpe near Margarita. Now, as Zeddie had just said, Ty had reason to believe that her father was on the *Black Dragon,* held for ransom by Thorpe and Levasseur. The payment would be her cooperation at the buccaneers' meeting, where she would tell Henry Morgan that she had willingly left with Rafael and still wished to go with him. If she did not, the fate of her father aboard the *Black Dragon* would remain precarious, left to the cruel whims of Lex Thorpe.

"I don't see how you can be optimistic, Zeddie. If Thorpe has my father, it's because he's working with Rafael. Together, they're not likely to have left any way for me to escape."

Her heart ached as she thought of Baret. Would he understand that she must cooperate with Rafael?

No, he would not. And how could she deny him before the host of buccaneers?

Remembering her past ordeal with Thorpe on the Venezuelan Main, when the pirate had boarded her father's ship and taken them captive, brought a rush of despair.

What if Baret didn't come at all? What if she were alone here among all these scoundrels?

No! She must not allow her heart to create fears and her mind to persistently mull them over. Her trust remained in her heavenly Father, who was all-powerful and ever faithfully in control.

As she walked up from the wet sand, she looked cautiously about, still hoping to see Baret.

He wasn't there!

What if—her mind screamed with sudden panic—what if they had overcome him last night? And where was the *Regale* anchored? Why hadn't Zeddie and Ty been able to point it out this morning when they had spotted the *Black Dragon*?

Her feet sank into the soft dry sand as she continued to walk away from the beach. A few hundred feet ahead, perhaps a dozen buccaneer captains and their men were gathered beneath an awning of faded sailcloth, watching and waiting. Her heart fluttered. She must be brave.

A buccaneer was walking toward her. She paused and shaded her eyes, staring intently. He wore a gaping white shirt of cool cotton, dark breeches, and the inevitable brace of pistols. The breeze played with his blue wide-brimmed hat and curling ostrich feather.

Zeddie and Ty stopped, and Emerald broke into a smile. Picking up the hem of her skirts, she ran toward Baret.

They met in a sweeping embrace, and she clung to him as their lips met. A shout of laughter arose from the buccaneers, but Emerald hardly heard them, for she felt as though she stood in the court of King Charles in Whitehall.

"You're all right?" Baret asked.

"I am now," she whispered, her eyes clinging to his.

As they looked at each other, an angry voice shouted. "Monsieur Foxworth!"

She stiffened at Rafael's voice but saw only irritation mixed with boredom in Baret's face. His eyes narrowed.

She gripped his arms. "No, please don't duel him. You know I love you. Is there no other way?"

"Maybe, but the man grows more burdensome by the hour."

Her eyes pleaded with his. "Please . . . you must understand what I'm about to do. I . . . I must go with him. For . . . for a short time is all. He has my father."

His eyes narrowed further. "You would deny me for *him* in front of the captains?"

Her heart wrenched with pain. "Oh! How can I?"

His eyes softened then. "It is unfair of me to even suggest you must." He held her close. "But you've a happy surprise coming. Your father is with me, but Rafael and Lex don't know that yet. Shall we surprise them?"

She sucked in her breath. "With *you?* But how? I thought—the *Black Dragon*—"

"You were right. But we were able to get aboard last night and free him. He's recuperating aboard the *Regale* with another notable prisoner that Lex was too blundering to realize was a friend of Governor Modyford."

Her heart swelled with laughter. She threw her arms around his neck and drew his head down toward her face. "I love you, Baret Buckington!"

"Enough to marry me now?"

Her lips parted with surprise, but the longer his gaze held hers, the more confident she became that it must be this way. It was inevitable, and she wished it to be so.

"You're serious?" she whispered.

"Of course." His eyes teased her. "Do you think I'd give up my cabin *again?*"

Her laughter died as Levasseur strode toward them and stopped some twenty paces away. The wind pulled at his hat, and his black eyes blazed.

"Monsieur! She comes with me! Step aside!"

"No, Rafael!" she shouted. "No!" She started to step between them, but Baret took her arm and whirled her behind him.

"I have had more of you than I can take, Rafael. What will it be, the blade or pistol?"

"Pistol!"

Emerald's hand flew to her mouth. "No—"

"Stay your hand, you rogues!" shouted Morgan, striding toward them with a black scowl on his rugged face. "Miss Harwick has yet to choose her man! We've agreed the choice is hers alone. You, Rafael, and you, Baret—you agreed to the terms aboard my ship only last night. Will you keep the bargain of faith or nay?"

Levasseur smiled confidently. "Let her choose. I will abide the answer, but will Foxworth?"

Baret smiled too and offered a brief bow. "It is a bargain, Rafael. The demoiselle will choose, and we will both abide her decision." He turned toward Emerald.

She walked forward, looking from Baret to the scowling Morgan to the smirking Rafael.

"Remember, Mademoiselle Emerald," said Levasseur, "what we discussed at Foxemoore the night you willingly left with me."

Her eyes chilled as they raked him. "I remember well, Rafael."

He stood cockily, one hand on his hip, his booted foot out in front of him on a rock, and looked at Morgan. "You have heard her, Monsieur Colonel Morgan."

"Aye, I heard her," snapped Morgan and looked at Baret.

Baret gestured with a jeweled hand in airy dismissal. "Proceed, my captain!"

Morgan turned and beckoned for the captains, and eight or ten sauntered forward through the sand.

Their gaudy outfits reminded Emerald of a flock of strutting peacocks. There was a flash of purple, blue taffeta, gold lace, and a round of hats—all were decked with pirated Spanish gems and plumes, each one seeking to outdo the other in gallantry and dress. They bowed, somewhat clumsily, and a number of accents filled her ears in a garble of French, Dutch, and blunt English.

Morgan cleared his throat. "As you know, Lady Harwick, we are all about the king's business. And the fair Governor Modyford of Jamaica has given me commission to take Spanish prisoners and find out what devilment Madrid is up to when it comes to landing Spaniards on sweet English territory. We'll be gone some months, and it's no fair place for a lady to be—unless, of course, she's with her husband. And even then," he warned with a glower, "she'll keep from flaunting her fair face among the seven hundred buccaneers sailin' under my commission. Is that clear?"

Emerald retained her cool dignity. "Yes, Colonel Morgan, of course. And I assure you, the last thing I wish is to become a problem among seven hundred ogling buccaneers."

The captains laughed until they looked at Baret and saw the glitter in his steady gaze.

"Which means," belabored Morgan, "that you'll choose your man now and that you'll marry aboard his ship, on which you will promise to remain."

Emerald swallowed nervously, and her damp hands clutched her skirts. "I have decided those to be fair terms, Captain Morgan."

He looked suspiciously from Baret to Levasseur. "Fair enough. Then which of these two dawcocks do ye wish to marry?"

Emerald, with heart pounding, walked over to Baret, keeping her back toward Levasseur. "I wish to marry Captain Buckington."

Baret's arm went around her, drawing her toward him. But she saw that his gaze remained upon Levasseur, where it had been all along, as though he expected him to react violently. She saw Baret's hand resting on his pistol.

Levasseur cursed. "No, Monsieur, no! It shall not be. She cannot!"

"*Har!*" Morgan shouted. "We all heard Lady Harwick's choice. Ye've vowed ye'd stay by the decision, Rafael."

Emerald stood with anxiety, fearing there would yet be a duel. *Please,* she kept praying, *make him leave peacefully. Please protect us.*

"Mademoiselle Emerald! And what of Uncle Karlton? Have you forgotten? I will do as I have said at Foxemoore!"

Emerald took confidence from the squeeze of Baret's hand, and she turned her head to look over at Rafael.

He was livid with rage, yet there was bewilderment in his face. He glanced from her to Baret as though he had begun to guess all was not as he had thought. Then his sharp eyes swerved out toward the *Black Dragon.* His lips thinned.

"Treachery, Monsieur Foxworth?"

Baret's dark brow lifted innocently. "Of what treachery do you speak, Rafael? Have we not played the game fairly? You have heard the decision from the lips of Emerald herself. She has spoken freely without duress or pistol or sword—or even the influence of Sir Karlton."

The mention of Karlton seemed to further infuriate Rafael. He hurled his hat down onto the sand. "So! There *is* treachery!"

"Wait a minute," Morgan snarled. "What goes here?"

"Perhaps Rafael would care to explain," said Baret smoothly. "I for one will abide by her decision."

Emerald looked at Rafael's smoldering eyes. He could charge Baret with boarding the *Black Dragon* and seizing a prisoner, but that would mean admitting to Morgan that he and Lex Thorpe had held her father prisoner to force her cooperation.

"Well?" demanded Morgan. "What are you squawking about, Captain Levasseur?"

"I think," said Baret, "Captain Levasseur has nothing more to say."

Rafael glared, but he stood without moving. His hands opened and closed with dammed-up anger. His jaw flexed. Moments ticked by in which his gaze locked with Baret's. Then he let out a breath. "You win, Monsieur Foxworth. But I will not forget your treachery."

"*You* dare speak of treachery, my captain? You best ask yourself whether *I* will forget *your* offense."

"It is not over, Monsieur. Of that you both can be sure."

Morgan stepped forward. "Are ye saying you'll not abide the decision Lady Harwick has made before us all?"

Rafael appeared to reconsider as he glanced at Morgan, then at the sober faces of the captains looking on. He smirked, then bowed elegantly. "Ah, Monsieur Morgan and Monsieur Captains—of course, I will abide."

Emerald was gripping her skirts. He couldn't be trusted.

Baret knew that as well.

But did Morgan?

17

THE RENDEZVOUS

After the confrontation on the beach, the fiery emotions lulled, but like a storm not yet past, Emerald's tension remained. She knew that neither Captain Levasseur nor Captain Lex Thorpe had genuinely accepted their defeat at Baret's hand. It was in their interests to show a false face, even after discovering that Karlton had escaped the *Black Dragon*.

As the final day of Morgan's rendezvous approached, Emerald attended her father aboard the *Regale*. He continued to recuperate from his ordeal and regularly vowed that Felix would pay for his treachery when he returned home.

As for Ty, eventually he would sail with her father as a crew member on the *Madeleine*, but until Karlton returned to his ship, Ty was to stay on the *Regale*. Baret sent him to Yorke and Jeremy to learn the ways of the sea.

A few days after the encounter on the beach, she and Baret stood at the ship's rail at evening, looking out at the vessels at anchor.

"Yorke and Jeremy are better seamen than buccaneers," he told her. "They'll discourage Ty from seeing the glamour of the ways of men like Morgan. Your father has discussed with me his intention of giving the *Madeleine* to him one day on the condition he sails as a privateer merchant rather than a pirate. But he doesn't want him to know yet. Yorke once captained a merchant ship out of Bristol, so he's the best man to teach him."

She turned toward him. "You'll have a hard time convincing Ty you're not a buccaneer hero. After you humiliated Levasseur on the beach and rescued my father from the *Black Dragon*, he wishes to follow you instead of Rafael."

He smiled. "I'll need to put a swift end to his dreams of the Brotherhood. Believe me, once my father is free of Porto Bello and we're in England again, I'll have had enough of the lot of them."

Emerald wondered if he would ever completely walk away from the lifestyle or from the ship he loved, but she remained silent. She glanced at him.

He was watching her. Her eyes grew warm and limpid as they looked at one another, and he reached out for her. As yet, they had not decided when the marriage ceremony should occur.

"This is where we first began, aboard my ship. It seems a fitting place to end one relationship and begin another that will last a lifetime." He enfolded her in his arms. "How long are you going to make me give up my cabin? This is the third time I've had to pack my bag and sleep below deck."

She laughed. "Maybe it's just your captain's desk you don't want to give up."

He held her gaze, looping his finger around the ruby pendant. "Will it disappoint you to be married aboard the *Regale* with Morgan's buccaneer ships anchored around us? I could wish to marry you at Whitehall with His Majesty in attendance. You deserve better than this."

Emerald didn't think anything could make her unhappy now. She glanced at the various vessels in the purple twilight and felt the gentle, warm Caribbean breeze.

"I wouldn't consider denying you your cabin again," she teased. "It's a long way to Porto Bello. And as I told you that night at Governor Modyford's residence when you gave me this pendant, I am as much in love with Captain Foxworth as I am with the viscount."

"I was hoping you'd say that. When?"

She sighed and rested her head against his chest. "After we actually set sail . . . when we're well at sea with the Caribbean around us as far as the eye can see . . . at twilight, like now, with my father performing the vows."

"I can promise that much. And when we get to England, I'll marry you again at court if you like. Though I'm not at all sure the company of royalty will be much better."

Their lips met, and she felt loved and secure in his embrace, knowing that in the end the one thing that truly mattered was that the Lord would bless their union and fill their hearts with His presence. Of that she was confident, because she was certain that Baret had submitted to His lordship.

The next day, as Emerald set about to wash and mend her betrothal gown for the upcoming wedding ceremony, she thought of Minette and felt a pang that her cousin wouldn't be present. Still, Minette was safe at Foxemoore with Jette and Sir Cecil, and Emerald preferred her there rather than on the dangerous voyage to attack Spain.

She was surprised by Hob, who had managed to come up with a needle and thread as well as other odds and ends she needed to mend her dress.

"Miss Carlotta done left some things, an' I be thinkin' ye could use 'em," he told her and set a large box down on the cabin floor.

"Hob, you're an angel," she declared, stooping and going through the feminine items with delight.

He chuckled. "Been called all kind o' things but nae an angel. Comin' from ye, Miss Emerald, I be likin' it."

Zeddie poked his head in. He held another—smaller—box, and his one good eye twinkled. "A gift from the captain, m'gal. But he says ye'll need to give it back to him before the ceremony." She stood and walked over to take the box, bewildered. "A gift I need to give back?" and she laughed.

"Aye, says he'll be needin' it."

She opened the box, and then she understood. It was the Buckington ring. She smiled and closed her palm about it tightly. In a week she would be Mrs. Baret Buckington.

That same morning, Erik Farrow rowed over from the *Warspite* and boarded, bearing a summons from Morgan to row out to the *Golden Future*. "The captains are arriving now. There's to be a council."

Baret cared little for an attack anywhere on the Main except the one place that drew him like a magnet. But he knew Morgan was wise enough not to reveal their destination until after they had set sail.

Erik glanced about. "Is Captain Harwick coming to the meeting?"

Baret frowned. "No, I've asked him not to. I want no further

174

trouble with Rafael and Thorpe right now, and Karlton's in a riled enough mood to draw pistol against both of them."

"What about Flynn?" Erik asked of the other survivor from the Dutch slave ship.

Baret had brought the man aboard the *Regale,* and he was recovering below. "Flynn's our good fortune. He has valuable information Morgan must hear. Lex didn't realize what he had that they were about to send to the bottom of the sea." He turned to Yorke. "Bring Flynn. Is he able?"

"Able and anxious, Cap'n. And he'd like to draw pistol on Cap'n Thorpe."

"Then make certain he doesn't have one," said Baret dryly.

"Aye, Cap'n, and I'll be makin' sure."

"Pinnace is ready, Cap'n," Jeremy announced.

Ty was waiting by the ship's rail to hand Baret the rope ladder. Baret could see by the feverish gleam in his fine dark eyes that he wanted to come, but Baret was determined to keep him as far away from the buccaneers as he could.

"Wait with Jeremy," he said, adding gravely, "I'll be needing you both at Porto Bello."

"Yessir!" said Ty, and his strong shoulders went back.

The crew rowed Baret and Erik across the blue-green water to Morgan's ship. As Baret stepped aboard, his hard gaze flickered over the ruthless breed who had gathered, wearing their velvets and Mechlin lace, sometimes stained with brine and blood. The less fashionable Englishmen wore faded calico and head scarves, but even so, they took pride in their long rat-tailed mustaches.

Beneath the sailcloth was a table and several chairs. The chief seat waited for Morgan. Most of the buccaneers lounged against the ship's railing or sat on the quarterdeck steps. All wore their weapons, since no one completely trusted the others. Captain Jackman, a Morgan lieutenant and now a captain of his own brigantine, was there. So was Captain Morris of the *Dolphin.* Pierre LaMonte was perched on the rail, scanning the others in silence, along with Jean David Nau, better known on the Main as Captain L'Ollonais, whose reputation along the Mosquito Coast brought terror to the Spanish colonists. It was said his family had died by the hand of Inquisitors from Cadiz. Rather than turning to God, he had turned insanely hateful of all Spaniards. Dutchman Roche, with blond hair and blue eyes, was there, as well as Captain Michael le Basque, who was perhaps one of the best swordsmen present.

Baret's glance also found his enemies. Captains Levasseur and Lex Thorpe saw him at the same moment. A tense, expectant silence hovered over the meeting as the captains wondered what would happen. There wasn't a buccaneer present who didn't now know that Baret had boarded the *Black Dragon* and released Sir Karlton.

Levasseur stood with mocking gallantry and bowed. Baret and Erik did the same, doffing their hats. Lex Thorpe laid his dirty hat against his chest. A jeering smile was on his wide mouth.

"Why, a fair morning to you, my captains. I assume you both slept well?" Baret inquired innocently.

"Me crew slept cozy," said Lex. "So cozy a thief coulda come aboard me ship and they wouldn'ta heard his puttering li'l feet." And he looked at his lieutenant Hacket, his smile gone. "Ain't that a fact, Hacket?"

Hacket nervously shifted his stance.

Lex nudged him with an elbow. "I asked ye if ye slept cozy-like."

"I slept well, Cap'n, aye. I did to be sure."

There were a few chuckles, but they died away when Henry Morgan appeared on the quarterdeck.

However dark the hearts of those present, the view from Morgan's ship presented unsurpassed beauty. Baret looked upon the blue sea and the anchored vessels, all in fine colors, while pelicans dove for fish, making pleasant splashes.

Morgan was wearing a flat-topped, flat-brimmed Spanish hat and a simple thin cotton shirt over which he carried a heavy-studded leather brace of fancy boarding pistols. His brown mustache had grown longer, and the blazing Caribbean sun had turned him as brown as a walnut. A pair of plain gold rings dangled from his ears, and his hair blew in the breeze.

He wasted no time with announcements. "The fate of the English garrison sent from Jamaica to reinforce Old Providence has met with the mercies of the *guarda costa*. The island has fallen to the Spaniards. After promising them quarter, they killed them all except two or three."

The captains muttered their dismay.

Levasseur unleashed his rapier, his black eyes snapping, but even as he spoke, it wasn't clear to Baret whether he was upset with only the Spaniards.

"They will pay! *Oui!* How they will pay!"

Baret exchanged glances with Erik.

They both knew well the background of Old Providence. It had been settled by a group of Puritans who were later driven out or killed by the Spanish. The island had recently been reclaimed by the previous leader of the Brethren of the Coast, the Dutch pirate Captain Mansveldt—"Mansfield," the English called him. Mansfield had sailed from Jamaica with an authorized commission to attack Dutch Curacao. Instead, he returned to Port Royal with the announcement that he'd captured the Spanish island of Old Providence and raided Cartago. He asked for an English garrison to be sent there to keep the Spanish from retaking the island.

Now, Governor Modyford's friend Sir Thomas Whetstone, Maj. Samuel Smith, and Captain Stanley, who had headed up the new garrison, were thought to be prisoners in the dungeons of Panama. A woman who had just sailed there to meet her husband was also missing.

Governor Modyford hurriedly arranged for a garrison to be sent, but he could not draw on the newly organized militia that was intended for the defense of Port Royal, so he called for volunteers. Among them was Sir Thomas Whetstone, who had been speaker of the House of Assembly for the past two years.

Almost halfway between Jamaica and Porto Bello, Old Providence was a rocky, rugged island almost completely surrounded by barrier reefs having good anchorages. A smaller island, Santa Catalina, was separated westward by only a narrow boat channel. Baret knew the buccaneer names—Jones Point, Split Hill, The Brothers, Crab Cay, Iron Wood Hill, Boat Rock.

Mansfield's idea of making the island a permanent base for the buccaneers had been a good one. It was much closer to the Main and shortened the distance the buccaneers had to voyage to attack the Spaniards. From Port Royal to Porto Bello was 625 miles, but from Old Providence it was only 300 miles southeast.

"They've broken our back at Old Providence this time," Morgan said.

"Then we'll sail to purge the island of their hides," said L'Ollonais.

Morgan's eyes glittered cold. His hard brown face was like stone. "We'll not waste our time there, no, not by a bloody eye. We'll hit hard where they'll hurt the most. The soft belly of the treasure cities. As you say, Rafael, they will pay!"

A cheer went up.

Baret was uncomfortable and remained silent.

"All right, ye gallant captains, we'll waste us no more time, seeing as how all of you will have in mind the place to attack the Spaniards. The discussion's open. And then we'll decide and vote." He lowered himself into the chair, lit a *seegar,* and listened without comment while robust discussion broke out in voices that mingled French, English, and Dutch accents.

"Attack Havana! A night attack. An' we'll take us a few sweet papists as prisoners. *Har!* That'll make em' sweat!"

"Havana?" Baret said. "It's one of the strongest towns on the Main. At least fifteen hundred men would be needed—representing at least another dozen ships. We don't have them, and we won't get them."

Lex Thorpe stirred with a leer on his face. "Ye be speakin' as if ye know a thing or two, Captain Foxworth. Now, I be wonderin' why. Don't ye be wondering 'ow he knows, Hacket?" he asked his lieutenant.

Hacket looked nervous and shrugged.

"Maybe this man can enlighten your wit, Captain Thorpe," Baret said. "All things are conceivable."

And as Lex's malevolent eyes narrowed, a few of the captains laughed.

"Wit from Lex? Do you not ask too much, *mon ami?*" said Pierre LaMonte.

Lex stalked forward, snarling. "Ye yellow-livered French shark! For a piece o' eight I'd skin ye alive 'ere an' now and toss your remains to the bottom of the Caribbee."

A gold doubloon landed on the deck from somewhere, and more laughter broke out, including Pierre LaMonte's. He remained where he was, sitting loosely on the side of the ship's rail. His swarthy French face mocked Lex.

"Get on with it," Morgan shouted. "What were ye sayin', Baret? You have proof Havana can't be taken now?"

178

"I've a man here who was previously imprisoned in Havana. There's no chance of taking the town unless you can come up with another few hundred men. You yourself were present when Modyford told us of the *armada de barlovento* arriving from Madrid. Two of those galleons operate from Havana harbor. They may be clumsy, but they have more guns." He turned. "Flynn, you were a prisoner in Havana?"

A thin and ailing man came forward, casting an uneasy glance toward Lex Thorpe. Baret could see that Lex recognized him as the prisoner he'd kept with Karlton, and Thorpe shot Baret another dark look.

"I was there, Colonel Morgan. It is well fortified, and the harbor is safeguarded with guns. Ye could take it, yes, but not with the fleet you have now—and if I were you, I'd not risk it."

The captains considered in silence, and then Morgan declared, "'Tis one of the strongest towns in the West Indies. We've not enough men."

"One would think ye've already made up your mind," Lex murmured.

"Do you have a better suggestion, Lex?" Morgan snarled.

"Aye, I has me a place. Santiago—we's can all remember how successful ol' Commodore Mings was when he attacked there."

"Santiago's been strengthened since Mings's raid. We want a place that's grown fat and lazy with greed and pride, a town that sleeps like a glutton, overconfident-like," said Morgan.

Baret's glance crossed with Morgan's. They already knew what they wanted.

Another captain mentioned Trinidad; someone else, Sancti Spiritus, where the early Spanish settlers had found placer gold. There was also Bayamo and San Cristobal on the south side of the island, and Baracoa and Santa Cruz on the north shore.

"Trinidad's too close to us here at the South Cays. The Spaniards keep their pieces of eight hidden, and a sharp lookout."

"What say we attack Santa Cruz?"

"It is too close to Havana," said Erik. "The capital's troops would be there before we could get away."

There was a lull. Morgan drew on his *seegar,* looking from one dangerous face to the other.

179

"All right, ye've all spoken, and now it's my turn." He stood and walked the deck. "Ye can be wise and follow me to the likes of treasure such as ye've never laid eyes on before, or ye can return with empty holds to Tortuga, preying on fishing boats and gatherin' rusty coins and allowin' the Spaniards to mock us!"

He had their full attention.

"And what do you promise, Monsieur?" asked Levasseur.

"Promise?" scoffed Morgan. "Ye know better than that, Rafael. 'No prey, no pay.' But there were will be gold doubloons enough for us all."

"And where will we attack?"

"Ye've all got stout hearts, or I wouldn't suggest it. Ye've seen what they did to Old Providence. Ye all know, better than most, the fate of any man brought to a Spanish dungeon. We'll sack Porto Bello."

Silence encircled the deck as the buccaneer captains looked at each other.

"Ye jest, Colonel darlin'," said an Irishman. "Ye'll nae get in the harbor. An' there's three forts with cannon to blast our boats from here back to Tortuga."

Morgan smiled. "Aye, me lad, but who says we need to attack the Spaniards the way they expect us to?"

"Ye've got other plans?"

"Now would I be laying it all out in front of ye? Aye, we've plans, all right. An' we're not foolish enough to go sailin' into the harbor to confront the fortresses and guns. The Spaniards will have a few unexpected visitors."

A cheer arose. They would teach the Spaniards a lesson. "To Porto Bello!"

While the laughing and jeering went up, Baret looked at Erik. They smiled.

18

A VOW TO CHERISH

The *Regale* was far out at sea, alone, and free, the wind in her sails as a spectacular sunset exploded in crimson and gold. Twilight followed in the sun's setting trail and softly enveloped the broad Caribbean sky. A slice of the young moon appeared above the rippling water, and the horizon came awash with deep turquoise and ruby.

Emerald Harwick, born on Tortuga, was about to become Lady Emerald Buckington, and the ruby pendant about her throat undulated with passionate color. As she stood before Baret on the lofty quarterdeck of the *Regale,* her betrothal dress shimmered like pearl in the mild breeze. The silky hem of her gown brushed lightly against Baret's buccaneer boots.

Their eyes held as her father read the marriage vows from the Calvin prayer book. As Sir Karlton paused, Baret placed the Buckington ring on her finger and held it in place while he confessed his vows of faithfulness before the canopy of heaven, sighing with stars.

Emerald whispered her own promise, then grew still as her eyes lifted to his, and a breathless expectancy settled over them. Full with promise, the warm scented wind blew in from the coastline of the Main.

"Then I have me the honor of announcing to one an' all that ye are bride and groom," said Sir Karlton in a husky voice. His own eyes were moist with tears. "And may the Almighty aid thee. And may He enable ye both to be faithful and true to one another. So be it."

Baret smiled. "At last." He drew her into his arms.

Emerald raised her lips toward his and was swept away in a long moment of bliss.

He looked down at her face, touched by the moonlight.

"You are exceedingly beautiful," he whispered.

Her eyes whispered her own devotion to the man before her. Baret lifted her and carried her away.

19

THE ATTACK
ON PORTO BELLO

A row of conical gray-green mountains, typical of the Isthmus, rose above the sea. According to Hob's veteran calculations, Emerald learned that almost directly abeam should lie the little fishing village of Puerto de Naos in the province of Panama, called La Castillo del Oro. She stood with Hob at the rail, cautiously swaying to the ship's mild pitching.

Hob handed her the battered telescope that he'd had "since I stole 'em."

"Hob!" she said, affecting shock.

He rubbed his chin. "Them was the days aboard me first pirate bark. I were, methinks, all of ten." His eyes twinkled. "I repented since then, Miss. Sir Mathias and Sir Cecil, and especially his lordship, done sceered the wits outa me so I was afraid to die. But me sins be all forgiven is the Lord's good promise. This spyglass be sanctified now."

She smiled and focused it on the ships ahead. There were two. "Whose are they, can you tell?"

"Oh, aye, that be Morgan's *Golden Future*, to be sure. And that be Captain Morris's *Dolphin*. An' behind us—" he gestured "—be Captain Farrow's *Warspite*. An' the others follow. An' that—" he waved his hat toward shore "—be what the yellow-livered Spaniards call the *Tierra Firma*, or the Main, as we says. An' they thinks they owns it all 'cause Rome made an edict sayin' so." He chuckled. "England and France and Holland don't be agreein'. An' the buccaneers be out to prove it to Madrid. Think we been doin' a fair thing of it, says I.

"Time ol' Morgan and his buccaneers get done attackin' and robbin' the treasure cities, ol' Spain'll be on its back like a dead turtle.

"Europe owes a lot to the buccaneers and pirates, but ye won't be hearing 'em say so. By the time we sacks Porto Bello,

Panama, and the other towns, they'll be busted and won't be able to pay their Inquisition armies." He chuckled and rubbed his hands together. "Been waiting for this day a long time, Miss."

Emerald lowered the spyglass and looked at him, troubled. "I can't say I approve of the bloodshed, Hob. Not all Spaniards are cruel."

"No? I be disagreein'."

"Hob!"

He jutted out his chin defensively. "Nae, the Main be full of blood, and it ain't all from pirates like L'Ollonais and his evil ways, neither, but the Spaniards. I can tell ye this, when the *guarda costa* takes prisoners—'heretics' they calls us—they has their ways. Had me friends that was pulled limb from limb on the racks of the Holy Inquisition, and I not be exaggeratin'. Others was made to swallow boiling lead, or they was roasted alive in stone ovens. Me, I got away.

"I tell ye, I be worried about his lordship's father. Can't see how he lived all these years. Afraid what he'll find there, Miss. Had one friend set free, but ol' Tom had empty sockets 'stead of eyes. His lordship be saying his father's alive, but I ain't so sure. Who can tell him he's wrong? I hate to wound his heart."

Emerald sighed. She knew all this about Spain, of course, and the cruelty was something one didn't like to think about. But truth was truth even when it was unpleasant to hear. As for Viscount Royce Buckington, she knew Baret remained convinced he was alive. She stared silently ahead. "How far?" she whispered at last, "to Porto Bello?"

Hob drew in a breath. "'Bout twenty leagues, mebbe, southward. 'Tis one of the richest cities on the Main. Belongs in what the Spaniards call the Viceroyalty o' Lima, Peru."

She turned her head to watch a flock of dark brown booby birds sweep up and away from their resting places upon a lime-streaked reef.

"They feeds on sardines," Hob said. "Good sweetings when soaked in turtle oil, sardines."

"And what is Porto Bello like? You say you've been there?"

"Aye," he said darkly. "I was there once, long ago."

"The name sounds lovely."

"Aye, it do, and the port be uncommon pert. 'Bout two miles in length it is an' half a mile across. The town be another thing. Rests at the bottom o' the harbor, curvin' the shore like the moon was lookin' the other night. Them tall galleons o' Spain, like the *San Pedro,* they find good ridin' there while waitin' for the silver ingots from Peru to be hauled over the mule team road. Ye've heard o' Sir Francis Drake and how he took that great mule train of silver? Well, the old road we're like to march on be the one. It's called the *Camino Real*—the 'Royal Road.' Me? I calls it 'Blood Road,' 'cause thousands of Indians, Africans, and Europeans was the prisoners who dug all that silver! Spain stole it all and shipped it to Madrid. And then King Philip used it for his armies. Still using it in Holland and France, too."

Baret had told her this as well. She grew uncomfortable. How could Morgan and the buccaneers possibly take Porto Bello, such a great city?

She asked again, more of herself than of Hob, but he answered.

"*Har,* ye don't know Captain Henry Morgan—an' he has the best of the buccaneers with him."

She left Hob cooking supper and returned to the great cabin. She went in quietly, not wishing to disturb Baret. He'd been at the desk working at charts and maps for the last day. He was studying his father's journal and making painstaking calculations of distances on another map that he'd drawn from the information given by Don Miguel Vasquez, who, as far as she knew, was a prisoner in one of the cabins below. Baret wouldn't tell her.

Emerald walked up and set his coffee mug on the desk and placed her arms around his neck. She kissed him, then peered over his shoulder to see what he was doing.

"Am I disturbing you?"

"Yes. With you around I can't keep my mind on my work."

He reached to pull her into his lap, but she slipped away, smiling.

"I'll go talk to Hob again," she said. "He's been telling me all about Porto Bello."

She turned, but his hand on her wrist pulled her back. "I like to be disturbed. Sit down, and I'll show you Morgan's plans if you promise not to breathe a word."

Emerald sat on his lap as he traced the route on the map.

"This is the harbor. It's defended by three fortresses. They cover the entrance and anchorage with more than sixty cannons. It's the third most strongly defended port in the Indies."

"Havana being the first?"

"And Cartagena. The castles have regular garrisons. This fort guards the entrance to the harbor. It's the *San Felipe de Todo Fierro,* the Iron Fort. If we sought to fight using ships, they'd soon blow us away."

She shuddered. "Then how is attack possible? Are you sure Morgan knows what he's doing?"

A brief confident smile was his only answer. "And this is Triana. It's environed with houses. This is where the dons live, some of them anyway. The governor is the same Don Jose Sanchez Ximenez who recaptured Old Providence and did not honor the surrender terms. We hope to teach him a lesson."

"And the third one on the west end?"

His gaze hardened. "Ah! That, my dear, is Fort Castillo de San Geronimo, large and strong. It may be that the prisoners from Old Providence are being held there in chains."

"How do you know all this? Through Don Miguel Vasquez?"

"Yes. I now know my father is in a dungeon beneath Governor Sanchez's castle. Miguel will be used as ransom. Miguel's life in exchange for my father's. I've little doubt the governor will choose his nephew."

"What if Miguel is lying?" she asked uneasily. "What if your father was moved to Peru and the silver mines?"

"If he's lying, Miguel will never set foot in Porto Bello to see his family alive. He knows that."

She glanced at him through lowered lashes. "Somehow I don't think you'd kill him even then."

"He thinks I will. And if it's a trap—meaning our own imprisonment—then, yes. I will kill him."

Her eyes searched his. She felt a chill and looked back at the map. "But he wouldn't lie. Not if he wishes to live. Does he know how Carlotta ran away with Sir Jasper?"

"If I told him that, he wouldn't cooperate. I confess, I don't know which man is worse. I'd prefer she didn't marry either of them. But by now she's Mrs. Jasper Ridley."

"I wonder where they went?"

"Barbados."

She handed him the coffee mug and studied the map while he drank, frowning to himself.

"I still don't understand," she said. "If it's suicide to enter the harbor and face the bristling cannon, how does Morgan expect to take the city? How will you get inside?"

"That, my sweet, is the brilliance of Henry Morgan—and your ever-loving husband. We'll fight on land, not at sea. We're attacking as soldiers."

Emerald turned to search his face.

Under her worried gaze his expression grew enigmatic, as though he was musing over his new role as husband. He had told her last night that he knew he no longer had only himself to consider. Daring and bold behavior must be carefully considered.

"And what will you fight with? You have no muskets! No horses!" she protested.

"Muskets!" He stood and swung her up into his arms. "Who wants them?"

"All soldiers fight with—"

"We're armed with a variety of weapons, but muskets would be unpopular even if we had them. Whether matchlock or wheel-lock, they're too heavy for a long overland march through the jungle. Both are cumbersome and frustratingly slow to load."

He set her lightly on her feet. "The wheel-lock mechanisms are unreliable. The spring of the lock gives us trouble—and the pyrites often don't spark. It's the humid weather." He looked toward the window as the sudden sound of pouring rain again filled her ears. "It's heavy along this part of the Main. Once the powder gets damp, it's useless. Pistols are more convenient in open boats or walking through jungle. And sword and cutlass are always dependable."

Emerald felt anything but relieved. Even if they did take Porto Bello, at what loss of life?

She placed her palm at the back of his neck, her eyes searching his. "Have I married the only man I'll ever love only to become a young widow?"

"No, I expect to keep you a good many years," he said lightly.

"Then I'll come with you on the march."

He laughed at her, and she fumed. "Why not? If anything happens to you, I want to die with you."

"Sweet, but unrealistic."

"Better to die than live without you!"

"Emerald," he said swiftly and drew her head against his chest, soothingly. "Nothing is going to happen to me."

"You can't say that. You *don't* know what a day will bring forth. Weren't those the very words we read this morning from James?"

"Yes, and if it comes to that, if my life is to be cut short, then it can happen anywhere. We'll trust God to keep us."

"I won't stay!"

"Yes, you will," he said airily.

She stared at him.

He met her challenging gaze evenly. "If anything did happen—" he began.

"You see? Even you think so."

"No, but if it did, I don't want you captured by the Spaniards!"

"And—and what if Rafael is planning to sneak aboard while everyone is gone and take me a prisoner again? When you get back, I could be aboard the *Venture!*"

"Don't you think I've thought of that? Levasseur and Lex are marching with Morgan. But I'm leaving some of my best swordsmen as your guards. And your father will be here with you as well—and Ty."

"Ty? He'll die if you don't take him with you."

"He stays. And so do you. And when I get back, darling, if God so wills, I'll have your father-in-law to introduce to you. And now," he said gently, "no more fears. I've been waiting for this hour most of my life, it seems. It's finally here. And with the Lord's help, I'll find him."

She held him as though he would be torn from her arms forever. "Oh, Baret, I hope so—for your sake."

He kissed her, and the sound of the drumming rain filled the cabin.

After the fleet had been many days at sea, the coast of the Spanish Main was sighted ahead. It included a single, isolated mountain rearing up like a flattened sugarloaf. Emerald could tell that the buccaneers recognized it.

"*Pilon de Miguel de la Borda,*" Baret informed her in his clear Castilian. "It's nearly seventeen hundred feet high and is close to the Chagres River."

Emerald guessed they were getting close to Morgan's choice of last anchorages before reaching Porto Bello.

Standing on the quarterdeck toward late afternoon, she shaded her eyes and saw Morgan's flagship abruptly alter course. Then she heard Baret fling an order to his own quartermaster. She looked up at the creaking yards of slatting sails and listened to the screeching of running gear as the *Regale* heeled over and set a new course, to be followed in succession by the other vessels, including Levasseur's *Venture*. She still did not trust her cousin.

She watched the blue, white, and red Union Jack snap and pull in the sea breeze. At least this time Baret was sailing under a legally authorized commission from King Charles.

She had learned that since Baret was British, he was considered a "privateer"; but because he belonged to the Tortuga Brotherhood, he was also a "buccaneer." The French and Dutch carried the same legal commissions from Governor Modyford through Morgan, but they were only rated as "buccaneers." It was all somewhat confusing.

Baret had smiled and hinted that it was intended to be confusing. "Even the legal commission granted Morgan did not authorize an attack on the Main but rather against shipping— and taking Spanish prisoners to learn whether or not Madrid intended to attack Jamaica. Of course, Morgan had only to explain away his attack as being 'needful.'"

She watched the afternoon sunlight give off richer tones, bringing the canvas to a golden luster as Morgan sailed toward Naos Bay on the northern end of Panama and then into an inlet formed by some small islands. There he signaled his fleet to anchor close to *Longa de Mos.*

Later, as the sun set, Emerald waited for Baret to appear at the table for dinner, but he had unobtrusively disappeared.

"How can a man disappear from off his ship?" she asked Zeddie, but he straightened his golden periwig and looked as though he might know something that he was forbidden to tell her.

"I'm thinking, m'gal, he don't want you to know, but ye can be sure the viscount knows what he's about."

Which did not explain where he had gone.

She awakened late that night to hear him enter the cabin, obviously trying to be quiet.

189

"Where did you go?" she whispered.

"Oh—to visit a small fishing village farther up the coast, borrowing canoes."

"Fishing canoes?"

"Big ones. At least twenty-five."

"From whom did you borrow them?"

"From the Spanish, of course."

She sensed the smile in his voice but couldn't see him in the darkness as he flung off his boots and came to bed.

"Why canoes?" she whispered, but his lips silenced hers.

She awoke next day to the sound of hundreds of parakeets squawking and chattering.

At breakfast Emerald learned that a *patache,* a Spanish boat, had seen them and fled south before any of the ships could overtake it and stop the Spaniards from giving the alarm.

"Doubtless they'll spread word that Morgan's 'heretics' are again on the coast."

Emerald's dry throat wanted to choke as she tried to finish her ripe melon.

If the dons were warned that Morgan was coming . . .

But Baret was not at all gloomy. "They'll never suspect us of having our eyes on Porto Bello."

"When will you go?" she whispered, trying to look as calm as he did.

"Tomorrow morning," was all he would say.

She laid down her spoon, her appetite gone.

Baret came around the table to where she sat and pulled her gently to her feet. His dark eyes were grave even as he smiled, trying to convince her.

"It will soon be over, Emerald. After Porto Bello we'll break away from Morgan. I'm not pleased with the character of the men he has with him. Neither is he, but we've no choice now. There will be no more of this style of living once my father is free. We'll sail with Karlton to Margarita, retrieve the treasure of the *Prince Philip,* and be off for London to King Charles—war or no war with Holland. In England I'll dazzle you with civility. How does that suit you?"

"If you are with me, it will be wonderful. Without you, nothing will matter to me again."

"Then I'll make certain I come back. We'll enjoy today. I'll take you ashore if you like. The foliage and wildlife are worth seeing."

The June morning was dark and ominous when some four hundred buccaneers under Henry Morgan lowered canoes into the wide stream and began their long and arduous rowing journey upstream beneath thick overhanging vines. The overhang was an additional threat, since poisonous snakes and other creatures were abundant.

Morgan crouched in the lead canoe. With him was a crewman from the *Golden Future* who had in years gone by been a prisoner in Porto Bello. Though an old man, he was here to validate the words of Don Miguel Vasquez as to the route to the castle of San Geronimo.

Baret captained his own canoe of trusted buccaneers, as did Erik, who sat with the large-muscled Jeb from the *Warspite.*

Baret was garbed as the others, in rough rawhide jerkin and cool cotton shirt, but while most liked head kerchiefs of various colors to hold back their hair and also absorb perspiration, he preferred the Spanish soft-brimmed hat, which gave more shade from the sweltering sun.

Like Morgan, he wore a wide leather belt holding several lightweight pistols, plus a peculiarity of his own—a leather chest bandolier slung over his shoulder from which hung what the Spanish soldiers called "Apostles" (a name that displeased him since he deemed it irreverent). These were small cylindrical containers, each holding sufficient gunpowder to load a pistol. Yorke and Jeremy were with him, carrying extra swords and cutlasses.

Don Miguel rode in Baret's canoe. Baret looked at him and saw that sweat dripped from his handsome forehead. His brown eyes shot toward Baret, but they did not plead; they cursed.

"Remember, Miguel, if you have lied to me about my father being in San Geronimo, I will not kill you myself. I will merely leave you to Captain Senolve or to the Frenchman Gascoigne."

Miguel's smile showed white against his deep tan. "It is no more than I should expect from *hereticos Luteranos!—ninos de diablos!*"

Baret grabbed the front of Miguel's frilled shirt and held him angrily. "You are deceived, Miguel. It is the cruelty of the

Spanish throughout the world that has brought about the hatred that is now evident in the hearts of the buccaneers. Every one of them, including me, can tell you of atrocities committed against innocent relatives and friends. The church that God establishes does not carry a cross in one hand and implements of torture in the other. Spain is a cruel beast that must be stopped. You sorely tempt me even now to toss you to the crocodiles!"

In the dense and humid jungle, colorful macaws screamed from overhead branches while warblers sang sweetly. Golden orioles had built their nests on the tips of overspreading branches for protection from snakes. He recognized the bansanuco plant, used for treating bites from the dreaded taboas and coralis vipers. Mammoth butterflies flitted. Monkeys chittered nervously as they swung from limb to limb, showering Baret with dew from the green leaves. Farther into the jungle, a peyote squeaked. He saw wild pigs and little honey bears—all in contrast to the pall of violence and death that waited the break of day over Porto Bello—the "Beautiful Port."

Baret watched Don Miguel Vasquez, sullen but frightened of the other pirate captains, especially Hans Senolve from Holland. Hans was notorious for vengeful atrocities against Spaniards that even L'Ollonais didn't measure up to.

Baret could agree with Miguel about the brutal character of many of the men with Morgan. They were pirates through and through, and these were some of the worst. In a meeting before they had departed, they made Morgan swear that, if they joined him to attack Porto Bello, afterward he must grant them freedom in the city. Baret and Erik voted against it but had been overruled.

"We all know your fair reputation, Captain Foxworth. But we have our own ways!"

"Cruelty for its own sake is damnable folly and accomplishes nothing but the staining of your own hands and heart. When this is over, I intend to return to civility. I don't want the torture of a city of people on my conscience."

"Then you can depart when you've rescued your father," Morgan told him. "And when I am ready, I will leave for my ship."

"And leave these devils free rein?"

Morgan's eyes turned hard and cold. He began to say something, then whipped about and strode away.

The pirates had won, and they laughed over their victory. Their hatred of Spain was intense, and because they had grown brutal along with the time and place in which they lived, vengeance flared like fire in their bones.

This disturbed Baret more than he would admit. That morning before they departed in the canoes, he had risen early and read from the Bible. The Scripture that he had "by hap" opened to was Proverbs chapter 1, verses 10-19. The words still rang in his mind like the warning toll of a bell:

> My son, if sinners entice thee, consent thou not. If they say, Come with us, let us lay wait for blood, let us lurk privily for the innocent without cause: let us swallow them up alive as the grave; and whole, as those that go down into the pit: we shall find all precious substance, we shall fill our houses with spoil: cast in thy lot among us; let us all have one purse: my son, walk not thou in the way with them; refrain thy foot from their path: for their feet run to evil, and make haste to shed blood. . . . So are the ways of every one that is greedy of gain; which taketh away the life of the owners thereof.

Baret wanted no part in their acts of vengeance, drunkenness, and rape. He must be cautious to locate and deliver his father, then retreat from the city. "The heart is deceitful above all things, and desperately wicked: who can know it?" But memories of his mother, and now his father, sprang up like hot flames in his heart! Apart from the Spirit of God within him, apart from his new nature in Christ, he was as capable as the others of ripping Porto Bello into shreds with his cutlass.

Remembering Christ being nailed to the cross and His words "Father, forgive them: for they know not what they do" helped extinguish those devouring flames that could so quickly leap out of control. He continually had to remind himself that God alone was final judge and that the personal injustices that stung his life were to be entrusted to His care.

By dawn they had landed on the sandy beach and were hiding their canoes in the foliage. Then began the march on foot. Crewman Dent, serving Morgan, who had been imprisoned in Porto Bello, led the way, but Baret had plans for using Miguel.

His hands bound behind him and quieted by a gag, the Spaniard walked just ahead of Baret and Erik.

When they came to a road, Baret had Yorke untie him and remove the gag. Miguel slumped down beneath a tree and drank thirstily from a canteen while Baret checked his map, drawn from Miguel's descriptions. He studied the layout of the three fortress castles and the postern gate near San Geronimo.

"Your map does not show this trail." Baret gestured ahead to where Dent had led Morgan's men.

Miguel shrugged. "I do not keep cattle. I am a soldier."

Yorke sneered. "Ye don't know what soldiers are. Look at ye —we've got to stop to let ye rest while Morgan's men march on!"

Miguel's black eyes smoldered like coals. "Spanish soldiers of His Most Catholic Majesty are not driven dogs!"

"No," said Baret, "they use others as their dogs. How many slaves in the castle?"

He shrugged. "I have told you before, maybe eleven."

"Where is Governor Modyford's son?"

Miguel smiled. "Where he belongs!"

Baret backhanded him, thinking of his father's being put to the rack.

Miguel spit blood. "If it is the walls of San Geronimo you want, they are ahead. You have but to stay on this road."

Baret gave him a cool measured look. "And if it leads elsewhere?"

"Where would it lead, *Capitan*?"

"To your Spanish soldiers. And if it does—"

"It does not. At this time of dawn, maybe one soldier on the road."

Baret reported to Morgan.

"Aye, his words match Dent's." Morgan turned and gave quiet orders to move ahead and seize the Spanish guard.

Within a short time, a handful of men returned, leading a Spaniard wearing a close-belted leather doublet, a loose-sleeved red shirt, and yellow-and-red pantaloons.

"Throw him down," growled Morgan and turned to Baret. "Ye speak their fancy language. Tell him I'll skin him alive if he don't cooperate."

Baret stooped and looked at the sweating brown face, the eyes that stared up fearfully. Then he spoke in precise Castilian.

"The password and countersign of your garrison at San Geronimo —what is it? And if you are foolish enough to lie, this pirate Morgan will turn you over to these English fiends. Believe me, señor, they are nothing to rile. I, myself, have a conscience, but these men have none."

The soldier tried to speak, but his throat seemed dry. Baret gave him water. He blurted out the information Morgan demanded.

Baret stood. "He has spoken the truth."

"Aye, you speak that language as smoothly as butter. You'll call up to the guard and tell him to open the postern gate."

They crept forward through the trees fringing the fort's walls and waited, eating dried *boucan* and drinking water until dawn revealed the castle walls.

Standing directly below the gate, Baret looked up at the tall crenelated tower topped by a flagstaff. Beneath it, eight-foot machicolated walls were flanked at their corners by stone lookout towers.

Baret thought again of his father. At last—had he finally reached the hour of seeing him free, or had he deceived his heart by believing any man could survive the dungeons of the Inquisitors?

A cock crowed within the city. The buccaneers waited in tense silence, their cutlasses ready, their pistols primed.

We must be mad, thought Baret. *How could four hundred buccaneers take a city that held thousands of Spanish soldiers?* Yet the men who followed Henry Morgan boasted that they were each worth twenty Spanish soldiers, and maybe they were. At least they were crazy enough and wild enough to believe they were. Their courage and ruthlessness were well-known and feared up and down the Main.

Baret looked toward Morgan. He gave the signal.

Baret left the trees and walked alone toward the wall, shouting up in Castilian: "*Ole, arriba!* Tell your *Capitano* that Henry Morgan is here with all his *Luteranos!* Save your lives, señors. You will receive quarter. Open the postern gate, and you will live!"

Morgan and the buccaneers waited out of sight, gripping their weapons.

The Spaniard's answer to the call to surrender came swiftly. Baret hit the ground as a wheel-lock's ball crashed into the trees, severing branches and spitting dirt into his face.

Morgan shouted, "Then take the Spanish dogs! Forward! Forward!"

A fiendish clamor broke from the pirates as they rushed toward the walls of San Geronimo, drums beating and cutlasses waving. While the first band stooped, the second group climbed to their backs, and then the third. Soon their feet were on the ramparts, and they were climbing over the wall.

Within, an infantry trumpet blasted a tinny warning, but only a few volleys were fired from the guns on the walls before Morgan's shouting men were clambering over the embrasure rims.

Baret and Morgan were the first over the parapet. The buccaneers, sweeping right and left were soon among the unattended cannons. Baret swung his cutlass, attacking the guards, and soon seized the postern gate. Moving aside the heavy iron bars, he flung it wide, and the pirates came storming through.

Bewildered infantryman ran from the barracks onto the parade ground.

"Take them!" shouted Baret. "Cut off their escape!"

The sundry forts and batteries shot off alarm guns to awaken the city as the pirates surged forward, slashing and hacking at anything moving in Spanish pantaloons.

Baret ran to where Erik guarded Don Miguel.

"All right, the dungeon where my father is. You'll lead me there now!"

He pushed Miguel forward, trying to avoid the fighting.

Miguel stumbled along, looking about with horror as soldiers fell in heaps and the pirates walked over them, moving steadily forward to secure the ammunition storage chamber.

Inside the city, church bells clanged. Citizens poured into the streets, dazed and running in panic in all directions.

Could it be this easy? Baret wondered. Porto Bello was like a rich slumbering giant about to be gutted! And Miguel was leading him swiftly to the governor.

"Watch out!" Erik shouted.

Baret had only a moment before he saw Lex Thorpe coming at him, his cutlass drawn, venom in his wild eyes.

"D'ye think you're any better to me than these Spaniards, Foxworth? Ye'll die wi' the dogs for marooning me! I'll run ye through and through, straight to your gullet."

Miguel broke away from Baret's hand. Baret made a move to thwart him, but Lex sprang between them, snarling his hate.

Miguel ran, stumbled over a body in his haste, scrambled onto his feet again, and plunged ahead.

Erik ran after him.

Miguel, glancing back, saw Erik, changed direction, and ran into a pirate with a ready cutlass.

"Where ye be runnin', ye yeller-livered cur?" He hacked savagely.

Miguel sprawled in a heap on the cobbles as the pirate snarled, "Death to Spain!"

Gone! Dismay seized Baret's mind and wouldn't let go. His guide and ransom to free his father was gone, all because of foul Lex Thorpe—

Thorpe lunged, hissing a curse between his teeth. A swipe of his cutlass whistled past Baret's throat, and Baret narrowly deflected the blow with his own blade.

In outrage over the loss of Miguel, Baret turned on Thorpe with cold determination. He fended off Lex's cutlass with a series of blows so powerful that the pirate, startled, fought defensively, backing away, with opportunity to do no more than avert immediate death.

Again and again, Baret's blade jarred with the merciless impact of his strength as it slashed and hammered against Lex's weapon.

With each blow, Baret was not seeing Lex but his dreams, dying and blowing away like rotting leaves in the wind. All of his intricate planning with Miguel! The taking of the *San Pedro!* All wasted, ending prematurely in catastrophe. His frustration energized his attack on Thorpe.

Lex stumbled back, retreating, fighting wildly for his life. Baret drove him against a stone wall, and Thorpe, his eyes wide, leaned there, undone. Baret, gritting his teeth, rammed him through without pity.

He withdrew his Toledo blade, glaring at Lex as he slid slowly downward.

The pirate sat leaning against the wall as though taking a rest, his eyes staring blankly ahead in startled amazement.

Baret, too, stared, looking down at the dead man, dazed by his own fury and what he had done.

197

From behind, the cry of the pirates filling his ears brought sudden loathing and disgust. As swiftly as his rage had caught him up, it ebbed. He turned from Thorpe to look at his own hand gripping the hilt.

Baret backed several steps away, colliding with Erik. Their eyes met. Then Baret, turning away, made his way through the throng to where he had seen Miguel fall.

His boots sounded over the bloodstained brown cobbles. Sickened, he stooped beside the Spaniard, while Erik stood guard.

Don Miguel Vasquez was dead.

The first castle fort, San Geronimo, was now securely in the hands of the buccaneers. Most of the Spanish soldiers had died, including the Castilian don.

"Check the dungeon for prisoners," Morgan shouted above the noise.

"Aye, we did," said Tom and spat. "There's no one to save. There were two Arawaks. One had no eyes, an' the other had no arms."

Baret clenched his teeth, still bending over Miguel.

"What'll ye 'ave us do with the Spaniards in the *dungeon,* Harry?" asked Tom.

"Drive 'em into the magazine and bolt the door. Blow it up!" Then Morgan shouted to the pirates, "Our work isn't done yet! We've two more guard castles to take before Porto Bello's riches open up before us! Onward! We take the Fort Castle of Santiago de la Gloria!"

Baret, taking rest in the harness maker's shop, which Morgan was using as his command post, pushed himself up from the bench and walked to the door to look out onto the noisy street. Ugly sights were seen, and hideous sounds came to his ears. Baret muttered something under his breath and swung toward Erik.

"This is like hades. These pirate dogs are no better than the Inquisitors!"

Erik emptied a jug of water and made no reply.

"Easy, Cap'n," Yorke said to Baret. "Your father could be in one of the other two dungeons."

"Unless," said Erik grimly, "it is as Sir Cecil has long suggested to you—that he has not survived."

"Miguel swore that he was alive!" said Baret, refusing to accept the possibility.

"And he may have lied, thinking it would save his skin."

"Will ye go on or turn back, Cap'n?" Yorke asked.

Baret believed he had little choice. He had come this far, he thought. There was no turning back. "Where is Morgan now?"

"Attacking the second fortress. The *castillano*," said Erik of the Spanish commander, "is holding them off bravely enough. Morgan's built ladders to scale the walls."

The fort stood just north of town. Its yellow-brown walls, quarried from local stone, boasted of a series of salients, curtains, and bastions about ten feet high. A crenelated *donjon* tower, packed with crossbowmen and harquebusiers, fortified the various barracks and storehouses.

Buckets of boiling oil and cannon balls were being launched against the buccaneers scaling the walls of the Santiago Castle keep. Bullets hissed from all directions as Baret climbed the parapet. He gained a foothold and pulled himself over the wall.

He and Erik joined Morgan, wielded their blades to take the gun platform, then fought their way into the courtyard, where Spanish soldiers in yellow and red tried to hold them back. Their swords smashed and struck without pity. Soon overwhelmed, the Spaniards sought to escape into the underground vaults and storerooms already crowded with civilians who had fled to the keep after the fall of San Geronimo.

The Spanish commander was deadly with his Toledo blade as he directed the defense of the castle keep with cool precision. But after having killed several buccaneers, he at last retreated with the remnant of his garrison into the refectory of the officers' quarters.

"Get that battering ram!" shouted Morgan. "Strike hard, and the castle is yours!"

Soon the refectory door was sagging from its hinges.

As the buccaneers clambered down the steps, they confronted a handful of soldiers, panting and sweating. "*Santiago! Santiago! Viva el Rey!*"

"I call upon you to surrender," Morgan shouted to the commander.

But the *castillano* spat, "Never, *diablos!* An honorable commander of His Most Catholic Majesty does not surrender to heretics! Better to perish fighting them!" He raised sword hilt to his lips and kissed it.

Captain Hans Sensolve snarled, "Let me finish him off, Morgan!"

"No!"

But the *castillano* started forward, and someone's boarding pistol exploded with a deafening sound. The commander half turned, then collapsed upon the bodies of the soldiers who were sprawled dead on the floor.

Baret had one purpose in mind. He and Erik, Yorke and Jeremy, lit firebrands and went down into the humid and light-less foul dungeon below the fortress castle.

Once there, for a moment Baret didn't move. The sight was repulsive. Light from his fiery torch illuminated the Maltese cross crudely incised into a stone lintel above the torture room door. The Holy Office had recently been at work, judging by the shiny state of the torture instruments. Neither rack nor pulley had gathered dust, and no rust stained the iron frame of that brazier upon which branding irons were heated.

"The cells are this way," said Baret, his voice emotionless.

"Wait," said Erik, laying a hand on his arm.

Their eyes met.

"Let me go first."

"He's right Cap'n," Yorke whispered.

Jeremy was trembling. "So this is 'ow me brother died—"

Erik sent three heavy bolts crashing back from their sockets. The door opened as if to the gate of hell.

For a moment Baret half expected Apollyon to come forth in a cloud of fire and brimstone. But only a nauseating stench surged upward.

"Nobody could be alive down there," Erik breathed.

"Wait—I've come too far. Do you hear anything?"

"Aye, Cap'n—like a whine—"

Baret brushed past Erik and, holding high his torch, started down the slimy steps with jaw set. "Anyone down here?" he shouted.

Feeble cries sounded and echoed in several directions.

"For the love of Jesus! Help—"

Baret went on down the steps, followed by the other buccaneers. He held his torch inside a low rock-hewn chamber no more than ten or eleven feet wide.

"God 'ave mercy," whispered Jeremy at the sight.

Baret stared. Eleven Englishman, naked and as gaunt as scarecrows, were secured by ponderous chains. Swiftly he cast the light of his torch across their faces, daring to hope, to believe again that a thousand prayers may have been answered by the grace of God.

His breath sucked in as the face of one of the men turned toward him. Baret had found what he had long searched for, and he let out a jubilant shout of joy.

"Father, it's me! It's your son, Baret!"

"Baret?"

He grabbed his father's feeble frame. "By the grace of God, Father!"

Royce Buckington let out a cracked and broken cry of incoherent joy. "My son! My son! I knew you would come one day! I knew you would come . . ."

Gradually a comparative silence fell over the castle of Santiago de la Gloria, but in the town bedlam reigned. Semidrunken pirates found merriment frolicking on Madeira wine while they mockingly dressed in fancy women's hats, gowns, and other silks discovered on their spree of vice and debauchery.

By the end of fifteen days, Porto Bello had been thoroughly ravaged and looted. Morgan's catch was 250,000 pieces of eight, plus a hoard of glittering goods and slaves. The ships and boats had been brought into the harbor and the goods loaded: boxes of silver, gold, jewels, fabrics; chests and coffers. The guns that could be transported to Jamaica or Tortuga were loaded as well, while the others were spiked. The buccaneers and pirates then boarded their vessels and set sail for Port Royal, their decks and cargo holds filled with treasure and shackled slaves.

Baret had taken nothing from the city except his father— and hideous dark memories that would not be easily forgotten. Royce had been carefully attended during those two long weeks, and although he was very thin and could walk only with crutches, his olive green eyes, so like his son Jette's, began to sparkle with life and energy.

"I have everything to live for," he said with a laugh. "I have two sons—one of them Jette, whom I have never seen! What more could an old buccaneer pray for?"

"You speak too soon, my father," said Baret. "You've forgotten the treasure of the *Prince Philip*. We sail first to Margarita—and *then* to England to salvage our reputations before His Majesty."

Royce smiled wearily as he was rowed out across the bay toward the *Regale*. "Who told you about Margarita?"

"We will have a thousand tomorrows to discuss the past. Now you must only enjoy the freedom of this day."

As planned, Karlton Harwick had sailed on the *Regale* to Porto Bello harbor along with the other ships, and he was waiting to receive them aboard.

Baret's gaze searched for Emerald. Then he saw her standing on the quarterdeck steps, a vision of purity and beauty as the breeze touched her hair and the silken skirts about her ankles.

Her anxious eyes scanned him for injury. Then she smiled and came running toward him, her arms outstretched.

He held her within his strong embrace, and his lips found hers. A minute later he said quietly, "It's over. The long search, the anger. We can be free in England or Jamaica, wherever we choose."

"And the son of Governor Modyford, is there news?"

"Unfortunately, the freed prisoners believe he was sent to the mines."

"Oh no. . . ." Her eyes looked deeply into his. "What about the treasure?"

"It waits. We'll deliver it to the king along with the journal. I've proof my father is innocent of piracy."

"And Lord Felix?"

"We'll not think of him now."

"Then—then Geneva and Jette weren't in Porto Bello as we feared?"

"No, thank God. Sir Cecil and Lavender must have convinced Geneva of the insanity of Felix's wishes to take her there." He sobered. "Don Miguel is dead, but his uncle will return to much more loss than his nephew's death. Porto Bello is ravaged."

He saw her wince in revulsion, and his embrace tightened. "I'll not be sailing with Morgan again."

"I didn't think you would."

He looked at her with longing. "Do you know how beautiful you are? And after what I've seen, you look as pure as an angel. Come, Lady Buckington, I want you to meet Earl Royce Buckington, your father-in-law."

He said nothing to her about one troubling thought: *Where was Captain Levasseur?*

20

AT THE COVE

While Morgan's buccaneers and pirates continued to hold Porto Bello ransom, a Spanish horseman escaped from the city and crossed the Isthmus to Panama. He reported at once to Viceroy Don Juan Perez de Guzman, who earlier had sent Governor Sanchez of Porto Bello to recapture Old Providence. Now, faced with the alarming news that a large force of "Inglish" buccaneers was besieging the port, the viceroy mobilized 3,000 troops and set out immediately to relieve Porto Bello.

And while the attention of the Spanish garrison was fixed upon stopping Morgan, the *Regale* slipped away unnoticed past Nombre de Dios and Cartagena and sailed up the coast to Santa Marta, or "Margarita," as the English called the island.

Emerald looked on proudly as her new husband—who wanted to steer his own ship through Margarita's double line of reefs—tacked as confidently as though sailing in Port Royal Bay. She watched the shortening of the ship's canvas as Baret maneuvered behind a steep headland choked with a tangle of vegetation, where a dozen varieties of palms grew in clusters among rocks of volcanic origin. Margarita's beach inched steadily toward the *Regale*'s prow.

They set anchor out of sight in a cove on an isolated section of the Main. There they would await the secret arrival of Captain Farrow's *Warspite* and her father's ship, the *Madeleine*.

Emerald was concerned that, before leaving the harbor at Porto Bello, her father had insisted that he was well enough to captain his ship. Ty was sailing with him. He had looked equally proud at being aboard the family vessel that he had recently learned would one day be his.

That night, anchored in the moonlit cove, as they waited for the others to arrive, Emerald met with Baret and his father, Royce Buckington. She paced the floor of the round room, then stopped before the windows where she could see the surface glimmering with silvery wavelets.

"He should have been here by now," she murmured to herself.

Baret, who was briefly going over with his father his plans for retrieving the treasure, glanced in her direction.

"Don't worry. There isn't a seaman in the Caribbean able to handle a ship better than Erik. I've asked him to keep the *Madeleine* in sight. They'll arrive by morning."

She turned from the window, hoping he was right.

Baret, wearing a cool white shirt, stood by the round mahogany table where his father sat explaining a sketch of the Spanish church where the treasure was hidden. The confidence in Baret's eyes relieved some of her concerns, and she managed a brief smile and went over to join them.

Royce pushed a drawing toward him, and as Baret drew forward to study it, Emerald could see what looked to be an old adobe ruin among palm trees.

"We'll don Spanish uniforms taken from Porto Bello," he told his father. "And Karlton will conduct himself as a sober and dignified Franciscan monk. You chose an interesting location, Father. The treasure's been there these five years, and neither Felix nor the Brotherhood knew where to search."

Royce's hard green eyes studied his son. "You're certain you can trust Erik Farrow?"

Baret lifted the silver drinking vessel, watching his father. "As certain as a man can be."

"Yet Farrow's reputation on St. Kitts is that of a pirate."

Baret affected thoughtfulness. "Yes . . ."

"And his reputation with the sword is noteworthy."

"He's shared his skills with me. I first met him in England while a student. I hired him as a personal trainer at the armory. He's proven a friend, Father, though admittedly there was a brief time when he served Felix. He had expected the hand of Lavender in return for his loyalties."

"And now he expects a share of the treasure?"

Baret's brow lifted. "As does Karlton. It seems only fair, Father."

"I agree with you there. And if you say Farrow is a friend, we will discuss it no more. Yet I cannot help wondering when and how it was that my son from Cambridge Divinity School became close with a man of Farrow's character. Cecil and I shall have a long discourse when I see him next. He was supposed to keep an eye on you."

Baret smiled ruefully. "My father still sees me as a boy in velvet knee pants, taking music lessons in Paris."

"It seems I have much to catch up on concerning the recent changes in your life. I'm sure you will make them quite clear."

Emerald recognized the humor and glanced at Baret, who laughed.

"Do you think a divinity student could have won the tongues of the Tortuga Brotherhood? There was only one way to glean information on your whereabouts, and that was to become one of them."

"Yes . . . so I see." But Royce smiled when he said it.

"There is the honorable matter of Barbados," Emerald spoke up, hoping to dispel the roguish cast that had settled over Baret's reputation. "Your lordship will be pleased with your son's defense of the island against the Dutch. Once the treasure is returned to His Majesty, both of your good reputations will be restored. Earl Nigel says your son will be knighted by King Charles."

Baret's dark eyes met his father's, and he smiled over his goblet. "As you see, Father, I've chosen my bride well. She'll defend me even before Charles."

Royce smiled at her. "I've a notion, my dear, that when we get back to England, you'll have your hands full defending us— and Baret and I will both need some reforming."

She dimpled. "A pleasure, m'lord. But are you sure I'll have sway with the king?"

"Perhaps more than Baret will appreciate." Royce glanced at him.

Baret's smirk reflected some understood irony between him and his father that she missed.

"As for the treasure, I promised Karlton and the others a share when we took the *Prince Philip*," Royce mused, and as though his thoughts had taken a turn that troubled him, he sobered. Using his walking stick, he pushed himself up from his chair and looked toward the window where the moonlight shone peacefully on the dark water.

"When I made that promise I had no idea it would take so many years before I could keep it," he murmured as if to himself.

Emerald recognized what was behind Baret's expression as his gaze drifted over the once-strong man now weakened by torture. But the scars and the thin, malnourished body apparently only increased Baret's love and pride. Royce remained on a crutch and was still recovering from malaria as well as from skin infections that had remained untreated for months. But despite everything, Baret had told her, his father was too resilient not to fully recover his health and stalwart demeanor with time and proper treatment.

She hopefully agreed. A long rest in England would set him back on his feet. Even now his eyes gleamed, and his rugged face, though scarred, retained its handsome appearance. The inner scars were another matter. They were likely to heal more slowly, as Royce's hatred for Spain seemed to have intensified.

"I didn't know it," Baret told her before they came to the round room, "but my father and Geneva were once in love. That's the reason she took such an interest in Jette and went to France to find him. I often wondered why she behaved almost as a mother."

The news had shocked Emerald. Geneva and Baret's father in love! She had a notion that the matter between him and Felix would grow even more bitter because of Geneva.

She was relieved that in spite of all the evil Uncle Felix had done him and his father, Baret now seemed satisfied to allow legal justice to take precedence rather than involve himself in personal revenge. He had his father again, the treasure was within reach, and he had also told her he wanted to do nothing that would mar their future—or the future of their children. He seemed confident the king would eventually arrest Felix and place him in the Tower.

Emerald's thoughts returned to the moment at hand as Royce turned his head, his green eyes snapping. "You are certain the others are all dead?"

She saw Baret's jaw flex. "Thanks to Uncle Felix, yes. Maynerd was hanged in Port Royal. I have no grief for him—after he left your ship he became little more than a bloodthirsty pirate—but Lucca was another matter. Felix was to blame for his death as well."

Royce's lip twitched as he looked back toward the window, and his fingers tapped his walking stick. "Brother Felix . . . he has much to answer for."

Baret made no response, and Emerald guessed that the emotions ran too deep for either of them to deal wisely with them now. She knew Baret's father had refused to believe Felix's treachery in his efforts to gain his half-brother's right to title and fortune—until Baret had shown him the information provided by Sir Jasper and Carlotta. At least she could think of one good result emerging from his father's weakened condition: he was unable to search out Felix and confront him. The matter was best left to the High Admiralty—and King Charles.

Baret spoke now. "Most likely the order for Lucca's death came from Felix, but unless Jasper tells this to the king, we've no proof."

"There's nothing in the information he gave you about Lucca?"

"Unfortunately, no. But I think I can make him talk. He's more reason to cooperate now that I've helped him and Carlotta escape to Barbados. One way or another, Felix will face justice."

Emerald glanced at both men and wondered at the uneasiness that crept over her.

"Isn't Carlotta's uncle the governor here on Margarita?" she asked suddenly.

As they favored her with a silent glance, she could see they didn't care to make anything of it.

"What if the governor is *expecting* you to come for the treasure?" she persisted.

She saw a flicker in Baret's dark eyes, but his smile remained.

He kissed her forehead and gave her arms an affectionate squeeze. "Enough questions." He turned toward Royce, who was frowning as he looked down at the drawing of the San Felippe church.

"When do you expect Farrow and Karlton?" he asked.

"By morning," came Baret's vague response. And again a look passed between them that only heightened her concerns.

"You must do nothing, Baret, until they arrive," Royce said.

"It's unwise to delay. The longer we wait here, the more chance some passing Spanish fisherman will spy our ship. I've good men aboard—men I trust implicitly, who are expert swords-men and bowmen. It would be far wiser to go ashore now—tonight—load the treasure before dawn, and slip away. The *Warspite* and *Madeleine* will surely be waiting in the Caribbean."

"You are sure you know where to find it, then?"

In a low voice Baret went over the location. It was stored in five heavy chests in a crypt deep below the old San Felippe church.

Emerald listened, imagining the wind whining about church ruins, in her imagination hearing the sand blowing. What if there was a trap waiting for Baret? But Baret was not unwise. Surely he knew the possibility of that. *Where was Levasseur?*

"The uniforms and cleric robe were a good precaution, but you probably won't need them," his father was saying in an equally low voice.

"Not need them! There may be at least a dozen Franciscans there! You're not suggesting the churchmen are friendly!"

Royce gave a bitter laugh. "Hardly, my son, but the church is abandoned. There are no clerics there to deceive with your robes and uniforms."

By now, Emerald was as surprised as Baret, and Royce had their full attention. She watched the men, wondering at Royce's smile and Baret's questioning brow.

"You mean there's no one there?" Baret asked.

Royce gave a chuckle. "No. How else would I ever be able to hide such rich fare beneath their noses before the Spaniards arrived in their *barca longas*?"

"Karlton never told me that . . ." He snatched up the draw-ing and looked at it again as though seeing the ruins for the first time.

"He could not have told you. He didn't know the story Lucca told me. We kept it between us. Karlton, bless his soul, knew only that there had been Franciscans on the island."

As Baret frowned slightly at his father, apparently believing something important had been kept from him all these years, Emerald mulled over the disclosure that her father hadn't known all the story. Had this been because neither Royce nor Lucca had completely trusted him?

"Ah, my son, I can see you too do not know the tale of Don Felippe," Royce said with a smile. He gestured to the drawing.

"San Felippe Mission was first built nearly a hundred years ago by a noble Spanish soldier from Madrid. Later he turned to the Reformed faith, but when he was killed in battle, the Franciscans who kept the church and the burial ground did not know this. Naturally, they made a great to-do over the don and laid him to rest in the crypt. For many years after his death they meticulously kept the mission grounds and the grave site. Then, as fortune would have it, they found out that this great man had become a heretic. They pronounced the place 'Ichabod' and packed up and went into town, where a new San Felippe church was built, using the silver and gold dug by 'heretic' slaves working the mines in Peru.

"This location—" he gestured again to the drawing "—was abandoned. As God would have it, my son, there were no Franciscans there at the time of the shipwreck." His eyes smiled at Baret. "It proved the perfect place to store the treasure, since I knew no decent Spaniard would ever go there again. And no one in the Tortuga Brotherhood knew the church was abandoned. Had our good fortune held out a week longer, we might have secured help from the local Indians and been able to sail away. But, alas, the *guarda costa* discovered the wreckage of my ship and landed troops."

"We now know why they were out in force searching for you," Baret said bitterly, "and who alerted them before the storm ever sank your ship."

Felix, thought Emerald sadly. He had betrayed his own brother.

A few minutes later Yorke came in. "We spied a *barca longa,* Cap'n. We was all set to blow 'em out of the water till they gave the secret signal. It's Farrow and Harwick. They're coming over the ship's side right now."

Relief swelled in Emerald's heart. *Thank You, Father,* she prayed.

"We're in good fortune, then," Baret told his father. "We'll take the best men and leave for shore as soon as it's dark. We'll be out on the Caribbean sailing for England by sunrise."

The *Warspite* and *Madeleine* waited in broader waters since neither Erik nor her father would risk navigating the reefs at night. They had come to the *Regale* by small boats, bringing several of their crewmen and having left trusted lieutenants in command of their vessels.

"What took you so long?" inquired Baret when they were aboard.

"A galleon was spotted coming from Cartagena. We wished to avoid suspicion and waited till she was out of sight," Erik said.

"See anyone else?"

"No, nothing."

Emerald believed Baret was quietly inquiring about Rafael.

Her father was more open with his words: "If that French nephew of mine shows his face, I'll carve him for dinner. Well, Emerald!" He threw his sturdy arms about her and pinched her chin, his robust face wearing a bright smile. "And how's my little lass feeling?"

She looked at him blankly. "Feeling, Papa? Why—I feel well enough. Why do you ask?"

His silvery eyes glinted in the moonlight. "I'm thinking of me upcoming grandson! I'm an impatient man. Any news yet?"

Exasperated, she blushed. "Oh, Papa!"

Baret laughed.

Karlton looked disappointed and sheepish. "Aye, lass, I suppose you're right. I'll soon have treasure enough to buy the boy all Foxemoore as a present." He rubbed his hands together.

Emerald smothered a laugh. "Papa, as Baret's wife I already own most of Foxemoore."

"Aye, and a bit of Buckington House too, eh?"

She glanced at Baret and saw his faint smile of amusement.

"Ah . . . a fair place to settle in me old age," he said with a sigh.

"If we don't go ashore to get the treasure and then get away from here," said Baret lazily, "we may all retire on Margarita— permanently. Why don't you wait here with my father?" he asked Karlton.

"Ah no, me lad. I've been waiting for this day too long to stay aboard now."

While Erik was overseeing the lowering of the longboats, and the choice men were gathered to row ashore to Margarita, Emerald walked with Baret to the ship's rail. The stars shone in the deep black sky, and below them the water sparkled like diamonds.

His arms went about her, and they stood listening to the waves lapping against the ship's hull. Despite the confidence he showed, she remained tense and troubled. So many things could go wrong. It was always difficult to be left behind when the one you loved went to the forefront of danger.

She looked up at him, watching the starlight fall on the handsome cut of his jaw. "Even though Lex Thorpe is dead, that still leaves Rafael. How do you know he didn't follow us from Porto Bello?"

"More than likely he did."

"You never mentioned that possibility until now. He could ruin everything!"

"My dear, I am well aware of that. But he risks his life just by being here, the same as I do. Rafael is no friend of the Spaniards. He's attacked numerous galleons, and they would enjoy trapping him and hanging him on the square. He wants that treasure, but he's clever enough to plan carefully—and that's what troubles me. I would have expected to see the *Venture* in these waters, since he must come the same route as we have. Yet he's nowhere to be seen."

"What do you mean, you would have expected him?" She plucked at his sleeve, her eyes searching his.

"There's only one other way onto this island, and that's openly—by way of the harbor."

Whatever troubled him was lost to her. "But as you say, he's no friend of the Spaniards. He would need to come as secretly as we."

"Yes. Unless something has happened I don't know about."

"You mean, he may be lying in wait at sea, even closer to the Atlantic?"

"I don't know. It's a thought. I've tried to think what I might do if I were in his place. There was a time when Spain's treasure galleons were not attacked by pirates in the Caribbean at all but near the Canary Islands or off the coast of Portugal as they neared Spain."

"You don't think he's set sail for Europe, do you—to lie in wait? Is that what you would do?"

"Probably . . . but there is one difference between his thinking and mine. Rafael is impatient. And that's what makes me think he *must* be on the island. But I keep wondering how he could have gotten here undetected."

"Baret, maybe we should wait—and come back for the treasure another time. After all, no one knows where it's hidden. What are a few more months, or even a year?"

He smiled and cradled her head in his hands. "Only your worry would cause you to even suggest that. No, darling, we've got to do it now. Our future in England depends on it. Though I do wish I had a few more days. I would like to search for the *Venture*, but there is no time. What we do, we must do now. Tonight. Word from Porto Bello will reach this section of the Main soon."

She held him as though afraid he would slip through her fingers forever. "Maybe Rafael's ship sank in a storm."

He laughed. "And maybe he decided he would return in peace to Tortuga and be content to let us sail away to England."

She laid her head against his chest and closed her eyes. "Oh, Baret, I'm afraid."

He held her tightly. "The One who has brought us together at last, He remains our one true hope and confidence. We'll trust Him to see us through this final hour. It will soon be over, and we'll sail home." He kissed her long and passionately, then gently pried her hands loose and held her away from him while his eyes spoke his love.

Emerald looked up at him, her eyes moist, not trusting herself to speak. She watched him go over the side of the ship alone, and shivered as though a cold wind blew against her. She gripped the rail and, closing her eyes, prayed fervently.

She listened as the oars sliced through the dark water and the two longboats rowed in the still darkness toward the mainland.

21

TREASURE
OF MARGARITA

The boats slipped quietly across the water as oars dipped through the shiny darkness. In the moonlight Baret could make out the outline of the gently curving white sand shoreline. Farther back, palm trees formed a ridge.

Once ashore, while the others dragged the longboats into a tangle of vines to conceal them, Baret climbed a sand dune and stood looking about, the breeze tugging at his Spanish hat. He could see the sloping rise and the outline of what he knew to be the old adobe structure of San Felippe Mission.

A few minutes later his boots were sinking into the dry sand as, accompanied by Erik and Karlton, he walked toward the ruins. All carried their weapons. Yorke, Jeremy, and several others followed.

San Felippe had been built to face the sea. Even as they neared the place, Baret heard the head wind whine like a whimpering dog among the nooks and crannies of its crumbling walls. The once-white cross had long ago tumbled from the sunken roof and lay untouched among the other debris, overrun with vines and bramble.

Karlton's face tightened. "Many a good man of your father's crew was cut down on this beach and left to die," he murmured, and his slitted eyes reflected the distant memory.

Erik, also, took in the still, ghostly scene. But his handsome face revealed none of the emotion that must have passed across his mind.

Baret's hand rested on his leather baldric. "And to think I've been hindered all these years from coming here, not knowing where my father hid it. I could have come and carried it away nearly single-handed, docking the *Regale* but a quarter mile off the beach."

Karlton glanced about, then looked toward the ridge of trees. He gestured. "That's where we hid from the Spaniards . . .

214

your father left his pistol yonder, then bravely walked to meet the swarming soldiers over there—" He gestured down toward where the water rippled against the flat shoreline.

Baret imagined what it must have been like, but there was no time to muse over the past now. "Come," he said.

The mission had two-foot-thick mud walls, and they entered through what had been a wooden door frame. Baret half expected to see Levasseur step from the shadows, but only silence greeted them.

He walked across a rough stone floor, avoiding areas where the roof beams had fallen. He came then to a stone lid, which was elevated about six inches off the floor. He knew crypts to be small subterranean vaults often built beneath the main floor of churches, used as burial places and also for secret meetings.

"That's the entrance, all right," said Karlton in a low voice. "It took three of us to lift this cover."

While Yorke and Jeremy stood guard outside, Baret, Erik, and Karlton crouched down and lifted one end of the heavy stone cover, then managed to slide it to one side to reveal the opening. A black cavernlike hole greeted them with stale air.

Baret looked down into the dark environs. Then he and Erik used a flint to light the few candles they had brought with them. They set some on the stone steps as Karlton led the way downward. A golden glow cast light on the walls and stair.

"If my memory of this place serves me as well as my nightmares, five chests wait by the Spaniards' bones."

The three entered the airless cavern of shadows. Karlton's boots sounded on the stone flooring as he cautiously made his way along with Erik just behind. Baret drew his pistol.

"The chests are here just as we left them!" came Karlton's relieved voice.

Baret joined him, walking past smooth bones. His boots avoided a skull. More than the don had been buried here! And without proper respect.

Karlton and Erik set up the two remaining candles on a low ledge. Baret seized one, then stooped to inspect a metal hasp. It bore the insignia of the *Prince Philip* and the crown of Spain. The lock of one chest was already broken, and he lifted the lid. Smooth bars of Peruvian silver gleamed invitingly.

Baret found himself remembering the slaves and Indians

who had died in the mines to produce it for the Spanish crown. But as he lifted a bar and held it, he also saw his own freedom reflected in its glow—and his father's reputation fully restored with the king.

Erik broke the lock on a second chest, and he and Karlton dipped their fingers through the gold, pearls, and shining jewels —including large bright green emeralds from Brazil.

Baret glanced at Erik's face, then Karlton's, and he could see the fire of passion in their eyes. He stood and firmly shut the lid. "Call the men," he ordered. "The sooner we get this temptation out of sight, the better we'll all be for it."

Erik stirred, as though awakening from a trance. "If I had but a handful of this," he murmured, "I could build a plantation on Jamaica for Minette."

Baret knew what he meant. Erik had told him he would be going back for her, that one day he would marry her. Baret smiled. "Don't worry, you'll have your plantation. Call for Yorke."

Erik strode to the steps, shouting, "Yorke! Jeremy! Get down here!"

Karlton had turned away, as though bothered by some thought that shamed his conscience. "You're right, Baret," he said. "The sooner this is aboard the *Regale*, the better off we'll all be. Temptation is something a wise man doesn't wish to dwell with."

Within twenty minutes the chests had been hauled up out of the crypt and were being moved by the strongest men down the sandy slope to the beach where the boats waited.

Baret was the last to leave—a boat would wait for him. He felt the need for time alone to meditate on what had happened in this place so long ago. He stood on the rise, looking out toward the sea, enjoying the trade wind that cooled the perspiration on his face. The water rippled in the moonlight.

It seemed that a great burden had at last been lifted from his heart. He watched the figures of the men moving about on the beach, loading the chests. Out in the cove's quiet water sat the *Regale* at anchor.

Only one thing seriously troubled him: Where was Levasseur? It seemed incredible that he hadn't followed them here. Was he waiting at sea between here and the Canary Islands? Had he been killed at Porto Bello? Even if he were dead, what of his crew? There were cunning, greedy men aboard the *Venture* who

knew as much about the treasure as did Levasseur. His lieutenant, for one—a French pirate named Pierre—would surely
have trailed them when they set sail from Porto Bello, if . . .

Baret turned to look back at the church for the last time.
He had no wish to visit Margarita again. He'd started to leave
when a voice called from the crest of a dune behind him.

So!

Levasseur stood in sharp silhouette against the sky, an ostrich
plume swirling on his hat as the sea breeze made it dance cockily.

"Bon soir, Monsieur le Capitaine," he called. "I have waited all
these days for your arrival. You see, we did not sail to Porto Bello
but came here, knowing you would arrive. Ah, we watch every
cove. And now you have led us to the treasure. Yet, I did not
think I would have the great privilege to come upon you alone,
no. So you killed Lex?"

"Why would you think that?"

"That fool," he said contemptuously. "What other end
would he have? He would not listen to me. He went with Morgan
just to kill you. But I had great faith in you, *mon foi.* I knew you
would best him! Ah, but alas! You have met your match in *me!"*

"Do not be a fool, Rafael! For Emerald's sake, I do not wish
to kill you. And for what would you duel? The treasure? The treasure is gone, being safely loaded aboard the *Regale* even now. Let
us make a bargain and part—if not friends—at least with our
rapiers sheathed."

Levasseur came sliding down the sand dune, his lean tawny
hand resting on his baldric. He stopped. "Aboard the *Regale,
Monsieur le Capitaine,* but not for long. Only until I tell the Spanish governor where to find you, yes? Still, what kind of a bargain,
Monsieur, do you offer?"

"A share in the treasure—as agreed upon in the articles we
both signed."

He laughed. "Ah, but already I will have a share. And, also,
your father would not agree."

"Why not? The king shall have his plenty. And after all, the
booty did belong to Madrid, did it not? You have made arrangements with the governor to locate the treasure for him? You shall
have more than he offers you. Come, Rafael! Bury your animosity once for all. I have a gift for you, as well—the jewels that your
cousin Minette took from your cabin so many months ago—"

Levasseur laughed again. "You expect me to be content, Monsieur, by the return of that which you have stolen from me?"

"Along with the generous share agreed upon. Think what you might do with it all—plus an extra share of the treasure of the *Prince Philip!*"

Rafael's black eyes snapped. "An extra share, Monsieur?"

"Yes. I will take it from my portion, to which we signed articles. The rest of my portion will be divided among my officers and crew. A double share, Rafael—plus your jewels. And," he added quietly, his dark eyes flickering with warning, "your life, my captain."

Levasseur smiled slowly.

"You would be very unwise, Rafael, to duel me. You may boast to your men, you may boast to Emerald, but you and I both know I can best you. Why die in the sand on Margarita when you can take great treasure back to Tortuga, marry a pretty demoiselle, and settle down to become governor?"

Rafael watched him for a long moment, then threw back his head and laughed harshly. "*Monsieur le Capitaine!* You speak smoothly enough. Very well—we shall have our secret bargain. Still, I will not come with you down to the beach. Ah, *mon ami,* I know the treachery that may await me."

"Then I will bring your bounty here—tonight."

"You and I alone?"

"You and I alone, Rafael."

Levasseur eyed him. "You would not be so foolish as not to return, Monsieur. If you do not, I pledge I shall send the *Regale* to the bottom. And the *Warspite.* And the *Madeleine.* With all on board."

The wind blew and stirred the sand between them.

"I am a man of my word, Rafael."

"I will expect you, Monsieur, when the moon begins to rise."

Baret came alone to the church ruins and stood in the open, listening to the wind whine through the mud walls and rubble. He waited. The sky was wide and black. The nearly full moon was at the horizon.

Then he heard echoing boots, and Levasseur walked from beyond the church.

Baret dropped two heavy bags of jewels and coins and, reaching into his shirt, drew out a small leather pouch. He tossed it on top of the two bags.

Levasseur came cautiously forward, hand on his rapier, and Baret stepped back, his own hand on his hilt.

Rafael stooped, untied the drawstrings, and opened each bag. He scooped up a handful of shimmering gold and silver pieces, letting them fall through his fingers. Satisfied, he opened the small pouch and checked the pieces within.

"It is all here," he admitted and stood.

Baret's smile was sardonic.

Levasseur doffed his hat.

Baret did the same. Then, straightening it, he placed it back on his head as he backed away.

"*Au revoir, Monsieur Capitaine!*"

There was a hint of malicious amusement in his voice that alerted Baret. But he was too late. A dozen or more Spanish soldiers emerged from the shadowy trees with swords and muskets. Another voice, unpleasantly familiar, ordered, "I want him alive!"

Felix walked forward, tall and spare and as swarthy as a Spaniard. His bone-colored shirt dripped with lace at the wrists, and there were stylish ruffles on the front of his shirt. With startling blue eyes he measured Baret. The thin mouth and hawklike nose gave him an air of royalty, but he revealed his true nature now, as he smiled his malicious triumph. "So. I now have father *and* son to send to the Spanish governor." He gestured with a slim hand toward Baret. "Seize him!"

Rafael's treachery!

Baret whipped out his sword and stepped back. He was hopelessly outnumbered. Not even Erik knew where he was, for he and Karlton had rowed back to their ships to set sail for Port Royal, where they would rendezvous and each man get his share before the *Regale* set sail for England. Baret had wanted to come here alone, not wishing to involve them in his feud with Levasseur. And since the treasure was safely stashed in the *Regale*'s hold, no one would miss him until morning . . . no one, that is, except Emerald.

Rafael snatched up his booty and offered a mocking bow. Then he straightened, holding hand at heart. He wore a rueful smile.

"Ah, Monsieur, you are but too trusting! Tomorrow at this

time I will also have Emerald and be far at sea. Perhaps I shall not return to Tortuga but to my native France." His smile turned savage. "She will learn that I do not forgive her treachery in marrying you."

Levasseur gave a sharp gesture toward the armed soldiers. "It is a sad thing that your father will again be turned over to them. Alas! But this time he will at least have *you* for company in the dungeon."

"Take your pay and leave," ordered Felix, showing who was in charge. "The *capitan* and his soldiers will go with you to seize the *Regale*. Then you will leave the island by morning, understood?"

Levasseur smiled unpleasantly. "But of course, Monsieur Buckington. I will take the woman with me as planned, and you will see me no more."

"See to it. Take her and go. And do not show yourself in Port Royal—ever."

Rafael bowed, smiled, then walked away with apparently no concern over the soldiers who accompanied him. His plans had been realized. Baret wondered if even Felix could trust him to keep his word. He watched the Spanish captain and his men follow Levasseur toward the now-dark, abandoned beach, where they presumably had boats.

What of the Regale? Baret was furious with himself. He had left men on watch. Yorke and several of his crew were awake and prepared to fight if need be, but they did not expect trouble now. No doubt they were enjoying discussing their success in stealing away the chests from underneath the sleeping noses of the governor and his soldiers. They would be dreaming of the fat share they would receive once back in Jamaica.

He was trapped. And what could he do? He looked again after Levasseur and the soldiers, then met the level gaze of Felix.

"So, Felix. You planned this with Levasseur?"

"Even an untrustworthy shark comes in handy at times. I knew you would come here after you left Morgan, and Levasseur was willing to play his part to trap you—for a price. I knew that once your mind was fully on him, you'd forget any possibility I might be here as well."

"You were right," Baret admitted. "I did forget you were friendly with the governor. It was a foolish mistake. I suppose you overtook Carlotta and Jasper?"

"Yes, and Jasper is dead. He couldn't be trusted. Nor would her marriage to him gain me a thing in the Spanish territories."

"Miguel is also dead."

Felix shrugged. "She told me how you abducted him to learn where Royce was kept. In the end it did you no good. I'm afraid your father cannot return alive to Nigel. I want that title—and I want the fortune."

"At any cost, of course. You've proven that."

He waved a hand airily. "As for Miguel's death, it matters little. The governor here on Margarita is Carlotta's uncle and will send her to Spain to marry. The family has ties to Seville. It will aid me."

"I knew it was foolish of Modyford to discuss Morgan's attack on the Main with you at that meeting."

Felix's smile revealed he was quite satisfied with himself. "There are few British secrets kept from me. I knew the treasure was on Margarita, of course, but I needed you to learn of its precise location from your father. I naturally assume you have done the daring and noble thing in rescuing him from Porto Bello, else you wouldn't be here now. He's aboard your ship, I suppose."

Baret remained silent, wondering how he could get out of this, if not for himself, then for Emerald and his father. If he could fire his pistol, it would alert Yorke and put him on guard. If he could stall Felix . . .

"By the time the sun rises, Governor Sevastian will have a vessel out looking for Farrow and Karlton. They won't come back to try to rescue you, if that's what you think. The governor has cannon, and the harbor walls bristle with guns. I have promised Levasseur the life of Emerald, but the others will be taken prisoner."

Baret knew that eventually Felix would not leave anyone alive, for fear that even one man might escape to tell the ugly tale to Modyford. Once successfully eliminating Royce and Karlton and Baret, he would return to Jamaica and England to resume his life as a spy for Spain.

But, strangely, Baret felt more anger toward Levasseur than toward his uncle. Felix he had always known to be a deadly and unfeeling enemy who could betray his own brother. However, although he had always disliked Levasseur, he had mistakenly believed Rafael could be reasoned with for booty. Evidently his jealousy over Emerald went far deeper than Baret had guessed.

There seemed no escape. Could he reach Felix, kill him before the soldiers standing about overpowered him? Could he hurl his knife? He chanced getting killed by doing so. But it was worth dying now, here on the beach of San Felippe Mission, rather than going to the dungeon with his father—his beloved father! No! They could not take him a prisoner again. He would not let them!

The remaining Spanish soldiers had spread out cautiously, forming a wide circle around Baret. Felix gestured for them to take him.

"You'll die first, Felix," Baret gritted. "I'll empty both pistols into your treacherous heart before my father is taken prisoner again."

As though his own situation had just dawned on him, Felix's black eyes dilated, then narrowed. His thin mouth twisted beneath his mustache.

"Would you kill your own uncle?" he mocked.

"As efficiently as I would blow off a viper's head," came the cold response. "You ceased to be an uncle when you sold your brother to Don Miguel Vasquez."

Baret knew that if he did kill Felix, the soldiers would turn on him with their muskets. Still, the gunfire would alert Yorke, and perhaps then there was a slim chance the *Regale* could weigh anchor and get away with Emerald and his father . . .

Before he could act, however, he heard a soft footfall behind him. Then a heavy thud sounded through the back of his skull. He felt himself dropping to his knees in the sand. The sand blurred as he fell face forward.

In the castle near the harbor, Governor Sevastian sat with Lord Felix and Carlotta at a long low table to a late dinner of roast pig and wild hen.

"I commend you for a job well done, Senor Felix. To have captured pirate Foxworth will bring the smile and reward of His Most Christian Majesty in Madrid." He raised his silver goblet and toasted Felix, then emptied it with a smack of his lips. His long glossy black curls dusted the broad shoulders of his burgundy jacket, which sparkled with gems at the broad black cuffs. His large fingers flashed with rings as he devoured a chicken leg and tossed the bones into a bucket, which an Indian slave quickly offered him. Sevastian impatiently gestured for another slave to fill his goblet with more Madeira and reached for more chicken.

"Tell me, Senor Felix, if you knew these heretic dogs would take Porto Bello, then how it is you did not warn me sooner or send word to my fellow governor at Porto Bello?"

Felix looked across the table at him with tried patience, yet needing the friendship of this man to further his own plans for wealth in trading slaves on the Main. Then he lifted his goblet. "I assure you, most noble Hector, that the man I sent from Jamaica was killed before he could reach you. And then, I was also delayed. I was obligated to overtake my daughter, who ran away with the help of Foxworth. Fortunately, I was able to deliver her from the biggest mistake of her life—marriage to Jasper."

Felix set down his goblet with sharpness. "That fool! He nearly ruined everything." He looked across the table at Carlotta. She sat in mute rebellion, her dark eyes on her untouched plate, her arms folded stubbornly. She was too much like the fiery woman who had been her mother in Cartagena, thought Felix. Stubborn, feisty, uncooperative!

"You are better off without Jasper," he told her again. "He could not be trusted. You would have been unhappy in Barbados."

"You trusted him for years!" she snapped.

Felix gave a bored gesture. "A necessity. But I never fully trusted him. I had him watched constantly. It is a good thing I did, else I'd not have known that the two of you had slipped away. Baret is to blame for that fiasco as well."

"This Foxworth sounds as slippery as a greased pig," Sevastian said. "I will have him placed under double guard."

Carlotta turned to him. "Uncle, what have you done with my cousin?"

Governor Sevastian, a robust man in his forties, arched both bushy black brows. "Your *cousin*, my fiery little leopard, is an English heretic. I could almost believe you worked with him to abduct Miguel from the *San Pedro*. The English pirate will be torn limb from limb on the rack for Miguel's death."

She gasped and jumped to her feet, looking from the governor, who reached for more food, to her father.

Felix stood. "Calm yourself, Carlotta. There is good reason

to indeed believe Miguel is dead because of Baret. Your uncle is doing his duty to Spain by seeing to his punishment."

"If Miguel is dead, then I suggest you killed him just as you did Jasper!" Her dark eyes smoldered.

"I had nothing to do with Miguel's death, nor did Governor Sevastian," answered Felix calmly. "It was Baret who killed him, the cousin you show such alarm for now."

She paled and slowly sank back into her chair. "Baret would not kill Miguel."

"No? He abducted him from the *San Pedro*, did he not? He blamed him for the incarceration of his father. Why wouldn't he kill him once he had Royce free?"

She turned her head away with a jerk. "I don't want to see him tortured!"

"If you cooperate with your uncle, maybe it won't be necessary."

Governor Sevastian sighed and wiped his hands clean on his large red linen napkin. "She will see matters differently with time, Felix. A few weeks here in my castle, spoiled and entertained, and she will soon become convinced to forget both Jasper and Miguel." He turned to her. "Ah, my dear senorita, a trip to Seville to meet many other handsome and wealthy dons will ease your loss."

"Both of you are to blame for my husband's death," she spit. "I will never forgive either of you." She stood and threw down her napkin, then flounced from the large hall and up the stairs to her bedchamber, followed by her two guards.

Governor Sevastian stood and looked at Felix. "The business of Carlotta must wait. She will forget all this in a year or two. She is so spoiled she does not know what she wants. There are other matters on my mind. Where is the treasure of the *Prince Philip*? Why has that French dog not returned with it?"

"There is no need to worry. Your captain and his soldiers are with Levasseur. It will take time to secure the ship and haul the chests here to the castle. By morning we will both be exceedingly wealthy men, Sevastian."

Sevastian faced the stairs and smiled. "If anything can soften a grieving widow's heart, it will be a bag of jewels. And now! I would see this heretic dog Foxworth, who sailed with Morgan in sacking Porto Bello!"

22

A TIME TO KILL
AND A TIME TO HEAL

Baret was shackled to the rack in the dungeon under the governor's castle. The chains dug mercilessly into his wrists and ankles. He was pulled taut, unable to move. At times, he could hardly breathe. The guards had tightened the chains and kept him in this excruciating state from the time he had first been brought here—when?—an hour ago? Six hours? Time had ceased to exist.

When the soldiers were finally done with their sport, they departed, leaving on guard duty someone called in from another section of the prison.

The torches flared on the stone walls. Sweat ran into Baret's eyes. In the silence he could hear rats puttering below the rack, where filth had accumulated for months, perhaps years. If he turned his head a little to the right he could see other implements of torture used to make prisoners talk—or simply to vent hatred for one reason or another.

He squinted at the guard. As stone-faced and cold as the surrounding dungeon, the man stood at the foot of the flight of steps leading upward to the door. The guards were savage, bitter men, trapped in their own hate and servitude to the governor. *One guard now,* he thought. But whether one or a dozen mattered little, since his situation was impossible to escape from.

Lord help me escape, he prayed, *for Emerald's sake. Spare her from falling into the lustful hands of Rafael!*

Baret had already noticed that the guards were not all full-blooded Spaniards. This one stood out from the others as looking to be part native Indian. He considered this.

He knew the Indians usually hated the conquering Spaniards as much as did the buccaneers. Indians had aided Morgan at Porto Bello, notifying him of the approach of a garrison of soldiers riding from Panama. Some of the pathetic prisoners they had loosed from the Porto Bello dungeons had been natives.

Baret tried to recall what he knew about the Indians on Margarita. He spoke to the man in English, but he didn't answer.

He tried Spanish. "You must find it a great honor to serve the great Spanish lords who have come from across the sea in ships. They have conquered your people and turned you into slaves. You must look upon Governor Sevastian as a god!"

The young man's brown eyes darted to his. For a moment he looked at Baret as though he were delirious, then his face became immobile again.

Baret managed a smirk. "Ah, your Spanish lords are worthy of your loyalty. How many of your people, like sacrificed chickens, died diving into the pearl beds? A thousand? Five thousand?"

"Too many to count."

A response from the guard was the sign he was hoping for. "They appreciated your sacrifice, of course. No cost is too great for the lovely Spanish senoritas to wear fat pearls around their throats, while your women are enslaved, sleeping with Spanish soldiers, bearing their children—like you."

"Keep silent!"

"Where is your father? Do you know? Did he own you as a son? And your mother—how was she mistreated? Did she tell you?"

The guard walked over to the rack, baring his teeth like a wolf ready to snarl. He reached for the crank to give it a turn. But when his angry gaze met Baret's, he stopped and stared down at him. For a moment he seemed not to see him, then he swallowed and gave him a measured look.

"You are French?"

"English and Dutch. My mother died in a torture chamber in Holland. Only days ago I rescued my father from a place like this in Porto Bello."

A strange smile formed on the guard's lips. "I heard what the English Morgan did to Porto Bello. And I have heard of the treasure you have taken from the mission ruins."

"Help me escape—and a portion of it is yours."

The guard looked sullen. "I cannot help you. They would kill me."

226

"A thousand pieces of eight—and your freedom away from here. I will bring you to Tortuga to join the Brotherhood. There are many there like you and me. Buccaneers, they call us. We have one thing in common—a desire to see Spain humbled."

The man cast a glance toward the steps that led up to the door. "They come."

"Just unloose me," Baret gritted. "I will do the rest! Quick! Just unloose me!"

The half-breed hesitated, but then swiftly unfastened the chains and retook his place as guard by the foot of the stairs, his face immobile once again.

The door opened, and Baret heard the voices of Felix and Governor Sevastian.

He lay still as though chained, but he flexed his hands, trying to regain the circulation where numbness had set in. They would soon discover he was loose. If he didn't act now, he would be secured again, and the Indian guard would die. But without a sword, what could he do?

His brain worked rapidly, thinking, trying to plan his next move.

Felix led the way down the stone steps, followed by the ponderous Sevastian in his burgundy dinner jacket.

Baret's eyes dropped to their scabbards. Both wore weapons. He remembered that Felix was an excellent swordsman.

"Ah, our thief and pirate is awake again," said Sevastian, drawing his sword and walking to the foot of the rack.

How soon would he notice that the chains were loose?

"What do you say, Senor Felix? Perhaps we can convince him to be more friendly and tell us where the diabolical Morgan is going to attack next!"

"Margarita," Baret retorted flippantly. "And I'll be the first to enter your bedchamber and pluck your beard, Don Sevastian!"

"You'll not retain that cynical tone when I've ordered the soldiers to split your tongue! Instead, you'll be making gobbling sounds!" He came around toward Baret as if he would do it himself, then and there.

Baret doubted that the governor had the stomach for performing such a deed, but it didn't matter. As he came close, Baret sprang off the rack and wrenched the sword from his startled grip.

Sevastian, though a big man, was no match for Baret. As circulation flowed back into his hands, Baret grabbed the governor and hurled him backward, crashing him into Felix, who fell to the dungeon floor.

"Quick!" Baret ordered the Indian. "Let us put our illustrious governor on the rack! Let him taste his own cruelty for a change."

The Indian rushed to perform the order as though executing long-awaited justice.

"No! No! Let go of me, you ape! I'll have you torn in pieces for this—"

"Not this time, Sevastian," said Baret, as the Indian swiftly locked down one arm and Baret the other. The governor shouted for guards, but Baret counted on any cries from this place being ignored.

Felix, however, was on his feet. He whipped his blade from its sheath and was inching backward toward the steps.

Baret intercepted him but kept a sword-thrust distance away, his dark eyes glinting with restrained anger.

"Now, now, dear Uncle, not so quickly," he mocked. "Surely you'd not want to send your beloved nephew away without a bit of refreshment and some warm, encouraging words?"

Felix's blue eyes turned as hard and cold as sapphires. "I don't need the governor of Margarita—or his soldiers. I will silence you myself! For years you have blundered into my plans. You will not do so again!"

"I was hoping you would say that." Baret stepped back, lifting his borrowed blade. "I can tell my father I was forced to kill you!"

Felix lunged at him, his lean body as agile as an angry and frightened cat. His sword struck Baret's and was swerved aside.

"Our illustrious governor has good taste in Toledo blades!" Baret goaded.

He struck swiftly, his sword ringing against Felix's and forcing him backward toward the wall. But Felix defended himself skillfully, and each of their blades checked and repelled the other again and again.

Baret swung harder, his inner turmoil feeding his sword with a force that savagely turned Felix's aside again and again.

He nicked Felix's wrist to loosen his grip, causing the man's hand to become slippery with blood.

"Six years he was a slave!" Baret gritted. "I have had but a few hours of your Spanish hospitality! He uses a crutch! His face is scarred! He is old now!"

Felix was gasping.

Baret pressed relentlessly until Felix fell back in retreat against the slimy dungeon wall, and the borrowed blade rammed him through.

Felix's eyes turned hard, cold, and lifeless. His sword clanked onto the stone floor.

Baret turned away. He looked over at the governor.

"Look at him," the Indian mocked. "He's fainted!"

"Leave him," said Baret. "There's no more time."

Footsteps sounded on the stone stairs.

Baret snatched Felix's sword from the floor and sent it clattering across the dungeon toward the Indian. He hoped he could use it.

The young man snatched up the weapon.

But as Baret looked to the steps, thinking soldiers were coming, Carlotta stared down at him with wide dark eyes. In the torchlight her face showed pale and frightened. She looked at Felix, and her hands went to her mouth. But she said nothing, only staring at the corpse of the man who had sired her.

"What are you doing here?" demanded Baret. "Jasper—"

"Th-they killed him . . ." She pointed to the governor. "Now my uncle will send me to Spain—I don't want to go!"

"Then come quickly. Do you know a way out of here?"

"Yes, through my room, but hurry, Baret! Soldiers will soon be swarming everywhere."

"We need horses. Are there any?"

She nodded. "In the courtyard." She was turning to lead the way when she saw the half-breed following. Her eyes sparked with suspicion.

"It's all right. He's one of us now. Hurry."

Several horses were tied in the courtyard, and only one old groom was tending them. Baret snapped his fingers at Carlotta, and she slipped off her gold earrings and dropped them onto Baret's palm. He handed them to the old man, who gave a toothless grin.

The three mounted, as the old man pointed to a gate. They bolted away, and Baret opened the gate just as the sound of soldiers' running feet came from the garrison on the other side of the dungeon. Baret, Carlotta, and the Indian held themselves low in the saddles to avoid a possible barrage of arrows. Then they leaped over the green hedge and raced into the warm dark night to freedom!

All was quiet when they arrived at the ruins of San Felippe. Baret knew that barely an hour of darkness remained. He left Carlotta on the beach, guarded by the Indian, and told them he would send a boat when it was safe to board the *Regale*.

"If anything goes wrong and I do not return, remain in these parts. Erik and Karlton will surely come back when I do not keep the rendezvous. You will have your chance to escape then."

The Indian remained stony-faced, though his eyes flickered with concern.

Carlotta took hold of Baret's arm. Her own eyes were worried. "If Rafael is aboard your ship with his men and the soldiers, what chance will you have?"

"I don't know. Time will tell. My men will fight if I can free them—if they are still alive. But I must go. Rafael will have Emerald."

She nodded her understanding. She looked toward the ruin of the mission. "God help you, my cousin."

The small boat Baret had used to row out to meet alone with Levasseur was still hidden where he'd left it. He pushed off from the glittering white beach into the darkened water. The morning stars were blending into the horizon as he rowed silently toward the ghostly silhouette of the *Regale*.

Was Levasseur aboard? And where were the Spanish soldiers who had accompanied him? Had Yorke and Jeremy and the others been able to put up a fight, or had they had been caught unprepared? He had some of the best buccaneers on the Main, but not even they were sufficient for the number of men with Levasseur.

Carlotta had insisted that Rafael had not returned to the castle with the treasure chests. There would not have been time.

Nor could he have transported them yet to the *Venture,* docked in the town's harbor.

Then, Baret thought, his jaw flexing, *Levasseur* must *be aboard the* Regale. He would be waiting until morning in order to navigate the reefs safely. Once it was light, he would sail into the town's harbor to join the *Venture,* would unload the treasure to the safekeeping of the governor's soldiers, take his own share along with Emerald, and make for the open sea.

If he was still aboard, there was a chance.

As Baret rowed closer to the *Regale,* he could see several longboats tied to the ship. Then Levasseur and the governor's soldiers *were* there. Had his men put up a fight? Was anyone still alive? Why was it so quiet?

Remembering his past success at secretly boarding the *Venture* to free Karlton, Baret dropped anchor some distance from his ship and slipped into the warm water. He swam toward the side where the boarding ladder dangled near one of the longboats. He listened but heard no voices on the deck immediately above. Had Levasseur put everyone into the hold? He would not need many guards on deck, since there was no need to fear the Spanish. And he certainly didn't expect a surprise visit from Baret!

He climbed the ladder cautiously, pausing to listen before going over the rail. There were few sounds, and he detected no Spanish soldiers prowling the decks. It appeared that everyone was still asleep. He came over the side, crouching low, sword in hand.

Lanterns glowed above the quarterdeck steps, and a thought came to torment him. He rejected it. If Levasseur was in his cabin with Emerald—if his father was dead—

He steadied his nerves before moving on, breathing in the cool air and trying to think clearly without hot emotion stirring the coals in his breast. Perhaps Levasseur had not put all his crew to the sword yet. They could be imprisoned in the hold.

He had the advantage of knowing every inch of his vessel. He moved across the deck and down into the waist to the companionway, where a guard paced before the hatch leading to the hold.

Without a sound, Baret came up behind him, threw his forearm around the man's neck and wrestled him to the deck, then snatched a pistol from his bandolier. He used the pistol

231

butt on the back of the guard's head, then pulled him aside into the ropes and tackle, retrieved the second pistol, and stuffed it inside his leather belt. Then he returned to the hatch and opened it.

A dim light burned below. With pistols in both hands, he went down the ladder, blinking against the light.

"*Har!* 'Tis his lordship!" breathed a jubilant Hob.

"Cap'n!" came Jeremy's hoarse voice. "Thank God. You're a sight for hopeless eyes!"

"I knew it!" said others, and a low murmur swelled to a hum until Baret fiercely waved them to silence.

"How many aboard?"

"Levasseur and a dozen Frenchies!"

"What of the governor's soldiers?"

"*Har,* ol' Levasseur done made quick shark bait out of 'em," said Hob. "Didn't take much to get him riled. Once he saw the treasure, he was lickin' his chops like a *boucanier*'s huntin' dog."

"The Spanish captain insisted on taking the chests back to the mission until he could transport 'em to the governor's castle in the morning," Jeremy explained, "but Levasseur would have none of it. He killed him."

"Shot him square through his gizzard," said Hob. "Then had his Frenchies turn on the dozen soldiers. "They's all floatin' dinner for the sharks by now."

Baret had seen nothing when he swam to the ship, but perhaps the sharks had been satiated.

"A fine mess you're all in," he breathed. "I leave my ship for an hour, and you end up losing it without a fight to that French peacock!" He removed his knife from his belt and quickly begin cutting them free.

Once Jeremy was loose, he joined in the work. Soon most of the crew were free and boiling over with energy.

"We did put up a fight, Cap'n," said Jeremy. "Yorke's dead, and Hawley is wounded, and . . ."

Yorke . . . dead. Baret concealed the pang he felt. There was time to grieve for his loyal lieutenant later.

His dark eyes hardened. "Where's Levasseur now?"

Hob rubbed his chin and looked up at the ceiling. "With Emerald, says I—and maybe your father. He wanted 'em both alive till he made sure he was aboard the *Venture*."

"All right, lads, are you ready to take our ship back?"

"Aye!"

"With pleasure, Cap'n!"

"After me, then! And no one make a sound!"

While his crew dispersed to deal with Levasseur's seamen one by one, Baret came quietly up the steps to the round room. The door stood open to allow the breeze to circulate. Lanterns burned, and he could see Emerald, seated in a chair. The concealed anguish in her face would not be recognized by anyone but himself. She pretended disdain for Rafael and had never looked more noble than she did now, he thought. The love he felt for her consumed his heart.

Royce stood by the window, but his hands were bound. Zeddie was hog-tied in a corner, his periwig awry and his black eye patch askew.

"You're mad, Rafael," Emerald said. "You won't get by with this. My husband will gain his freedom, you'll see. And when he does—"

"By now he is on the rack, *mon cherie*, and the governor will see to it he hangs on the gallows by noon tomorrow. You best cooperate with me now. It may be I shall take pity on you and save you from the debauchery of the Spanish soldiers!"

Baret stepped quietly into the room. "That would be very *galante* of you, Rafael. But as you can see, that will not be necessary. I am quite able to defend my wife against Spanish soldiers and despicable Frenchmen!"

Levasseur whirled and stared unbelievingly, as though Baret were a mirage.

"You," he breathed.

"Yes, it is I, *Capitaine*. It is you and I, alone. And I vow, when I'm through with you, there will be nothing left to even tempt the sharks! Come, Levasseur! It is long past due to see which of us is the better swordsman!"

Emerald backed away toward Royce, her face pale and tense, but there were no hysterics.

Tense and deadly serious, Rafael unsheathed his blade, his black eyes measuring his opponent. He seemed to know there would be no mercy shown him this time, and he lunged to gain the moment's advantage.

Their blades whispered, cutting through the air with speed and force, then coming together in a solid clash of cold steel.

Levasseur gave a short laugh. "You see! I have taken your devilish lessons, Monsieur!"

"You have learned nothing yet as you ought to have learned!" Baret feinted, lunged, and caught Rafael off guard, nicking his throat.

Shaken and white, showing surprise and fear as well, Levasseur wiped away the blood and stepped back.

Baret stalked him, deadly determined. "Come, Rafael. It is not over so quickly. You will taste defeat first! For all the misery you have caused Emerald and me!" He lunged at him.

But Levasseur hurled a lantern, drenching the round room with a splash of flames and shadows. Then he leaped over a chair and bolted through the door.

Emerald grabbed a pillow and rushed to beat down the fire.

Baret went after Levasseur. He was heading toward the quarterdeck steps.

"He flees like a rabbit!" Baret announced, seeing some of his men.

"Har!" shouted Hob gleefully. "Behold the dawcock fleein' like a scurvy rat for his hole."

The *Regale* crewmen mocked Rafael with their laughter and jeers.

Baret caught up with him on the steps, and here Levasseur, his eyes flaring renewed rage, stood his ground. Then he sprang, his blade whipping past Baret's chest and drawing blood.

"Ah!" Levasseur shouted, as though the sight spurred him on to new levels of energy.

"Come back, then, dog!" Baret invited and drove him furiously again. "You shall soon meet your Maker. Are you ready? I think not!"

"I shall see you in hades first!" Levasseur came at him, beating back Baret's sword in a frenzy. "Ha! Beware, *Capitaine!*"

Baret sensed that Emerald and his father had come running from the round room. He glimpsed her clutching the upper deck rail and looking down, fear written on her white face.

Levasseur's energy now flowed like spewing lava. His lips were drawn back in hatred.

Baret remained dangerously cool, his concentration sharpening as the intensity of their duel mounted. There was the sound of steel clashing against steel—and then Levasseur was retreating down the steps to the lower deck.

The crew moved back, watching gravely. All wordplay died into silence as Baret stalked his enemy.

They circled on the deck. Levasseur lunged. Baret parried. The duel grew more careful, each man resorting to fencing tactics known only to the most skilled instructors.

Levasseur shook the sweat from his eyes. "You are dead, Monsieur!" and he rushed him.

"Ah! Vain hope!" Once more Baret parried skillfully, then turned his blade. His sword slipped past Rafael's defenses, and he thrust him through.

Levasseur stumbled back against the ship's rail.

Baret tipped him backward over the side of the *Regale* to splash into the dark, forbidding Caribbean.

"Alas, Rafael . . . a final adieu. You should not have played the game of treachery with me."

23

THE DAWN

Baret saw his beloved waiting for him on the steps of the quarterdeck. The wind was tossing her skirt and blowing her dark lustrous hair. She came toward him, and he walked to meet her. They met in a crushing embrace. For some time they held one another as though afraid some new enemy would emerge to tear them asunder.

At last, with arms about each other, they walked to the rail to watch the flaring dawn break with new hope and sweet promise.

His father and Zeddie had been cut free, Levasseur's crewmen were safely confined in the hold, the treasure was secure, and a boat was on the way to bring Carlotta and the Indian to the ship.

Baret asked Emerald, "Ready for England?"

Her eyes, reflecting her happiness, gave a ready answer, and together in heart they watched the dawn brighten with splendor, the sky deepen into royal blue.

Their new life was beginning. Only God knew where it would eventually lead them. But they possessed the greatest of treasures: they had one another, they had their freedom, and they had *Him.*

Moody Press, a ministry of the Moody Bible Institute,
is designed for education, evangelization, and edification.
If we may assist you in knowing more about Christ
and the Christian life, please write us without obligation:
Moody Press, c/o MLM, Chicago, Illinois 60610.